strong hand on his cheek.

Although Cord didn't move, he felt himself flow into the contact. As when they made love, he lost the distinctions between them.

He was full of words. Words that wouldn't come. All he could do was look into Shannon's eyes and wonder what emotions she was keeping hidden from him.

Maybe none. Maybe a lifetime's worth.

"What are you thinking?" she whispered.

That I want to bury myself in you until there's nothing except us.

They were words he didn't dare speak aloud. To acknowledge them would surely be his destruction.

Dear Reader,

Our lead title this month hardly needs an introduction, nor does the author. Nora Roberts is a multiple *New York Times* bestseller, and *Megan's Mate* follows her extremely popular cross-line miniseries THE CALHOUN WOMEN. Megan O'Riley isn't a Calhoun by birth, but they consider her and her young son family just the same. And who better to teach her how to love again than longtime family friend Nate Fury?

Our newest cross-line miniseries is DADDY KNOWS LAST, and this month it reaches its irresistible climax right here in Intimate Moments. In *Discovered: Daddy*, bestselling author Marilyn Pappano finally lets everyone know who's the father of Faith Harper's baby. Everyone, that is, except dad-to-be Nick Russo. Seems there's something Nick doesn't remember about that night nine months ago!

The rest of the month is terrific, too, with new books by Marion Smith Collins, Elane Osborn, Vella Munn and Margaret Watson. You'll want to read them all, then come back next month for more of the best books in the business—right here at Silhouette Intimate Moments.

Enjoy!

Leslie Wainger
Senior Editor and Editorial Coordinator

Please address questions and book requests to:
Silhouette Reader Service
U.S.: 3010 Walden Ave., P.O. Box 1325, Buffalo, NY 14269
Canadian: P.O. Box 609, Fort Erie, Ont. L2A 5X3

THE RETURN OF CORD NAVARRO

VELLA MUNN

Published by Silhouette Books

America's Publisher of Contemporary Romance

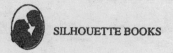

SILHOUETTE BOOKS

ISBN 0-373-07749-1

THE RETURN OF CORD NAVARRO

Copyright © 1996 by Vella Munn

Books by Vella Munn

Silhouette Intimate Moments

The Man From Forever #695
The Return of Cord Navarro #749

Silhouette Shadows

Navajo Nights #58

VELLA MUNN

grew up the daughter and granddaughter of teachers, and from childhood on was in love with the written word. She turned to writing when her first child was born, and now has twenty-nine contemporary and historical romance novels to her credit. She is the mother of two grown children and lives in southern Oregon with her husband.

Chapter 1

"**H**e isn't here."

Cord Navarro stood without moving, his work-hardened chest rising and falling in a smooth rhythm that nearly tore Shannon loose from her surroundings, and flinging her back to a time when that chest, that well-honed body, was hers to touch and caress. When she cared.

"Where is he?" her ex-husband asked in response to her short and obviously not satisfying explanation.

"With a friend." Willing herself to return his gaze, she concentrated on her own breathing; brought it back under control. He meant nothing to her and hadn't for more than seven years. It shouldn't be so hard to remember that. "Cord, we—he—had no idea when you'd be back. We certainly didn't think it would be this soon. If you'd called—"

"I left a message."

"You did?" Freeing herself from his obsidian eyes, she glanced over her shoulder at the house behind her. "When?"

"About an hour ago."

"An hour?" She pointed to the weathered barn to the left of the house. "I've been with the horses. I keep thinking I need an extension out there. As soon as I can afford—" She stopped herself. "Matt will be delighted to see you. It'll just take a little time to round our son up, that's all."

Cord nodded, then pressed his hand against the back of his neck. From experience she knew he wouldn't admit he was tired even if he was in danger of collapsing. She hoped he wouldn't, because if he did, she'd be forced to touch him, and she didn't—wouldn't—ever want to do that again. Still, he looked somehow vulnerable today, and that was getting in the way of her objectivity.

"You aren't out with a group?" he asked when she wondered if his silence would run on forever. "I thought you might be."

"No need, at least most of the time. My horses are plodders." Experience had taught her that she would have to supply the bulk of the conversation. "Most of them know exactly where they're supposed to go and how long they'll have to put up with the strangers on their backs, which is fortunate since sometimes, I swear, I have clients who've never been where there aren't gutters and sidewalks. If I had high-strung horses, it would be a disaster."

His gaze swept over her house/office, barn, three corrals, even the small flower garden that flourished only because she religiously covered it at night during Colorado's frequent spring freezes. "You've done well," he said.

He'd told her that last winter, and she'd spent too long wondering if he was surprised that she'd succeed at running her own horse rental business in a part of the state that lived for ski season. But her barn housed all number of horse-drawn conveyances, and there was nothing like a sleigh ride to cap off a day of skiing. In fact, she did more business in the winter than summer. She'd told him that the last time she'd seen him; she saw no point in repeating herself. The trouble was, she wasn't sure what to say next. She wished she'd put on makeup. More than that, she wished it didn't matter to her what she looked like.

He was here. Facing her. *Cord. Cord Navarro.* Despite the years and distance between them, the name, the reality of him, wouldn't stop. But she should be used to that, shouldn't she?

Once, a lifetime ago, his body had taught hers what it meant to be a woman, to want and need—and be fulfilled. Now, Cord, with his courage and competence and a mind filled with knowledge passed down through generations of people who existed in harmony with the land, stood only a few feet away and she hadn't had time to prepare herself.

He wore a thin chambray shirt and jeans that had to be at least five years old. His boots were faded yet soft, the result of regular rubbing with saddle soap. Funny that she would recall his devotion to his footwear. When they'd first married, she hadn't understood his concern with the way his boots fit. That was before she realized that next to his keen eyesight, the most important skill he brought to his work was his ability to cover vast distances as quickly as possible.

She couldn't say how long it had been since he'd had his hair cut, several months at least. Deeply black, the coarse hairs slanted across his forehead and bunched over his collar. Once she'd loved to bury her fingers in the thick mass. Once she'd... He needed a shave. His eyes were half closed against the swirling wind that had kicked up this afternoon, but that didn't prevent her from feeling their impact.

Lordy, but he could see, and absorb. At seventeen she'd thought his eyes the most compelling things she'd ever seen—them and his hard, compact, already deeply muscled body. Well, she wasn't seventeen any longer. It had been years since she'd felt anything simply because he looked at or touched her.

Years.

Although she should be saying something about the whereabouts of their ten-year-old son, her thoughts caught on the passage of time and what it had done to Cord. The elements had etched his features, furrowing lines around his eyes and mouth, darkening his flesh until it was impossible to know where his Ute grandfather's heritage left off and the power of the sun, wind, rain, and sometimes snow began. If she got any closer, she might catch his scent, but even with necessary distance between them, she remembered. He smelled like the wilderness, always. Except when they'd just made love and then her nostrils would pull in something primitive and basic.

How many mountains had he climbed? Maybe a thousand, each of them adding to the strength in his legs and the breadth of his shoulders. One reporter had called him magnificent. Another wrote that he was a cross between an oak and a bear, an odd poetry of words that must have embarrassed him. If he asked her, she would be forced to tell him that both reporters were right.

As a man, he was exactly that—a man. So rawly alive that it was impossible for her to know where muscle and strength and physical competence left off and what else he was began. Unfortunately, an undeniably masculine body wasn't enough. There had to be emotion, as well, that essential, missing element in Cord Navarro's makeup. Or if it existed in him, he kept it too deeply buried for her to tap. And she was tired of trying.

Tired but still aware.

With her body feeling as if it had been hit by an outlaw shaft of lightning, she stepped forward and extended her hand. "So, tell me how it went."

"The rescue?" He engulfed her hand with his but didn't take his eyes off her face. "She was easy to find."

"But there was some kind of problem, wasn't there?" she asked so she wouldn't think about the heat and power in those fingers. "Something to do with her health?"

"She's diabetic," he said, and released her hand. "Can you call him?"

She knew he was asking about Matt, who'd all but tripped over his lower lip when he'd heard that his plans to spend the summer with his father had been delayed. Cord, probably the country's premiere search and rescue expert, had been called away at the last minute to track a lost hiker in Yellowstone. She told Cord she'd try to get in touch with Matt, but it was possible that he and his friend Kevin had already left for the Wagon Creek campground. Until they reached the remote area managed by Kevin's uncle, she had no way of contacting him.

"I have to tell you, I wasn't sure what I was going to do with him," she said. "He was so disappointed. Thank heavens he and Kevin came up with a plan to spend a couple of days together. Apparently Wagon Creek is full, but Kevin's uncle offered to let them camp out next to his tent. You must have found that woman in record time. How did you get back here so soon? And that vehicle?" She pointed at the dusty Jeep parked in the graveled lot she'd probably never have the money to pave. "That's not your run-of-the-mill rental car."

"It belongs to a local pilot. He was at the airport when I landed. Since he was flying to Denver and going to be there for several days, he let me borrow it."

"Did he? That's good." They could carry on a civilized conversation. It might take effort, but they *would* do it. "You must feel like a bouncing ball, always being sent somewhere new, not knowing how you're going to get there."

"I'm used to it." He shrugged, as if relieving himself of a weight, and placed one foot on the bottom porch step, stretching denim over a hard thigh. "One thing about the traveling, I've seen a lot of places I wouldn't like to live." He looked around, and as he did, the strong wind tore through his hair. "I love this part of Colorado. The seasons, the vastness. I always have."

"I'd like a longer summer, but you're right about the vastness." She looked around, taking in the surrounding, sheltering mountains of the Arapaho National Forest. Sometimes, mostly in the middle of the night, they made her feel trapped. But maybe it wasn't the mountains; maybe the restlessness came from within her. "I've been wondering something. Why didn't you come back? After all, you grew up here, and it can't matter where you have your base of operations."

Cord blinked, his eyes strong on hers. "A lot of reasons, Shannon. However, I've been—" He stopped whatever he'd been about to say. "I flew over the high school on my way in. The football field looks the same. And the gym. Do you ever go back?"

She shook her head. "Maybe when Matt gets into high school. I'm not much into nostalgia."

"Hmm. I wonder if they still have your picture in the main hall."

"My picture? Oh, the homecoming one." He remembered. What was she supposed to do with that piece of information? "I'd forgotten. It seems so long ago."

"Yeah, it does," he said, and she wondered if there was a touch of regret in his voice. "Do you still have the dress you wore? The pale blue one."

"Dress?" *Don't do this to me, Cord. I don't want to go back in time.* "I think . . . I think my folks have it at their place. That and some other stuff I need to get out of their hair. I ought to tell them they don't have to hang on to that horribly dated thing anymore. I'll certainly never wear it again."

"No nostalgia where it's concerned?"

What did that matter to him? "Not really. I try not to live in the past."

"No, you've never done that. Besides, being homecoming queen's a little different from what you're doing now, isn't it?"

He couldn't be more right. She'd been a cheerleader, mainly because she was athletic and understood the rules of competitive sports. Being crowned homecoming queen had come as a shock. She couldn't say she hadn't enjoyed the attention, dressing up, having a professional photographer pose her. But now she lived in jeans and boots because, working with horses the way she did, that was the only attire that made sense. Still she asked herself if she would have worn something else today if she'd known she'd see her ex-husband.

When he again rubbed his neck, she invited him inside so she could make the call that would take him away from her again—him and their son. As he entered the front room that served as her office, she wondered if he would notice the changes she'd made since he was here last Christmas. Probably not, since he'd stayed only long enough to pick up Matt so they could spend the week between Christmas and the new year together. Still she hoped that on some level it would register that she'd put down new tile to replace the horrible old carpet that had come with the place and had given the walls a fresh coat of white paint so that her framed photographs of wildlife stood out. Success. Competence. Independence. That's what her surroundings said.

She hadn't bothered with drapes, which meant the office was flooded with light whenever the sun shone. Today, however, clouds were boiling on the horizon and would soon cast the room into shadows that played up the structure's age. That might mean a storm was on its way, something she didn't need with a full complement of tourists due to rent horses over the next few days.

"Would you like something to drink?" she thought to ask as the phone rang.

"Water. I can get it myself," he said, and headed toward the small kitchen at the other end of the house, his boots making a soft thud on her new floor covering. If she didn't know him as well as she did, she might have been put off by his assumption that he had full use of her house, but Cord Navarro wasn't a man who expected others to wait on him. No wonder. From the time he was a toddler, it had been only him and his reclusive Ute grandfather, Gray Cloud.

He returned a minute later as she finished talking to a representative of a group of high school seniors set to arrive the beginning of next week. Cord had a large glass of ice water held in a hand that had probably never cradled a long-stemmed wineglass. She'd always thought her office large enough to accommodate the press of clients that trooped in most summer mornings, but Cord's presence changed her perception. It was, she admitted, because he wasn't a man for walls. Even at rest, part of him always seemed to be reaching beyond manmade boundaries, seeking more space for himself. He was breathing in that easy way of his, a cadence that changed only when they were making love.

Had made love.

Had.

Fighting free of thoughts she'd spent the past seven years exorcising, she dialed Kevin's number, hoping to reach his parents. Although she kept her gaze trained on the massive old rolltop desk she'd refinished last winter and the pile of paperwork awaiting her, she was all too aware that Cord had stepped closer. She experienced a flash of resentment, and pain. Her ex-husband wanted her to tell their son that he wasn't going to be spending the night camping with his friend after all because his father was here and was going to take him God knows where until school started. She would be alone.

"Kevin?" she asked in response to the unexpected juvenile voice. "What are you doing there? I thought you and Matt were going to Wagon Creek."

"We were. Only..."

"Only what?" she prompted, punching the speaker button so Cord wouldn't have to stand so near.

"We...well, we had a fight."

"You did? I'm sorry. Look, Matt's dad is here. Could you tell him he should come home? I'm sorry if that's going to mess up your plans, but—"

"He isn't here."

"He isn't?" Sighing, she shook her head to let Cord know she wasn't responsible for the actions of ten-year-olds.

"No."

"Then, where is he?"

"I don't know."

"Okay," she said patiently. "How about your best guess? Where do you *think* he is?"

"On his horse."

"On his horse where?"

"Probably halfway to Yellowstone."

"What?"

"That's what he said." Kevin sounded exasperated. "He thinks he's so smart. He tried to tell me he's going on all his dad's rescues this summer, that his dad needs him. I told him, no way. He doesn't know nothin' 'bout searches and stuff. How can he when he doesn't even live with his dad? When I said that, he got mad and told me he was too going to rescue people."

"Yellowstone." She had to struggle to get the word out, but it was important to keep Kevin on track. "He didn't really say that, did he?"

"Just about."

"Kevin." It was Cord, his voice low and controlled, in command. "This is Matt's dad. I want you to tell me exactly what he said."

Chapter 2

Cord concentrated, not just on what Kevin was saying, but the boy's tone, as well. His son's friend was obviously more than a little miffed at Matt, maybe so focused on that that he was unable to remember the details of their conversation.

"Let me get this straight," he said after Kevin had rambled on for several minutes. "Matt had brought over his gear so the two of you could spend the night at the Wagon Creek campground, but you don't think that's where he went. He didn't say anything about coming back home, though, did he?" Kevin's family lived some two miles from here, an easy horseback ride for a boy who'd been around horses most of his life.

"No. He called me a butthead. Said I didn't know squat 'bout what you've been teaching him. Is it true? You're really gonna take him wherever you go this summer, even if it's to the top of the highest mountains in the world?"

Cord had never climbed the Alps, hadn't so much as mentioned them to Matt as far as he knew. However, he saw no reason to say anything that would lower Kevin's opinion of his friend any more than it already was. Besides, that wasn't the point of this conversation.

"Kevin, I started tracking with my grandfather when I was younger than Matt is now. What I told him was, since we're going to be together for the next three months, he'll be as much a part of whatever I'm doing as possible." He didn't mention that there'd be times when Matt would have to remain at base camps while he was on particularly arduous or dangerous searches.

"Wow! Can I come? My dad—I know my dad'll let me. And he can talk my mom—"

"Wait a minute," Cord interrupted with a chuckle. "Let's deal with one thing at a time. I can't believe Matt didn't say anything to you about his plans. Didn't he at least hint at what he was going to do?"

"Well . . ."

"Well, what?" From his twice weekly phone calls with his son, he knew there was almost nothing Matt didn't share with Kevin.

"He—is Matt's mom still there?"

"Yes, I am," Shannon said.

"I told Matt he was gonna get in trouble for this, but he said I didn't know what I was talking about, that you let him do it all the time."

"What do I let him do all the time?" Shannon asked. Out of the corner of his eye, Cord noted that she'd pressed her hands against her flat stomach, but her voice betrayed nothing of her emotions. Either that, or she had become too much of a stranger for him to know what she was feeling.

"Stay out all night."

"When it's something like your place, or a campground I approve of like Wagon Creek, yes," she said. "But you're saying he didn't go there."

"No," Kevin said, and Cord felt the weight and heat of Shannon's eyes on him.

"What did he say?" he prodded because Shannon was slow to speak. Besides, Kevin had a case of hero worship where he was concerned and this conversation might drag on forever if he didn't exert a little pressure. "It's very important that I know exactly what's going on. You're going to help me in this, aren't you?"

"Y-yeah. Sure. 'Sides, it's not like it's some big secret. I just don't know why Matt didn't tell his mom himself."

"Tell her what?"

"That he's going campin' on his own—I swear I don't know where—for a couple of nights. He said for me to tell her not to worry. He made me promise."

Not to worry. As if Shannon could do that. He again asked Kevin if Matt had given any indication of where he might be going, but although Kevin stuttered and stammered and then was quiet for too long, the boy swore he didn't know more than he'd already told them. Cord's thoughts all too easily fixed on their rugged surroundings, miles and miles of wilderness that had been his childhood backyard. Although Shannon's address was the little town of 'Frisco, there were massive mountains on all sides. It was said that Summit County, Colorado, boasted more outdoor recreational opportunities than almost anywhere in the country. The area included the Snake and Blue rivers, the Gore and Tenmile mountain ranges, Dillon Reservoir, and a history rich in gold miners and Ute Indians.

In short, there was a hell of a lot of space, most of it capable of hiding a boy bent on proving something to his best friend—and maybe his parents. Mostly his father.

"You're sure about this?" he pressed. "Matt definitely said he'd be gone two nights?"

"Yeah. He showed me his food. He's got a lot. Neat stuff he probably wouldn't have shared with me anyway. 'Sides, he said you weren't going to be back for a while and he wanted to get into shape for when you needed him."

"I understand. Being in shape's important. But so too is letting people know where you're going to be. I can't believe he didn't say anything about his destination. That's the first rule of wilderness traveling. Kevin, I need you to think. Is it possible he was going to go to Wagon Creek on his own?"

"No way," Kevin insisted. "He says that's for babies. Uh, is he going to get into trouble?"

Cord didn't answer for the simple and yet hard reason that Shannon was responsible for disciplining Matt. True, that would change once father and son were together, but right now Matt technically was living under his ex-wife's roof, and although he and Shannon hadn't sat down and had a heart-to-heart about shared child rearing, he'd never once questioned her competence in that department. After all, she'd grown up with parents. She, not he, knew how the roles were played out.

Although he sensed that Kevin was holding something back, Cord was unable to get the boy to reveal more than he already had. Shannon was no more successful, and after a few more minutes, she hung up the phone.

She walked over to her office chair and sank into it, staring and yet not staring at him. She opened her mouth but slowly closed it without saying a word. The mouth he'd once claimed for himself looked tight. Her hands lay on her thighs, the tips pressing into the flesh beneath her jeans. He might not know her thoughts, maybe he never had, but he could read her body language.

She was under control, barely.

Weariness hummed at the edge of his awareness, but he knew how to keep his body's need for sleep at bay. More times than he could remember, the difference between life and death for someone he'd never met and would never see again depended on his ability to run on nerves and guts and determination. He would rest when he knew where his son— their son—was. When he could wrap his arm around the boy's shoulder.

"There's something Kevin isn't telling us," he said. "Either Matt swore him to silence, or Kevin's still mad and that's how he plans to get back at Matt."

"You don't know that. Cord, you hardly know Kevin."

No, he didn't because he didn't live with his son, a fact he tried to think about as seldom as possible. However, he knew how to listen and more times than not that ability made it possible for him to hear things left unsaid—like the tension and fear in Shannon's voice, like her need for him after all these years. He didn't want to be needed.

Through the open window, he caught the clean, clear scent of pine and snow-tainted air. He walked over to it and stared out at what he could see of his ex-wife's world, thinking. Planning. The sky had been clear as he flew in, but that was changing. Clouds that looked like soft pillows tossed against the horizon were changing from white to gray. If they continued to darken—

"What's the weather forecast?" he asked without turning around.

"I'm not sure. I don't think I heard. What..."

When her voice trailed off, he waited for her to begin again and then listened as her chair squeaked softly in response to her rising. She was wearing boots, but they made almost no sound as she came toward him. He felt her just behind him, her slender body and long limbs making an undeniable impact even though he wasn't looking at her.

"It was a good winter," she said softly. "Enough snow to make everyone happy. There's still some high on Breckenridge, Copper, and Keystone."

"I know. I can smell it."

"Can you?" She now stood beside him, not touching him. "The clouds—it might rain."

"It might."

Out of the corner of his eye, he saw her lift her hand and place it against the screen. Because listening, *really* listening, came as second nature to him, he heard her soft intake of breath. "What do we do now? What—he's never done anything like this," she told him. "Never gone off without telling me what he's up to, without getting permission first. He's responsible. Responsible and, damn it, independent. Self-confident."

"I know."

"Do you?"

Just as he'd suspected that Kevin was holding something back, he knew Shannon's emotions were rising, expanding. He longed to return to the quiet and expendable conversations that defined their relationship these days.

"Do you really?" she repeated. "Cord, I don't think you have any idea how hurt he was to have you put him off the way you did. He kept saying you should have taken him to Yellowstone, that he could have helped you."

"I didn't have time to explain anything to him. He and I didn't even have time to talk." Would she agree?

"I know," she said after another of those whispering breaths of hers, a breath that had once felt as much a part of him as his own. "You had to go after that woman. I tried to explain to him that time was of the essence—he finally said he understood. But he hasn't seen you for months. That's what matters to him.''

''Of course it does.''

After that she remained silent, still. Another woman might ricochet off the walls, running off in one direction or another in an unorganized attempt to find her child. Maybe she was waiting for him to take charge—or maybe things were still sinking in for her. Her body language told him some of what was going on inside her, but not enough. He didn't expect anything different. After all, seven years ago he'd learned how little he understood this woman.

''He's riding Pawnee,'' she said. ''I didn't want him to. That gelding's only three, full of energy. But I felt sorry for him so I— He could be anywhere.''

''You really believe that?'' he asked as the phone rang. Two seconds after she said hello, her impassive features told him the call had nothing to do with Matt.

She didn't seem to notice he was studying her. She wasn't a tall woman, five foot seven to his five-eleven. She'd told him that she'd had to endure the nickname Twigs for several years because her arms and legs had been long and skinny. Her legs still went on forever, but then, he'd always loved that about her. He didn't think she'd gained so much as a pound since their divorce; the real change in her body had come as the result of two pregnancies. When she was a few months' pregnant with Matt, she'd pointed out—not that he'd needed her to—that she could finally put her bra to real use. Nursing Matt had kept her breasts full and firm and although they'd gone down a little when she weaned him, it hadn't been much. The same thing had happened with Summer.

Summer. Their daughter.

Belatedly he realized that she had finished her conversation and was talking to him. He was forced to ask her to repeat herself.

"He still doesn't know the meaning of the word fear, Cord," she said. "You know how he was as a baby, always exploring. He's so much like you in that respect."

"What places does he talk about the most?" he asked as an image of his black-haired, brown-eyed son formed in his mind. It was time to become what he was, a searcher. He didn't dare let himself be distracted, because this time it was his son out there. "Which ones fascinate him?"

"Which don't?" She looked around her as if having to remind herself of where she was. "He loves skiing—you know that. Unfortunately, he doesn't like taking the same run over and over again. He's always pushing to try something new. All winter he bedeviled me to take him to Vail." She smiled, almost. "I've tried to make him understand how hard it is for me to get away when I've got paying customers. And Vail's too rich for my pocketbook. Here I can get discounts, thank heavens."

"Shannon, I can send more money."

"I know you can. You're already more than generous. But that isn't the point. He has to understand the value of money." She looked down at her hands and blinked as if surprised to see that they were tightly clenched. "Places...places he could be," she said vaguely. "He's crazy about fishing, but that, like the skiing, has to wait until either one of his friend's parents or I can take him."

He knew all about Matt's passions in life, but let Shannon continue. One thing he'd learned over the years was that giving people something to do, even if it was just talking, kept their minds off the uncontrollable. And Matt had done something his parents had no control over—something Cord had done himself when he was even younger. The differ-

ence between him and Matt was that Cord hadn't had a
mother to worry about him—only Gray Cloud, who believed his grandson could accomplish everything he set out
to do.

"Skiing season's over," Cord noted when she ran down.
"What about his fishing pole? Did he take that?"

She shook her head, then pushed a strand of hair off her
forehead. She'd done her long, rust-brown hair in one of
those pigtail styles that started at the top of the head, and
although he knew she'd taken care with the project, she had
so much hair that it was nearly impossible to control all of
it.

Once, a thousand years ago, she'd let him help her and
they'd laughed together at his efforts.

"He and Kevin were going horseback riding and sleeping
under the stars at a family campground, not fishing," she
continued. "At least—at least, that's what I thought they
were doing. And now this. I don't like it, Cord." Her gaze
slid from him back to the building clouds. "I want him
home. That's all."

He didn't say anything, not because he didn't feel the
same way but because he didn't want to frighten her.
Whirling away from him, she stalked toward her desk and
picked up the phone. She began calling Matt's other friends.
She spoke quickly, matter-of-factly, concerned but not
frightened, and he remembered that he'd never seen her
panic.

He hoped her self-control wouldn't be tested before this
was over.

I'm going after him.

Cord's statement had been so calm and matter-of-fact
that for several seconds, she hadn't registered the serious-
ness of what he'd said. Cord Navarro, who maybe knew

more about the wilderness and people who ventured into that wilderness than any man or woman alive, wasn't content to wait for his son to finish his two-night solo adventure.

Shannon wasn't, either, of course; that was a given. Learning that none of Matt's friends had seen or heard from him today had left no doubt in her mind. But to hear Cord say what she'd been thinking forced yet another shiver of alarm down her spine when she was already enough on edge.

They'd been standing at the window, not talking, for no more than a minute while the sound of the wind in the trees increased. Her mind had been lost somewhere in the past; somewhere with Cord....

"Go after him?" she repeated stupidly. "You don't even know where to look."

"Kevin lives on Tenmile Road, doesn't he? I'll try to pick up Matt's tracks from there."

If anyone else had said that, she would have laughed. But Cord made his living finding the unfindable. In response to his question, she told him that Pawnee had shoes on his front hooves but not the rear ones because he had the bad habit of kicking at other horses. Cord nodded, told her that would help identify the gelding, and then asked which horse he could borrow.

Glad to have something to do, she stepped outside and led the way to the corral. Most afternoons there were people around, but the two college students she'd hired as wranglers were out with groups and she didn't expect anyone to return for several hours. She shouldn't have felt isolated and trapped—wouldn't have if it had been anyone except Cord.

She tried to gauge the wind. Would Matt notice the wind and clouds and rethink, or would saving face with his best friend and proving himself to his father come before wisdom?

Before she could lean her weight into the warped wooden gate, Cord swung it aside and stepped into the corral. Despite her resolve not to gaze at him any more than necessary, she did just that.

When they got married, he'd still been taking on the contours of maturity, but she hadn't known that. Back then, she'd thought him the most powerful man she'd ever met. Once her mother had asked if she felt safe around him. At first she hadn't known what her mother was talking about, but then it sunk in. Her mother was worried that Cord might someday use his strength to get what he wanted from her. But that had never been his way.

Never.

Even now he was speaking quietly and calmly to the curious horses who'd come up for a sniff as if being surrounded by animals who weighed over half a ton was as natural as breathing. Perhaps she should have helped run interference; but for too long she couldn't do anything except listen to him and remember how his voice had sounded as they'd made love, when the tones came from the depth of his being and words she wasn't sure he remembered or ever acknowledged were ripped from him. When he had given her so much of himself—maybe all he had.

She desperately wanted Matt to return, not just so the knot of tension in the pit of her stomach would go away, but so that father and son would leave and she wouldn't have to look at Cord anymore. Wouldn't have to feel. Remember. Remember too much.

Realizing he was watching her, she snagged one of the mare's halters and led the roan out of the corral while Cord closed the gate behind them. Strange. Without either of them having said a word, they'd managed to work together to accomplish a simple but necessary task. Too bad—

No! She wasn't going to go down that road again. She wasn't! After all, she couldn't blame Cord entirely for not being who she needed. Her college psychology courses had taught her how much of an impact one's parents had on how a person turned out. Well, Cord hadn't had parents. He'd had Gray Cloud. Only Gray Cloud.

She'd seen a faded newspaper picture of the old Native American after he had brought a trio of lost Boy Scouts down off Breckenridge. Its quality hadn't been particularly good, but because that was the only picture Cord had of his grandfather, she had no other way of putting a face to the man who'd shaped her ex-husband. Shaped and, in many ways, limited him emotionally.

"You've been letting Matt stay out after dark?" Cord asked as they headed toward the barn.

"Not beyond sleep-overs and campgrounds where I know the managers. I'm aware of how you feel about him gaining self-confidence, but I'm not ready for him to be any more independent than he already is. I'm much more comfortable playing the overprotective mother." She couldn't prevent sarcasm from entering her voice, then worked up a smile she hoped would blunt the edge of her words. Confrontation had never been her strong suit; she wasn't going to start today, with him. "You have to be around school-age boys all the time to understand that logic is not something they give a lot of thought. If it feels good at the moment, they do it and worry about the consequences later."

Cord rubbed the heel of his hand against the mare's forehead, saying nothing, waiting for her to speak, as he'd done too damn many times. She obliged only because she hated what was going on inside her. "Once, when he was in kindergarten, I got a call from the principal because Matt had upended another kid in the toybox. When I asked him about it, his only excuse was that it seemed like a good idea at the time.''

''What happened?''

She frowned. ''What do you mean?''

''Did he get into trouble?''

''No,'' she admitted as they stepped inside the cool, dark barn and the smell of wood and hay and horses engulfed her. ''At least, not from me. I acted pretty firm when we were in the principal's office. Sometimes it's easier to go along with authority figures than to get into long debates.'' Working from feel and experience, she chose a bridle. ''Afterward I asked Matt why he picked that particular kid. He said he'd butted in line ahead of him at the water fountain and he didn't want him to do it again. It seemed to me that the boys were handling their problems about as maturely as a couple of five-year-olds could be expected to. I pointed out some facts, like what might have happened if there'd been anything hard or sharp in the toybox, and then let it go. The next day Matt and that kid were best buddies.''

She shrugged and even smiled a little although she wasn't sure Cord could see. She wasn't sure how she felt about being in this confined space with him. ''I'm convinced that's how kids grow up, by working things out on their own as much as possible.'' Her smile faded and she knew her eyes were giving away what she felt inside. ''He's a good boy. Just young. Impulsive.''

''I know.''

Cord's words stopped her. For perhaps a half second raw fear tore at her, but because as a mother she'd battled worry for her child before, she knew how to smash it into submission and concentrate on a plan, what had to be done to return that child to her. What happened to Summer had nothing to do with Matt. Nothing! Matt, like his father, was healthy and filled with a zest for life's risks.

"It's going to be all right, Shannon," Cord said.

Can you promise me that? Can you? Instead of throwing her irrational words at him, she simply nodded and watched as he worked the bit into the mare's mouth.

"I've been thinking," she told him. "Matt's been talking about the south end of Dillon Reservoir a lot lately, asking me how big the fish get and whether there'd be tadpoles this time of year."

"I'll keep that in mind."

"You don't know when you'll be back, do you?" she asked, pointing to the saddle she wanted him to use.

"When I know something."

Another wave of fear washed through her. She spoke around it. "What kind of communication system do you use? I want to know as soon as you find him." *If you find him.*

Lifting the saddle effortlessly, he placed it on the mare's back. "Hand-held radios. I'll show you how to use them."

"Good," she said, as if she would have it any other way.

While she waited outside the barn with the mare, Cord walked over to the Jeep. He came back carrying a powerful flashlight, the radios, a denim jacket, and a small, personalized first-aid kit. It made her feel better that he hadn't bothered with a lot of equipment. If that was all he intended to carry, it wasn't as if this was a real search, just a necessary, time-consuming but routine chore by an adventurous child's tired father.

"Don't try to hold Misty back," she said as she turned the mare's reins over to Cord. "Let her run herself a little. Then she'll do everything you want her to."

"I understand."

Of course he did. There wasn't a thing she had to tell him about how to conduct his business—except that the boy out there was so much a part of her that there was no separating them.

Matt was a part of Cord, too, she reminded herself as Cord handed her a radio. The unit felt solid, yet too small. This black box was all that connected her with what might happen out there. She concentrated as he showed her how to use the instrument, then stepped out of the way so he could swing into the saddle. The mare flung her head high, a snort of excitement renting the wind-whipped air. Shannon felt exhilarated, momentarily blocked off from her unease simply because Cord was sitting astride a horse, looking a part of it and his surroundings.

Bring him back. That's all, just bring him back tonight. Could he sense her thoughts? she wondered as he ran his broad-fingered hand over the mare's taut neck. Did Cord ever try to put himself in another person's place? She'd thought so back when he'd pressed his hands over her swollen belly and looked at her with eyes that seemed to churn with a million emotions. But he'd been gone so much the last year they'd been married, she could no longer delude herself into thinking she knew anything about him. She hadn't understood why he'd been willing to risk losing a roof over their heads so he could be his own boss, and although he'd encouraged her, she knew he hadn't really understood why she'd wanted to go to college—or why, after Summer's death and the crumbling of their marriage, a formal education had no longer mattered. She didn't believe he'd sensed her resentment and loneliness when she had to be student and parent and tenant and bill payer and a thousand other things while he was off taking care of other people.

Most of all, he hadn't said what she'd desperately needed to hear when Summer died. She'd had to mourn alone.

"Cord? When my customers come back, I'll ask them if they've seen anything. And I'll call Wagon Creek, ask Kevin's uncle to keep an eye out for him."

"Good," he said, then, without looking back at her, he cantered out of sight.

Three long hours later, during which Shannon moved through the motions of her business, Cord called. "I'm at the south end of the reservoir. He isn't here," he said without preliminary.

She gripped the radio, speaking slowly in an effort to keep her emotions under wraps. It was no longer afternoon; the day was moving relentlessly toward evening—darkness. "How can you be sure? The reservoir is so big."

"I've been listening."

"Listening?"

"For something that sounds different. I know the wilderness, Shannon. Its rhythms. When there's something in it that doesn't blend in, I know that. There's nothing."

Nothing. "That doesn't tell me anything," she told him when what she wanted was to demand he stop scaring her. "Where have you been? I kept thinking you'd call."

"I didn't have anything to tell you."

Damn him, he didn't understand, would never understand that she couldn't live without communication. "And you thought three hours of knowing nothing wasn't going to bother me? Never mind. Where were you?"

"I went to Kevin's place first," he said, then explained that he hadn't been able to pick up Pawnee's prints because Kevin's sisters and several of their friends had been riding their horses all through the area. Kevin hadn't been there to question further, prompting Cord to act on her suggestion to check the reservoir. She strained for any hint of emotion in his voice, but either it was lost in the distance between them or was lacking—probably lacking. She couldn't stop staring at the now deeply shadowed sky.

"Shannon? I need you to think. Are there places you don't allow him to go, somewhere that's particularly intriguing?"

"I try not to rein him in any more than necessary. Arapaho—" *No!* "—maybe."

"That's miles from here and steep. The snow runs are for advanced skiers. There's no reason—"

"You took him there once—he's never forgotten that. He was so little you carried him on your back most of the way to the top. Do you remember that?"

"Yes."

"Cord, it's going to be dark in less than two hours. You can't possibly get there before that."

"I know."

I know. Why did so much of what he said frighten her? But even as she asked herself the question, she knew the answer. Cord Navarro's worth came from his ability to take away the unknown, the uncertainty; at least, that's what the press said about him. However, he was only human—a man who couldn't hold back the night or find one little boy who might be anywhere in the vastness she'd always loved.

Cord told her that he'd cover as much territory as he could in the daylight left to him and then do what he'd done at the reservoir—let his senses tell him whether he'd gotten any closer to their son.

Alone, she listened to the now angry wind beat itself against the side of the house and tried not to think of Cord riding into the dark, letting it engulf him, becoming part of that rugged world. The air smelled of rain. If Matt had gone to the reservoir, at least he'd be at a relatively low altitude and less likely to be caught by the unpredictable weather.

However, if he'd gotten it into his crazy head to climb Arapaho, he might even encounter snow.

Fighting frantic thoughts, Shannon prayed for her last customers to return. Finally they did. Trying to keep her voice calm, she asked if they'd seen a boy on a high-spirited pinto, but no one had. She considered calling her parents but decided against it. There was no reason, she told herself, to upset them if Cord returned with Matt. Her son was having an adventure, not lost or hurt. Why did she need to keep reminding herself of that?

Because she'd already spent too much time pacing in the house, she took the radio into the barn with her and killed time by meticulously arranging halters and bridles. She even brushed several horses who wanted nothing more than to be left alone so they could sleep. Every few seconds she willed Cord to contact her, to tell her something, anything. But he didn't and she nearly hated him for that.

It was dark; the mercury light that lit her small spread had been on longer than she wanted to think about. It hadn't started to rain yet, but from past experience she knew it soon would. The temperature was cold for this time of year and the blasted wind hadn't let up. What jacket had Matt taken?

She'd gone inside and was just walking into Matt's bedroom when she heard hoofs thudding against the hard-packed soil. Not breathing, she stepped outside.

Cord and Misty were illuminated by artificial light, their shadows fading off into the night. He rode the mare as if he'd been born on the animal's back. He was all Native now, both timeless and primitive. She needed her anger and the hard lessons of the past, but how could she wrap those emotions around her with the sight of him consuming her?

When he was close enough that she could make out his features, he locked eyes with her. His silence said everything. She pressed her palm to her stomach and watched as he guided Misty toward the corral. He dismounted with a liquid movement and reached up to remove the saddle. He would have to speak first; she couldn't.

He ran his hand over Misty's neck and then turned toward her. He looked older than he had earlier today, but that might have been a trick of the unnatural light. "Nothing."

Nothing. "You went all the way to Arapaho?"

"To this side of the base, yes."

The knot inside her tightened. She looked up at Cord, needing and yet not wanting to see the same mood in him. But whatever he felt, he kept it to himself as he had too damn many times in the past. "What happens now?"

"We'll have to wait until morning."

"Morning," she repeated, not caring that the word came out a whimper.

He nodded, then, without speaking, started toward the barn. Something about the set of his shoulders caught her attention; he was exhausted. "Go inside," she ordered. "I'll take care of her."

"You don't mind?"

"It's the least I can do. Go."

She remained behind long enough to feed and water the mare. Although she knew she was being foolish, she kept her senses tuned to the dark. If will alone could accomplish miracles, Matt would be coming into the light now.

When she entered the house, she noted that Cord had removed his boots and jacket. He'd slumped onto the couch and was staring, not at her, but at the rocker she'd once used to rock Matt to sleep. "I should have helped you out there," he said, his voice little more than a whisper.

Unexpectedly her heart went out to him. No matter how much he shuttered his feelings inside him, he couldn't completely disguise his body language. He leaned forward and ran his hand over the back of his neck in that gesture she had given up trying to forget.

"Darn him!" The words were out before she knew they'd been bottled inside. "Doesn't he know what he's doing to us?" She pressed her fingers against her mouth. "I'm sorry. That isn't the point right now, is it?"

"No. It isn't."

Chapter 3

"It's going to rain tonight."

Shannon didn't need Cord to spell out the obvious. Besides, he should realize she didn't want to think about what Matt might have to endure tonight. "This isn't the first time he's pushed his boundaries. Pushed himself I should say," she admitted. "He's a good boy. But . . . he has a lot of you in him."

Cord blinked slowly, the movement hitting her somewhere deep and unwanted. "I know he does."

"He needs space," she continued, feeling her way past memories of their years together, buried years. "He'd rather be outside than in no matter what the weather. And he'd rather die than sit still."

"Yes, he would."

Yes, he would. Words of understanding between parents. Darn it, she wouldn't let him get close!

"Cord, I've been thinking. That's all I did while you were gone. Think. The other day I heard Matt on the phone tell-

ing someone about all the places he was going to go with
you. That someday the two of you would—''

"I can't be with him all the time, Shannon."

"I didn't say you should."

"But if I'd been here today, he wouldn't have gone off."

"No. He wouldn't have. But we can't do anything about
that, can we?"

"Do you blame me?"

She wanted to. Heaping responsibility on him would take
it off her shoulders, but to what purpose? "I don't know all
the factors that went into his half-baked decision to do this.
Until I do... I just wish he wasn't on such a healthy, adventurous horse. The two of them together— Oh, well,
that's water under the bridge. Getting him back is the only
thing that matters." *The rest of life means nothing.*

When he didn't respond, she forced herself to walk into
the kitchen. Working automatically, she threw together a
couple of tuna fish sandwiches, her mind bouncing between unwanted thoughts of Matt having to sit out the night
in the rain and Cord retreating into the silence that was so
much a part of him. Once she hadn't cared whether Cord
went the rest of his life without saying another word. Let
him live in solitude! Let him drown in it! Now she wanted
to march back into the living room and shake something—
anything—more out of him.

Guilt stalked her for not having nailed Matt's foot to the
floor. Cord should feel the same way. She fervently wished
she could wring a confession out of him. Instead she put his
dinner on a plate and carried it to him. She stood over his
slouched, strangely vulnerable-looking form, wondering
which of them carried the most guilt and why that should
matter. He hesitated a moment and then took the plate.

"Have you already eaten?" he asked.

She could have lied. Instead she shook her head. "I thought about it, but my stomach—it has all it can do to manage the emotions I've thrown at it."

He lowered his gaze to his plate and picked up a sandwich but didn't bring it to his mouth. Was his stomach as knotted as hers? For some reason, the thought frightened her. Cord Navarro was supposed to be all strength and competence, not mortal like everyone else.

Not scared like her.

"He's going to be all right," she said, hating herself because she knew how trite and untested the words were. Still, she couldn't stop herself. "I—"

The phone rang. She reached for it, praying she'd hear her son's voice at the other end. Instead, her caller was Kevin's father. He and his wife had just gotten home from a late commitment and had heard that Matt's parents were looking for him. "I take it there are no updates," he said.

"I'm afraid not," she admitted, and filled Hallem Segal in on Cord's efforts so far. Hallem tried to be reassuring and offered his help. He said she seemed to be holding up well.

If he only knew! She was holding her fears at bay with an iron grip. After hanging up the phone, she glanced over at the clock. How did it get to be 11:00 p.m.? Leaving Cord with his meal, she stepped into Matt's bedroom. For too long she couldn't make herself turn on the light. Standing in the dark, she could imagine that her son was curled up in his bed, fist tucked under his chin.

But he wasn't here, just his essence, his energy and scent; his everything. Feeling overwhelmed, she snapped on the light and forced herself to concentrate on what had brought her in here. Matt's wool-lined but nearly too small wind breaker wasn't in its usual place on a hook behind the door. At least he had some kind of covering. Not allowing herself time to take in any more of her son's cluttered, comfortable room, she walked back into the living room and told Cord what she'd discovered. He nodded.

Before she could think of what, if anything, to do next, Cord finished his sandwich and wiped his hands on the napkin she'd given him. "I appreciate it. I didn't know I was hungry. That happens when I'm on a search."

He hadn't touched the other sandwich or the salad she'd pulled out of the refrigerator. "You lose your appetite?"

"I just don't think about things like food." He nodded toward where he'd left the Jeep. "I have my things out there. Do you mind if I grab a little sleep here? There isn't anything I can do until morning."

She was surprised he felt he had to ask. Certainly he understood they were in this together until Matt was safely back where he belonged. By way of answer, she walked into her bedroom for a spare blanket. She'd started to hand it to him when she realized what she was doing. Because her living room wasn't that large, she'd bought a rather small couch. There was no way he could get any rest on it. The youth bed in Matt's room wasn't any better.

She held out her hand, indicating she'd help him to his feet. "Take my bed. You'll need it."

He stared at her hand for so long that she thought he was going to ignore her impulsive offer. Then, with a sigh that came from deep inside him, he engulfed her fingers with his own. She braced herself against his weight—and more. "Shannon? Thanks."

"For what?" He stood maybe five inches away, smelling of the forest, of night, of life, of something deep and undeniable and compelling. She'd never been able to look at him without thinking of his substance. If she put her arms around him, as she had a thousand years ago, she'd find nothing except muscle. When he released her hand, she pressed her palm against her leg, wiping away his impression—trying to, anyway.

Cord yawned. "For being . . ." He indicated the blanket. "You don't have to do this."

"Yes, I do. That's our son out there."

He gave her a look that made her wonder if he was searching through himself for something—maybe an emotion, maybe certain words, maybe a way of reaching across the chasm between them. She wanted to reach for him and yet the years had turned them into strangers. She might not want to spend the night alone, but she didn't have the strength or courage to try to hack away at what had gone wrong between them.

Concentrating on every muscle movement, she took a backward step. "I hope, when this is over, we'll be able to talk."

"Talk?"

"About—" *Why it fell apart for us.* She didn't try to finish. He was right. Except for Matt, they had nothing in common. "About what the two of you will be doing this summer."

The tarp he'd stretched between four close-growing trees flapped wildly in the wind, the sound waking Matt Navarro from a light sleep. He heard the plop-plop of fat raindrops as they hit the heavy fabric, but so far none of them had reached him. Realizing that, he smiled. Then, although he hated moving, he forced himself to sit up. The night was awfully dark, pitch black in fact. Other people, sissies and cowards, would be inside a tent with a lantern burning. Someone like Kevin sure wouldn't be here alone; most grown-ups wouldn't, either. But he wasn't most people. He was Cord Navarro's son, brave, part Ute Indian.

Because, like his dad, he didn't wear a watch, he had no idea what time it was. But then, it didn't matter. His dad would know; Cord Navarro knew everything important.

Knew that there was nothing to be scared of just because it was dark and no one was anywhere around.

Nothing to be scared of—hadn't his dad told him that the last time they went camping together?

And he believed what his dad told him.

After listening for a few minutes, Matt decided that the flapping tarp and rain and not Pawnee or owls or some other night creature must have wakened him. It took him a few more minutes to convince himself to crawl out of his cozy mummy bag. Working by feel, he managed to tighten his makeshift roof so it no longer made such a racket. Still using his hands instead of his flashlight, which he didn't want to risk running down by using any more than absolutely necessary, he checked to make sure his bag hadn't slipped off the pad his dad had bought so he'd be protected from cool, damp ground. Then he dove back into bed and stretched out his stockinged feet. Only after he'd tucked the bag up around his shoulders did he realize he hadn't checked to make sure the heavy-duty flashlight was within reach. Darn it, if some animal snuck up on him—

Don't be scared! Don't even start thinking like that! Only babies—

I'm not a baby!

I know you aren't. You're Cord Navarro's son. You want him proud of you, don't you?

'Course I do. I'm not chicken.

Tired of the dumb argument going on inside him, he tried to listen for anything except the rain, but all he heard was Pawnee snorting and pawing the ground nearby. "I'm sorry," he told the gelding. "How was I supposed to know it was going to rain? Besides, you've been rained on worse than this. And snowed on, too. Remember. Why don't you just go back to sleep like I'm going to?''

Pawnee snorted again. Matt couldn't tell whether the horse was agreeing or arguing with him. Maybe he was thinking about thunder and lightning, two things that really made Pawnee show the whites of his eyes. He still felt bad that Pawnee had to be out in the rain while he remained dry, but he didn't know what he could do about that. He'd been a little unsure of how to tie Pawnee so he wouldn't wander away during the night, and was irritated with himself for not paying more attention to what his mom had said about how to keep horses from tangling themselves in ropes. When he got back, he'd ask her again and really listen this time.

Mom.

A sharp sense of unease kept him from relaxing enough to fall back to sleep, but then he reminded himself that his mom didn't know he wasn't with Kevin. She wouldn't be worrying. Hadn't she told him she wasn't going to call Kevin's uncle at Wagon Creek to check up on him because it wasn't as if he'd never gone there before? Kevin might be a king-size butthead, but at least he knew enough to keep his mouth shut. Despite being so mad at Kevin he'd nearly wrestled him to the ground, Matt had stuck around long enough to make sure Kevin understood he was not to tell his mom what his real plans were.

And if she somehow found out that he wasn't at Wagon Creek, Kevin was to say nothing except that Matt was going to spend two nights camping out and for her not to worry.

Two nights were enough for what he was going to do; at least, he was pretty sure they were.

His shoulders had gotten cold while he was fixing the tarp, but they were already warm again. He'd have to remember to tell his dad that the mummy bag he'd given him was absolutely perfect.

Dad.

Although sleep tugged at him, he tried to imagine where his dad might be tonight. He wasn't sure how far away Yellowstone was. A long way by car, but his dad had flown his plane. Soon—real soon—his dad would let him take the controls.

And track...track down people who'd gotten lost or hurt and were...

More asleep than awake, he barely heard the owl hooting overhead. His mouth twitched into a half smile as he imagined the round-eyed bird staring down at him. Owls were neat with their big, keen eyes and ears so good they could hear a mouse hundreds of feet away. Their ears—something his dad had told him about their ears.

He'd ask him...tomorrow. No. Not tomorrow, because Cord Navarro was saving some dumb woman, and he was going to climb a mountain all by himself so the next time he wouldn't be left behind like some baby.

A...really tall...mountain.

The smell of rain blew in through the open window in Shannon's bedroom. The scent, so much a part of Cord, cleared away the haze of sleep he'd only briefly managed to wrap around himself. Sleep was important. Although he'd learned to function without it for days on end, he knew how essential it was to replenish his body. If it had been any other time and the search ahead of him had involved anyone else—

His son was out there, a lean, growing boy with dark eyes that sparkled with excitement for life's adventures. Thinking about Matt warmed him, warmed him and made him resent how quickly his son was leaving childhood behind.

That's why Matt was out there on a rainy night, because he felt ready to take a giant step toward adulthood. Maybe he was ready. Maybe he wasn't.

Yet that wasn't what kept Cord awake tonight. In truth, if it wasn't for Shannon, he would have been tempted to wait for Matt to finish his personal test and return, successful and boastful. He'd done what Matt was doing and more when he was even younger, proving to Gray Cloud that the lessons learned at his grandfather's side had taken.

But Shannon's eyes and voice and body language told him she couldn't take Matt's absence in stride. She was a mother without her child within reach and nothing mattered to her except being able to hold Matt in her arms again.

He understood why it was that way for her. She—they— had already lost one child. That pain . . .

Turning soundlessly in the bed that seemed to have taken on her contours, he repositioned her pillow and pulled in the scent of her shampoo. Her hair was still glorious, rich and healthy. What had she said once when he'd admired it? She couldn't take credit for its condition and was grateful she'd been blessed with hair that didn't require a lot of care because she had better things to do with her life than to spend it at a beauty parlor.

Everything about her was natural, honest.

Eyes open now, he stared at what he could see of her room.

While getting ready for bed, he'd paid as little attention as possible to this space that said the most about his ex-wife. Now, caught in that quiet time of night when there was nothing to do except think, his mind drifted back to a time when he'd known, or thought he'd known, the mother of his children.

She wasn't the same seventeen-year-old girl he'd fallen in love with all those years ago. Although he missed the quick, shy grin that had first attracted him to her, he had no regrets that she was no longer a teenager. He might regret what they'd lost since that magical first year, but the woman she'd become—

That woman moved with a deer's grace, her lean, athletic body challenging him in a way he didn't want. But want it or not, the fact was, he still physically desired her. His heart might have put love behind it, but his body, his damnable body hadn't forgotten what it felt like to make love with her.

What had he called her smile, honest? Her body was the same. Yes, she'd been an uncertain virgin when raging hormones and curiosity and loneliness, at least on his part, had brought them together that first time. But that hadn't lasted long. Learning together, they'd tasted sensual experiences and, in the tasting, the testing, discovered that they were capable of igniting something in both themselves and each other that he now believed might never be extinguished.

Seven years after he'd left her bed for the last time, the flame still hadn't been snuffed out.

When his jaw started to ache, he realized he'd been clenching his teeth. He forced himself to relax. Once he'd accomplished that, he worked on the rest of his body. Using techniques Gray Cloud had taught him, he visualized every muscle, mentally easing tension out of one after another. He fought to keep his mind clear of any other thought, fought and only partly succeeded. Whenever he slackened his grip, his thoughts went back to her—the woman curled on the couch in the next room.

She could have taken Matt's youth bed, a bed the boy was rapidly outgrowing, but for reasons she kept to herself but he could guess, she hadn't entered their son's room again. Was she sleeping? He doubted that she had been any more successful at blocking out the world than he had been.

Only, it wasn't the world that kept him awake.

Their missing son was responsible.

And that son's mother.

A woman he'd once loved and made love to like a dying man clinging to life. A woman he'd lost somewhere in the tangle of the past and only wanted to forget.

Tonight wasn't for forgetting.

Instead his body burned and ached and remembered.

Not a word.

When the stupid phrase skittered through Shannon's mind for the umpteenth time, she stretched out her legs until her feet dangled over the arm of the couch, and she stared up at the darkened ceiling.

She'd managed to fall asleep, but that hadn't lasted very long. Concern for Matt had been a large chunk of what had awakened her. But Matt Navarro wasn't any ordinary ten-year-old boy. He was Cord Navarro's son, an outdoor child who believed night was as fascinating and comfortable as day. Just because she couldn't hold her son didn't mean he wasn't all right. She couldn't sleep because Cord and she were under the same roof during night's quiet for the first time in years.

Of course he was asleep, she told herself a little testily. The experienced tracker knew how to shut off his mind and get the rest he needed. He'd probably trained his mind as thoroughly as he trained his muscular legs and keen eyes and sharp hearing.

Muscular legs.

No! That was the problem; she couldn't stop thinking about his thighs and calves and chest and arms—and the rest of him. Why was he so strong? So physical? So...so primitively masculine?

A long and not-too-steady sigh escaped her lips. She gave up trying not to think about Cord. He'd always slept on his side; at least he had when he'd been married to her. He seldom moved in his sleep, one of those fascinating/maddening things about him she'd never forgotten. When he wanted her in the middle of the night, he would place his hand lightly over her rib cage and run his forefinger up and down her side until she either responded or turned away from him. Most of the time she'd responded.

Past tense. Damn it, past tense.

She hadn't known anything that first time, not a single solitary thing about what went on between men and women. Oh, yes, like most of her girlfriends, she'd spun fantasies about falling in love, making love. Doing "it." But those fantasies had had nothing to do with reality.

Now she knew the reality, and her body refused to forget.

It had been his hands. In some instinctive way, Cord had known how to take her smoothly and cleanly from virginity to womanhood. He'd come to her as inexperienced as she'd been. Because he'd been a loner, she couldn't imagine that he'd shared much locker room talk about what girls wanted and expected. She also couldn't imagine him discussing sex with his grandfather, either. Somehow Cord's hands had sensed what she'd needed. They'd played her, explored, taught, learned.

And she'd given herself to him with every fiber of her being.

A million years ago.

Before his silence had come between them.

Not a word. Don't forget that. He walked away from you tonight without saying a word.

* * *

Shannon's eyes felt as if she'd tried to wash them with sandpaper. Stepping out of the shower, she quickly toweled off and slapped a little cream on her face. After throwing on some clothes, she brushed her teeth, trying not to look at Matt's smaller toothbrush next to hers. The constant sound of rain made her want to climb on the roof and yell at the heavens not to pour down on her son.

Cord, who'd already used the bathroom, was outside doing whatever it was he needed to. It still wasn't light enough to see without turning on the bathroom light; at least, normal mortals like herself needed help to see. As for Cord, he'd showered in the dark and then dressed and gone outside without saying a word to her about his plans. He didn't seem to be hurrying, yet getting ready hadn't taken him any time at all.

Had he slept? she asked herself yet again. During those horrible hours while she lay curled up on the couch praying for the night to be over, she'd listened for the sound of Cord's breathing. She'd heard nothing, but then, he'd slept silently when they were married. Maybe that hadn't changed.

Sleep. Had he been capable of shutting off his thoughts so he could go about the vital task of preparing his body for today's work? If he had, then he indeed lived up to his publicity as the intrepid tracker. But to truly rest, with his son somewhere out there—

Reminding herself that there was something essential she and Cord had to discuss, she laced her boots and stepped outside. It wasn't cold. But neither was it as warm as she wanted it to be. As long as she stood on the porch, she could almost convince herself that the rain wasn't that much of a factor, but the moment she stepped out into it, she was lost.

Why, Matt? What were you thinking? Does proving yourself to your father really mean this much?

Cord, wearing a soaked T-shirt that hugged his wonderfully hard and competent body, turned from what he'd been doing at the Jeep. He came toward her with his backpack slung over his shoulder, his eyes steady on her. He looked ready to take on the world one quiet step at a time. Despite the rain and wind, he didn't so much as blink. The day was gray, dark, making a lie of summer. Cord was part of that world.

"Go back inside," he said as he came close. "There's no reason for you to get wet."

"Isn't there?" she retorted. She hadn't known she was angry until the words burst from her, but maybe the truth was that anger had nothing to do with what was happening to her. Unable to meet his intense gaze, she held her hands out palms-up so she could catch some of the raindrops. "He's out there, somewhere. Standing in this."

"Don't."

"Don't what?"

He balanced the backpack effortlessly on his left shoulder. His free hand hung by his side and yet she felt herself being drawn to it. "Don't do this to yourself, Shannon," he said. "Worrying about him won't change anything."

"What do you want me to do? Pretend he's at a sleepover with a friend? He isn't." She glared at him, felt his dark eyes begin to absorb her, forced herself to study what she could see of the horizon. "He might be lost. No matter how good he thinks he is, he might be lost."

"Don't," Cord repeated. Without asking, he grasped her wrist and led her back up the steps. Once they were on the porch, he set down his burden and pulled her around until she was forced to look up at him. "The night was hard for you. I'm sorry it had to be like that with nothing to think about except Matt."

She'd thought about a lot more than their son, but she wasn't going to tell him that.

"The inactivity got to you, but it's morning now. I'll find him. He'll be all right. I want you to believe that."

I want to believe in you, Cord. To trust completely. But it isn't that simple. Life never is. "Is that what you tell everyone?" she asked, struggling to keep her voice calm. "That you'll find whoever you're looking for?"

"No. Not always."

She should ask him to explain himself, but something in his tone warned her that this wasn't ground she wanted to tread on this morning. Although she knew it wasn't wise, she looked down at her trapped hands, her safe and secure hands. Cord Navarro, a man with a skill unrivaled by any other, had promised her that nothing bad would happen to her—their—son and she wanted to believe him.

"It's the rain," she admitted after too long a silence. "If it wasn't raining—"

"It'll make finding him harder."

Don't say that, she thought even as she nodded to let him know she understood. Looking up, she struggled to find something brave and optimistic to say. But his midnight eyes were on her, reaching into her.

Although it was the most dangerous thing she could do, she couldn't stop herself from leaning into him. She expected, half hoped that he would push her away. Instead, he folded her into him and held her tight and safe against his wet but warm body. An unsteady breath brought her the scent of shampoo and soap and something else, some memory of smells hidden under seven years of separate living.

Beyond all reason, she wrapped her arms around him and lay her cheek on his chest. Despite her heart's unsteady and unwanted pounding, she heard his own heart beating—beating strong. This man, who'd given her two children, a roof over her head, a reason—once—for living, became her world again. It wouldn't last; it was illusion and delusion, but she would grab it for what it was this stormy morning and take strength from him.

He ran his hand up and down her back, pressing when he reached the base of her spine. He must have meant the gesture to be comforting; certainly he wasn't interested in eliciting any other response from her. But she had no control over what was happening to her, no way of denying the deeply buried woman who, after all these years, wanted him.

Wanted?

No!

Hoping he wouldn't notice that she was shaking, she pushed away until he was no longer touching her. "I'm sorry," she managed. "You're right. I had too much time for thinking last night. It won't happen again."

Chapter 4

Shannon had gone inside ahead of him. By the time he'd placed his backpack on the office floor, she'd left the room. Forcing himself to concentrate on what was automatic and essential about his job, he inventoried his food supply, satisfying himself that he had enough of what could be eaten on the move. He gave the rest of his equipment a quick check. It wasn't full daylight yet, but he should already be under way. He would be if he had only himself to consider.

Standing, he cocked his head to one side and listened, but couldn't determine where Shannon had gone. Maybe she was deliberately keeping quiet so she wouldn't disturb him from what he needed to concentrate on. Or maybe she'd decided to distance herself as much as possible from him.

He wouldn't blame her. After all, she couldn't have wanted that embrace any more than he had. Except, he admitted with customary frankness, he *had* wanted to feel her against him. Had needed to touch and be touched. If he'd taken anything from the years he'd spent married to Shannon, it was the knowledge that he wasn't an island, a solitary human being, after all. He needed to belong to someone. Except for Matt, he hadn't found anyone.

There, a sound. Following it, he found himself standing at the entrance to Matt's bedroom. Shannon was in there, her back to him as she stared into the jammed and jumbled closet. Some emotion had wrenched the moaning sound from her a few moments ago; he knew that instinctively.

It was a boy's room, complete with sports posters, cowboy boots, a mound of clothes on the floor at the foot of the bed, a stack of nature magazines on a small desk under the window. Matt had told him that his mother had bought him the desk to do his schoolwork on but he preferred to work at the kitchen table closer to his mom. Now the desk held two footballs and a helmet, comic books, a hammer, screwdriver, and pliers. Cord saw something else—the compass he'd given him two years ago. Now Shannon was staring at it, too.

"I'm trying to determine what he took with him," she said, not looking at him. "The backpack frame you gave him is gone. So is his sleeping bag and ground cover."

He'd given Matt all of those things.

"But not the compass," she continued. "He didn't understand why you'd sent it to him. After all, he said, you never use one."

"No. I don't."

She spun toward him. In the shadowed room, he could barely make out her features and nothing of her thoughts. "He wants to be exactly like you, to find his way with the stars and sun. But he doesn't have your... your instinct."

It wasn't instinct. At Gray Cloud's side he'd learned to be at home in the wilderness, something he hadn't been able to teach his son yet because they weren't together enough. Besides, maybe Matt would never need the skills that were vital to his career. Keeping his voice level, he told her that Matt might not need a compass depending on where he'd decided to go. He didn't say that father's instinct was telling him Matt wouldn't stay on the beaten path.

"What else did he take?" he asked. "Can you tell?"

"Food, a lot of it. When he was getting ready to leave yesterday, I teased him about how much he was packing." She blinked and he thought he detected a hint of moisture in her eyes. "Cord, he had more than enough food for two boys for a couple of days. Alone..."

Alone he might be able to survive without hardship for the better part of a week, but Matt had told Kevin to let Shannon know he'd be gone only two nights. He reminded her of that now.

Shannon stood next to Matt's bed, her fingers resting lightly on the pillow. Now that he'd gotten used to the lamplight, he was able to make out much more of her, her practical jeans and boots, the loose cotton shirt that clung damply to her generous breasts and accented her slender waist.

"I can feel him in here," she said. "I know it shouldn't make any difference, but it makes me feel better. He's such a mix, part of him still my little boy, the rest trying to be a teenager."

"That's what growing up is about."

"I know," she said with something that wasn't quite a laugh. "But if he was still a toddler, he wouldn't be in this predicament."

And we wouldn't be standing here talking. I'd be out of your hair, your life. "You like challenges yourself," he observed.

"Yes, I do. But I'm also disgustingly practical. A tax-paying member of the middle class. I'm not a rock-headed

ten-year-old with more energy and dumb determination than
sense."

"Rock-headed?"

"Stubborn. Strong-willed. Whatever you want to call it.
Anyway—" She looked around, as if trying to reorient herself. "That backpack frame is his most prized possession. I
can't remember how many times he's had me watch him
walk around with it on. He says the fit and balance is just
right, that he...that he could hike all day with it on his back
and not get tired."

He wanted to comfort her and again reassure her that
everything was going to turn out all right, but he couldn't
concentrate on that with what she'd just told him making its
impact. Something he'd sent Matt was his prize possession.

"Cord, look."

She had gone back to the closet and was pulling out a
tightly wrapped tent—the domed model he and Matt had
picked out together the Christmas before last.

"And he didn't take his propane stove, either," she continued. "No tent. No stove. What was he thinking?"

Cord leaned against the doorjamb, easily imagining Matt
sleeping in this room. "I bought him the tent and stove so
he could go camping with his friends, but he knows I don't
use either of those things."

She seemed to sway a little. "In other words, he wants to
do everything you do the way you do. Walk around without a compass. Sleep under the stars—or in the rain. Eat
nothing but cold food. Damn you, Cord."

There was no anger behind Shannon's words, and he
didn't take offense. Instead, he was glad she'd been able to
discharge a little of the tension she must be feeling.

"Shannon—"

"Don't tell me he's going to be all right. I don't want to hear that when neither of us has any idea what he's doing. Or where he is."

He'd been about to ask if Matt had been wearing riding or hiking boots, but didn't. Instead he studied her standing in their son's room and knew he would never forget the sight. Then he turned and walked back down the dark hall. He didn't want to leave her in there alone, but she'd lived without him for the past seven years and didn't need him for anything anymore—except to return her son to her.

When she came out of Matt's room, Shannon was again struck by how silent Cord could be. She'd long known he wasn't a man for words, but it seemed that he could walk around in hiking boots without making a sound. For all she knew, he'd left the house.

A bolt of fear tore through her and she hurried outside, not taking time to close the door behind her. If Cord had left without her—

He hadn't; hadn't she all but tripped over the pack he'd left on her office floor? Even Cord had enough social grace and compassion and understanding not to disappear without telling her where he was going.

But he wasn't going anywhere by himself!

A new fear, laced through with heavy determination, settled inside her. They hadn't discussed today's agenda. Certainly he planned to resume last night's search; what she hadn't told him was that she was committed to going with him. She didn't care how much resistance he might throw at her. She was *not* going to endure any more of this doing nothing.

"Shannon."

Although Cord's voice came to her from some distance away, she still jumped. He was out in the corral, and she started toward him. The rain showed no sign of slackening, and if anything, the wind was stronger than it had been a few minutes ago. Soon she was soaked to the skin. For some unexplainable reason, she embraced the pure, lilting sound and the wind. "What?" she asked when she was close enough that she didn't have to raise her voice.

"What horses do you want to take?"

Horses. As soon as she pointed out the two geldings she had in mind, Cord went after them. She now felt chilled in her dripping, oversize shirt and berated herself for not grabbing a jacket. Cord, however, seemed impervious to the weather.

"You knew, didn't you?" she said as she led one of the horses into the barn to be saddled and bridled while Cord brought the other. "That I was going with you."

"Yeah, I knew."

Did he want her to come? It didn't matter. "What are we going to do? I don't know how you can possibly track him with these conditions."

"It'll make it harder—I won't deny that. But I've done it before." Picking up a large old towel she kept for such purposes, he started wiping off one of the gelding's backs prior to saddling him. His movements were so practiced that she had to remind herself that he hadn't been part of her business. He didn't belong in this shadowed, hay-smelling barn; he wouldn't be content spending hours in it the way she did. Still, maybe he now understood a little more of her world.

"I've been thinking," he continued. His voice echoed in the high-ceilinged space. "I want to run this past you and get your reaction. Matt told Kevin that he wants to prove himself to me, right?"

"Yes."

"If that's his intention, then he wants to give himself as much of a challenge as possible."

"I . . . guess."

"Guess?"

"All right!" When her horse shied, she forced herself to lower her voice. "Yes, I think you're right. But where—"

"You said he's fascinated by Arapaho. Last night I didn't have the chance to really explore it. I want to go back there, look at it through his eyes."

If it had been anyone else speaking, she would have laughed at the possibility of seeing a demanding ski area through the eyes of a ten-year-old boy, but this was a man who made his living getting into other people's heads before the terrain, elements, or their own limitations and stupidity killed them. He was also that ten-year-old boy's father.

"How long do you think it's going to take?" she made herself ask.

"I can't tell you that. No one can."

"But you've done this before. You must have some kind of idea."

He did. The way his eyes darkened told her that. But instead of telling her what she probably didn't want to hear anyway, he shrugged his competent shoulders and asked if she'd told her parents yet.

"No," she admitted. "Last night, well, I kept hoping you'd come back with him and there wouldn't be any need. It's so early. They might still be asleep."

"They have a right. And they'd want to be part of this, to help."

"I know. It's just—they love him so, Cord. I don't want to scare them."

"They're strong people."

Yes, they were. Although Cord had been somewhat distant around her parents, probably a combination of his natural reserve and the belief that they held him responsible for their daughter becoming a mother at eighteen, he understood them better than she thought possible.

In the end, he was the one who made the phone call.

"Elizabeth," Cord said while she stood a few feet away, "it's Cord. I'm at Shannon's house. Matt didn't come home last night. We're going after him."

He stopped talking and she could hear the murmur of her mother's voice. A few moments later he basically repeated what he'd already said and then asked if they could come over and handle her business while they were gone. Closing her eyes, Shannon marveled at his ability to think of that when she should have been the one to plan for her absence. She opened her eyes again when he spoke her name. Taking the phone from him, she managed to mouth the lie that she wasn't worried, just determined to get Matt home and dry. After some brief reassurances, she finally hung up.

"You're sure you don't want anyone else out there with you—with us?" Shannon asked Cord. "Every time I hear about searches, especially when children are missing, half the people in the county are involved."

He'd been standing off to one side with his arms folded across his chest while she spoke to her parents. Now he fastened his fingers around her elbows and pulled her close. She looked up at him, seeing what the past seven years had done to his once boyish features. "This is different."

"How? Because it's your son? If you're worried that your reputation will be damaged if people learn that your son is the one they're—"

"It's not that."

Of course it wasn't. She had no business saying that. "Then, what is it? Cord, I don't know how you run your business any more than you know how I handle mine. But I'm all too aware of how vast, how isolated this area is. I'd think you'd want as many eyes and ears out there as possible. Is it—you don't want to waste time getting people together?"

"Half the people in the county can't do any more than I can alone."

"You're that sure of yourself?" She couldn't keep the disbelief out of her voice.

"I know what I'm doing, Shannon. The question is, do you trust me?"

His question was impossible; surely he understood that. Hadn't she once trusted—expected—him to support her and Matt? But instead of keeping his factory job with its steady paycheck, he'd gone to the county sheriff, the state police, the forest service, anyone who might have a use for his skills. She'd been so afraid of the uncertainty facing them that she'd taken a part-time job in addition to her college courses. But he wasn't asking her to step into the past. He needed to know whether she believed he would find their son.

"If anyone can find Matt, it's you."

He nodded at that and released her. Although she was now free to back away from him, she remained where she was and breathed in the smell of wet cotton and denim. She wanted him to tell her that her trust was well placed and he wouldn't fail her. But he didn't. Instead he told her what she needed to bring in the way of clothes, and because they couldn't leave until she'd done that, she turned and started toward her room. Her back between her shoulder blades felt warm, as if they'd been touched by him. But then, maybe it was only because she needed the contact—a contact he couldn't give her.

Cord waited until he heard Shannon's dresser drawer open and then dialed the country sheriff at his home. Although it was barely 6:00 a.m., Dale Vollrath answered before the second ring. "Cord? What the hell are you doing? Do you have any idea what time it is?"

"Unfortunately, yes," he told the man who'd already been on the police force when he was still in high school. He quickly explained what he and Shannon were up to. Unlike Shannon, Dale didn't ask whether he wanted local search and rescue volunteers called out.

"This is your call, Cord," Dale said. "Just tell me what you need from me."

"Nothing right now. I'll be getting in touch with you from time to time to give you updates. I'd like the same thing from you."

"You got it. I'll contact anyone and everyone I can think of around Arapaho or the other wilderness areas. A nephew of mine is doing fire watch for the forest service this summer. He's still wet behind the ears, but he can see a hell of a long way from his tower. Who knows. He might be more reliable than I give him credit for."

"I'd appreciate it."

"No problem. The more eyes you've got working for you, the better."

The sheriff had given him his first break. Although Cord hadn't gone through the formal training most search and rescue personnel received, Dale had called him to lead an expedition to find skiers buried by an avalanche on Copper. The mission had attracted widespread media attention and when Cord refused to quit until he'd found the last survivor two days after the avalanche, the wire services had picked up the story. As a result, he'd started getting calls from all over the country.

"We'll have to get together for a beer," he told Dale. "Just as soon as I get Matt back where he belongs. What does the activity on the mountains look like?"

"Unauthorized activity. That's what you're talking about, isn't it?"

He said yes, alert for sounds of Shannon's return.

"Yeah," Dale said after a brief pause. "Yeah. Maybe. The only thing I've got is a report from a couple of forest service employees who were working on Breckenridge a few days ago. They heard shots, and when they checked it out, they spotted four, maybe five men with rifles. The men were pretty far away and on the move. By the time the rangers got there, the poachers were gone. My guess, they realized they'd been made and took off."

"You're sure they were poachers?" Cord asked, not because he questioned Dale's conclusion but because this was the last thing he wanted to hear.

"There's nothing I can take to court, but I've been a cop too long not to know the signs. Several men with rifles in the wilderness when it isn't hunting season. They wouldn't go all that way for a little target practice. Come on, Cord. You know how that adds up as well as I do."

"Yeah. I do."

"Look, don't go getting uptight over this. Like you said, your son could be anywhere. There's a hell of a lot of territory around here. Chances are, even if those characters haven't hightailed it, your son won't get anywhere near them."

"Dale? I've seen what poachers can do."

The sheriff let out a long, hissing breath. "That killing in Utah last fall. That's what you're thinking about, isn't it? I forgot."

Cord hadn't. Although he'd seen a lot of things in his career he wished he hadn't, the accidental killing of an elderly man and the wounding of his wife by a couple of drunken hunters stood out in his mind.

"I'll tell you what." Dale broke through his thoughts. "I'll get in touch with forest service employees all over the county as soon as we're done talking. I know a couple of local pilots who'll probably check out Breckenridge for me. Anything I hear, I'll pass on to you."

"Thanks. I'd appreciate that. And, Dale? I'd like to keep this between you and me. Shannon has enough on her mind without adding anything to it."

"You got it. Look, Matt can be anywhere. He might have no interest in Breckenridge."

Maybe. Maybe not, Cord thought after hanging up. What made this so hard was having to face the simple fact that he didn't honestly know what was going on inside his son's head. That, and vivid memories of what a bullet was capable of.

At the sound of Shannon's boots on the floor, he shoved thoughts of Matt's possible agenda and whether that might bring him in contact with poachers to the back of his mind. His ex-wife. No matter how many times he'd told himself that that was what she was, he'd been unable to exorcise the memories of when she'd been his wife.

Other people, even men aware of how attractive she was, would look at her today and see a competent businesswoman, a strong and mature woman capable of facing everything life dished out, even this.

But deep in her hazel eyes, fear lurked. She wouldn't talk to him about it, and he wouldn't bring it up. Avoiding anything of an emotional nature was one of the few rules that defined their relationship these days. They could talk about their respective jobs and lives, their son, her family, the price of gasoline, politics, anything casual friends might discuss. But as for what went on deep inside them—oh, yes, he knew how to avoid that.

"You were talking to someone?" she asked.

"Dale Vollrath."

"The sheriff? What did he have to say?"

"Not much. Just that he's going to do what he can here on the ground."

She gave him a sideways look but didn't say anything. When she dropped to her knees beside her backpack, he joined her. Still silent, she handed him her spare clothes and watched as he secured her belongings. Her hair hung wetly around her cheeks. He wanted to brush back the strands, wanted to flatten his palms against the side of her neck and hold her there while he kissed her.

Most of all, he wanted to tell her that their son was in no danger, and believe his own words.

Although her parents had said they'd be over right away, Cord wasn't waiting for them to arrive. Following his lead, Shannon stepped outside. She stood in the cool drizzle and tried to be grateful because both the wind and rain had slackened.

He hadn't said a word to her since telling her that he'd been talking to the sheriff, but he didn't need to for her to understand that he was in a hurry to be on his way.

Shoving aside her insane wish to be anywhere but here and doing this, she mounted and checked the pack she'd secured behind her saddle. She briefly wondered why Cord hadn't helped her, then realized he hadn't because he needed to know how she was going to handle the physical demands.

Fine, she told him silently. *Whatever you do, wherever you go, I'll match you.*

Cord, sitting tall and nearly motionless, rode ahead of her. She'd never seen him look more like his Ute grandfather, more in tune with his wet, green, brown, and gray world. He hadn't said anything about their needing to be quiet so he could listen to his surroundings or whatever it was he did at a time like this. She hoped he would be honest with her about what she needed to do to be the most help but until they'd picked up Matt's trail—*please,* she prayed, *let that be soon*—there really wasn't anything to talk about.

The sound of squeaking leather and shod hoofs plopping on wet earth kept her aware of where they were. After wiping moisture off her forehead and then deciding it was a useless gesture, she prodded her horse.

She wished she was on Pawnee, taking courage from his strength and energy, but the young, strong, and excitable gelding was with her son—taking him too far from her. There was nothing wrong with the horses she'd chosen, nothing except that they wouldn't go as fast as she needed them to. But it wasn't the horses' fault. Cord set the pace and he seemed to be in no hurry.

She wanted to yell at him and remind him that they had to get out of this high, wide meadow where she'd established her business and reach Arapaho as quickly as possible. But when she took note of the way Cord kept his eyes locked on his surroundings, his alert stance, how he cocked his head sometimes as if listening to something no other human could possibly hear, she understood that he'd thrown his entire being into this task.

What did he see, hear, sense?

Was it good? Bad?

And if bad, how, as Matt's father, did he deal with it? Maybe, if she told him how horribly hard this was for her, he'd be just as honest and they could draw strength from each other.

Maybe.

"Why couldn't he have at least picked a sunny day?" she asked, because she was going crazy listening to the thoughts clanging around in her head. "There's probably a law

somewhere that says kids are required to do the most illogical things in the most illogical ways so they can give their
parents the maximum number of gray hairs.''

Cord said nothing. Only slightly aware of the sound the
rain made as it sluiced through pine needles on the way to
the earth, she blinked water out of her eyes. She probably
should have worn her slicker instead of sticking it in her
backpack, but it wasn't that cold and too much clothing re-
stricted her movement. She fastened her attention on her
hands wrapped around the reins.

Finally they reached the first of the trees that marked the
boundary of her property. Feeling slightly claustrophobic,
she concentrated, or tried to concentrate, on the sounds the
horses were making, the taste and feel of mountain air.

She couldn't keep her eyes off Cord.

Her son's father was painted in earth tones. Even his jeans
seemed more brown than blue, a gentle fading of color until he'd become one with his environment. There were times
when life took him out of the wilderness, but even then, she
suspected, he carried his beloved world inside him. She'd
never seen him in a suit; she doubted that he owned one.

Good.

He should always remain part of the elements.

But emotionally apart from her when what they were doing was taking every bit of self-control and courage she had?

The past seven years hadn't changed anything. It was no
different from when . . .

She refused to let herself finish the thought.

Chapter 5

Cord ran his left hand down his pant leg. For one of the few times in his life, he didn't feel comfortable in his own body.

It hurt, not just being unable to reach out and touch his son today, but facing how much he was missing of Matt's growing up. In truth, he hated that most of all the things that couldn't be changed in his life—he hated the holes in his heart that he didn't fully understand. Closing his mind to the pain had always ensured his emotional survival. But life seldom felt as raw as it did today.

If they kept up this pace, they'd soon have to rest the horses. Still, although Arapaho was already dead ahead, he couldn't make himself slow down, and Shannon hadn't said anything about conserving her horses' energy. Shannon, with her long legs and active life-style, shouldn't have any trouble keeping up with him today and longer if it came to that. When he'd first seen her this morning, with her rich brown hair braided down her back, his defenses hadn't had time to lock into place and he'd come within a breath of telling her she looked like an Indian maiden, beautiful, desirable. But she wouldn't want to hear that from him any more than he wanted to give voice to his thoughts.

If, in spite of the damage caused by the rain, he could locate Pawnee's prints at the base of Arapaho, he would have a purpose, a plan, a goal. He'd no longer be susceptible to distraction, something that never happened when he was on a search. It had been dark much of the time he'd been here last night, which meant he could have missed his son's signs. The other possibility, one he hadn't told Shannon about but she must have considered, was that Matt wasn't anywhere near Arapaho.

Experience had taught him not to let his mind tangle in the unknown. Still, it wasn't easy to turn his thoughts from the very personal object of his search to what might happen today. If Matt intended to explore Arapaho, he would have to abandon his horse when the trail got too steep. Although the rain would wash away many of the signs the boy made, if he stepped where the ground was level and the dirt dense, he would leave footprints. If that happened and if Cord was very, very lucky, he might overtake his son before nightfall. He wouldn't have to go on looking at Shannon, thinking about what they'd once had and shared—and lost. They would go back to their separate lives and he'd find a way to stop thinking about the body of the woman who'd carried his children.

What if Matt was trying to hide?

There was another possibility. One he hadn't mentioned because he'd wanted to spare Shannon any more burdens. Lost people, especially children, typically zigzagged aimlessly through the woods, making it difficult to separate a path made earlier in the day from a more recent one.

He accepted that Matt might not understand enough about wilderness survival to know how to mark his trail so he would have a guideline in case he had to backtrack. And he wasn't sure Matt would be aware enough of his surroundings to tell if he was going in circles. From a distance, climbing a mountain seemed like a straightforward objective but, surrounded by trees or rocks, the goal could be easily lost.

He should have taught his son more about how to be at home in the wilderness, how to control his environment, instead of the other way around. He'd planned on doing that this summer. But maybe—no, it wouldn't be too late!

Straightening, he focused on what lay around him. The trees at this altitude grew in random, healthy clumps. In some areas, the pines were so close together that sunlight never reached the ground. Given the right motivation or camouflage, any animal or human being could blend into the dense shadows and even he might not see them. Still, every fiber and nerve ending in him said that his son wasn't nearby. *His son.* How he loved the words.

Classroom learning was important; he knew that. A structured setting, friends, familiar surroundings gave a child a solid foundation. That's why Cord hadn't asked Shannon to share custody of Matt, though he wanted his son with all his heart. With his work, he couldn't offer Matt true stability. How could a child keep up at school if his father constantly dragged him around the country, or left him with baby-sitters?

Shannon was a good mother. A wonderful mother. He had only to look into her eyes and see into her nurturing heart to believe that. She might be able to keep a great deal from him, but not everything.

Somehow he knew there hadn't been many men in her life since their divorce. Maybe it was in the way she conducted herself, her awareness of, or rather, her disregard for, her physical body. When she spoke of "we" it was always about her and Matt and sometimes her parents. She'd had a single male wrangler last year, a man Matt thought fascinating because he'd once been on the rodeo circuit. Matt said that the man sometimes asked Shannon to go to a movie or dinner with him but she never had. After three or four months, the wrangler had moved on, and according to Matt, Shannon had said she was glad to see him gone.

But someday a new man would walk into Shannon's life—and into Matt's, as well.

When that happened . . .

Like a well-trained tool, Cord's mind switched to his reason for being here and what he needed to see and hear and smell and sense. He was still aware of Shannon's presence behind him, but his attention was now fully trained on the ground. Despite the effects of rain, he could tell horses had recently been along the main trail that ringed the base of Arapaho. Whether the prints were made by Matt's mount or by any number of vacationers, he couldn't say.

He would put his training and instinct to use when the mountain started giving up its secrets—if it had any—to him.

Because he'd done it before, he easily put himself in the mind of a ten-year-old. At that age he'd already spent more than a week alone in the wilderness, soaking dew from rocks with a handkerchief and wringing the moisture into his mouth to slake his thirst. He'd eaten wild rose hips, the inner bark from pine trees, pigweed, and returned to his grandfather, not full, but not hungry, either.

Gray Cloud had praised his accomplishment and then told him he'd come within a quarter mile of a lynx den. Had Cord seen the signs? He hadn't, but by the time he slept under an old growth pine a month later, he'd trained himself to be aware of every predator and prey for a mile around.

Matt wouldn't be, and that worried him. The big cats and few black bears who lived around here wouldn't bother human beings, but although he'd taught Matt that, the lesson might not have stuck. After all, the boy had sat through a long, dark, wet night with nothing to do except listen and think. Who knew what his young, fertile imagination might have come up with? Somehow he had to give Matt peace.

He straightened, his free hand automatically reaching behind to check the pack that held the two-way radio, waterproof matches, a multitool knife, his sleeping bag and mat, the first-aid kit, food. There was good thinking and bad thinking. He had to stay in his son's head, not remember some of the things he'd seen in his years of trying to bring people back alive to where they belonged.

It was fully light now although the rain made a lie of the fact that this was June. Fog clung to the ground in a number of deep pockets, and Cord couldn't see the tops of the tallest trees. From the looks of the clouds, he didn't expect the drizzle to let up for several hours. By the feel of the air on his cheeks, he gauged the temperature to be about fifty degrees. Most people, if they were dry and wore a light jacket and remained active, could stay out all day in this temperature. Thankfully there wasn't enough breeze for a wind chill to factor in, but Matt was probably at a higher elevation and maybe wet.

That was why he hadn't worn a jacket. He wanted to experience the worst of what his son might. He felt a cool bite along the back of his neck and down his shoulders, but he was used to being exposed and had long ago stopped perceiving cold as discomfort. It wouldn't be the same for his son.

Turning in the saddle, he spoke to Shannon. "It's going to warm up more. Even with the rain, we'll get at least another ten degrees. That'll help."

She nodded and gave him a quick smile. Still, her eyes telegraphed her concern. He wondered if she knew how transparent she was. "I can't keep thinking," she said. "What if his granola bars get wet? I wonder if he'll eat them anyway."

"He will." He leaned forward to make it easier for his horse to climb a short hill and then explained that most people out like this wound up eating anything and everything that was remotely palatable.

"What happens when he runs out of food?"

"Then he gets hungry."

"Then, hopefully, he'll get serious about hustling back home."

It was more complicated than that. Still, he held back from spelling out those complications to her. The tightness around the corners of her mouth made it clear that she knew how serious things were. Yet, she wasn't making impossible demands on him or allowing fear to have the upper hand. He wanted to thank her for that, to compliment her self-control.

He also wanted to draw her attention to the wind's fragrance, the messages spread by birds and insects, the rhythm of nature to her.

He didn't ask himself why.

"What are you looking for?" Shannon asked when it seemed that Cord had been gazing around him forever.

"For patterns," her ex-husband said, the words coming slow and soft. "My grandfather called it *the spirit that moves in all things*. Once I've found the pattern, the rhythm here, I'll know what the spirit is telling me."

Did Cord really think she would buy that business about patterns and spirits? Yes, she'd heard him mention such things in the past and had tried to understand what he was saying, but he talked about insight and instinct, making what he did sound like philosophy, not tracking. And, she could now admit, for too much of the time they were together, she'd been so wrapped up in her own life that she hadn't truly listened. She—they—had been so young.

"What is *the spirit that moves in all things* telling you?" she asked as a gust of wind shook the nearby trees.

"That this is a people place, a part of nature that has been touched by many and changed."

She looked around her. As far as she was concerned, they were in the wilderness. There weren't any buildings, chimney smoke rising in the air, livestock. Yes, Arapaho had been scarred by ski trails and lifts, but there weren't any nearby and they were idle this time of year. The trees grew so thickly here that even without the rain and ground fog, it would have been impossible to see more than a few feet beyond the trail. She felt completely isolated from the rest of the world. How could Cord say that the wilderness had been changed by mankind?

But Cord knew things, sensed things no one else did; she had no doubt of that. And when he spoke this morning, she listened to the words, the sound, the energy in him, and used those things to keep from losing her mind.

"Does being in a people place make it more difficult for you?" she asked.

"It's going to make finding Matt take longer. His spirit is mixed in with the spirit of others."

"Spirit? I guess that's as good a name to give what you're looking for as anything. Is that how your grandfather referred to—to . . . I don't have a word for what you're talking about."

"Not many people do. Gray Cloud had a unique way of describing the wilderness, mystical almost. I've held on to his descriptions because that's better than anything I could come up with."

"Like the way he gave credit to the Great Spirit for everything," she offered, almost without knowing she was going to say the words, words she'd never forgotten. "I remember you telling me that Gray Cloud believed that in nature everything lives in harmony. That an ant is as important as a bear."

"And that we must see with our hearts and that the wind speaks to us and in the wilderness there is only the present."

"The present," she echoed. "Time, as we think of it, had no meaning for your grandfather, did it? 'The rhythm of nature is slow, steady, and has a beat all its own. The ground itself has a heart, and if one knows how to listen, he can hear it.'"

"You remember more than I thought you did."

She concentrated on the gentle, deep-throated question and asked herself why those lessons and more had stayed with her all these years. She wanted to tell Cord that she'd never forgotten Gray Cloud's wisdom and had, almost instinctively, incorporated some of it into her life. But they'd come to the first steep rise in the trail. Before much longer they'd leave behind the civilization Cord still sensed. Then, hopefully, he'd be able to put his unique skills to work and find their son. He'd hear the earth's heart and it would tell him what he needed to know. Maybe she'd be able to listen with him.

Listen to a heartbeat that didn't exist? What was she thinking? Had fear for Matt unhinged her? Or was Cord somehow responsible?

Repositioning herself in the saddle, she wondered why she felt uncomfortable when usually she could ride all day without becoming weary. The rain hadn't changed its gentle, almost lazy cadence, thank heavens. Because they were surrounded by trees now, she could hear the wind's song as it eased its way through the treetops.

She and Cord hadn't been married more than a few weeks when she first heard him speak of the sound the wind made as a ballad. Back then she'd held on to his every word, awed by his knowledge of what took place beyond roads and telephone wires. His understanding of her, at least her body, had been just as complete. He'd played her as the wind plays with the treetops and her body had sung to him.

When it went wrong between them, she'd forgotten that there were things he knew more about than any other human alive.

At least, she'd thought she'd forgotten.

Here, in his world, as she joined in his effort to find their son, too much was coming back to her.

She felt like crying, like singing. And she wished there weren't so many years and silences between them.

Cord stopped, reining his horse gradually and gently. He straightened, seeming to lift his body fully off the mare's back, then cocked his head to one side. The gesture was all it took for Shannon to know he wanted her to listen, as well. Gradually the sound came.

Frogs. Dozens and dozens of frogs. They sang their discordant notes with full-throated joy, proclaiming their delight at having it rain. Up until that moment she had been thinking about the creatures, and the boy, who must be seeking shelter from the drizzle.

But some, like frogs, embraced rain.

"Do you think the frogs know we're here?" she asked.

"They know," Cord explained. "But we don't represent a threat to them."

She chuckled at that. "Matt loves it when the ones who live in the pond behind our place start croaking. Sometimes, when they get going while he's trying to fall asleep, he leans out his window and yells at them to shut up."

"Do they?"

"For a moment. Then they start up again. He had a frog for a pet once. He brought it flies and kept water in its bucket."

"What happened to it?"

"It died. I told him it would, but he had to see for himself the consequences of his intervention."

When she looked at Cord, he was nodding, the movement slow and unconscious and so graceful that she felt it deep in her belly. "I'm glad you gave him the experience, although I doubt that the frog would agree. That's how we all learn. At least, the best lessons. Not because someone tells us, but from doing something ourselves."

"I agree," she said, shaken by the depth and breadth of his comment. "Since then, Matt's never wanted to control another wild animal. He doesn't even like it when orphaned or injured animals have to be penned up until they're ready to be re-released into their environment. I don't think he's ever going to hunt."

Cord didn't hunt. Once he'd been offered an incredible sum of money to guide some wealthy hunters with more determination than savvy, but he'd refused. He hadn't offered her an explanation of why he'd made that decision. She hadn't needed one because she knew he believed that no amount of money could atone for putting an end to a wild life.

Because she needed to free herself from yet another memory, she asked Cord if he knew that Matt wanted to be a search and rescue expert when he grew up. Her words turned Cord around again.

"He told me that, but I thought he might be saying it for my sake."

"He means it." Cord was backlit and nearly surrounded by forest. It was almost as if the trees had taken claim of him, as if he'd given them permission to do so. If she didn't keep her eyes on him, he might slide away into nothing like morning mist when the sun hits it. "He thinks the world of you—you must know that. Of course, he tends to idealize what you do."

Cord's mouth tightened. "And he thinks he knows more than he does."

He wouldn't if you'd taught him the way Gray Cloud did you. But that was unfair. Cord had lived with Gray Cloud. Cord didn't see enough of his son. As for whether that bothered Cord, she couldn't say. "Most children are like that. So darn cocky. He'll learn from his mistakes, unfortunately—we all do."

"Do we?"

"Yes," she said without giving herself time to think. "If I hadn't been so tied up inside myself when we separated, I would have done some things differently."

"Like what?"

"Like—" Was she ready for this? No matter. It was too late to turn back. "Like asking you to live closer so you could be with Matt more." Matt. That's who she needed to think about, not what couldn't be changed.

"You want that?"

"That's not my decision, Cord. It's yours." Because trees grew close to the trail here and he had to concentrate on where he was going, she found herself speaking to his back.

"I did what I had to," he said.

What did he mean by that? She hadn't pushed him away, had she? "I'm surprised you didn't go back to your grand-father's cabin." If he needed quiet, he'd tell her. Other-wise, talking was better than listening to what insisted on going on inside her. "Oh, I know it's barely habitable the way it is, but it could be fixed up. It shouldn't be that hard to get electricity to it, or phone service. Still—" She weighed the wisdom of saying anything, then plunged ahead. "I rather like it the way it is. Rugged. Primitive."

"Hmm."

Hmm wasn't enough of a reply to hang a conversation on. Still, although he would probably prefer it, she didn't feel ready to retreat into silence. "You heard from the local his-toric society, didn't you? I know they'd love to buy it and turn it into some kind of landmark."

"I talked to them."

"And what did you tell them?" she asked, although she'd bet everything she had that she knew the answer.

"That I can't give up the only thing that remains of the man who raised me."

That admission, so intensely personal from an intensely private man, sent a chill through her. Fighting to keep her reaction from him, she told him that was what Matt had said his response would be.

"I've taken Matt there a few times," Cord said. "What about you?"

"A few," she acknowledged. Her thoughts spun away from their conversation and settled in the past. Cord had taken her to his grandfather's cabin the day after she'd told him about being pregnant. A few days later he'd told her that she was the only girl he'd ever wanted to show the log walls and shake roof of the little place Gray Cloud had built. He'd admitted he'd wondered if she'd laugh at the not-quite-square sides, or if she could possibly understand why he'd been content growing up in a place without electricity.

She hadn't laughed. Instead, she'd run her fingertips over the sleek peeled logs his grandfather had lifted into place more than fifty years ago. She'd bent, taken a deep breath, and then told him she could smell pitch and pine and hoped that the aromas would never fade. Finally she'd touched the corner of the handmade kitchen table where Gray Cloud had carved an eagle in flight. "I wish I'd known him," she'd said. "There's so much of him in you."

They'd made love on the sagging old mattress Cord had always slept on, two kids still discovering the wonder and excitement and fear of sharing themselves with each other— and the consequences of surrendering to that wonder. He'd held her and pressed his hands over her full breasts, then brushed his lips against her belly. Although he said nothing, his eyes had told her that he was just beginning to grasp that his child was growing inside her.

When their lovemaking was done, he'd stood naked in front of her and it was all she could do to keep from losing herself in the sight. His long, dark hair had sheltered him somehow and those incredible eyes of his had looked both trapped and awestruck, and she'd known he couldn't decide whether to run for freedom or stay.

In the end, he'd pulled her against him and awkwardly told her that he'd be there for her and their baby. Nothing about that afternoon had faded from her mind. She'd given up hoping it would.

Today the memories were stronger than they'd ever been.

They were giving the horses a breather and Cord was giving Shannon a brief sketch of what country he'd covered last night when his walkie-talkie squawked to life. Afraid it might be the sheriff with news he didn't want to share with

her if at all possible, he thought about moving away from
her before answering, but that would only make her suspi-
cious, only drive more of a wedge between them.

"Cord. It's Hallem. Kevin's father. I wasn't sure how I
was going to get in touch with you. Thank heavens, you left
this receiver with Shannon's parents."

"That's where you are?" he asked. "You have news?"

"Maybe. Hopefully, although I'm not sure it's the kind
of news you want to hear."

He watched as Shannon moved closer. He read fear and
determination in her eyes. "We're both here," he told Hallem. "What is it?"

"I've been grilling my son. Unfortunately for him, I know
him better than he wishes I did. He was keeping something
to himself and it was eating him alive, something that's going to make things easier for you to round up that kid of
yours."

Shannon gripped his forearm with so much strength that
it tore his attention from what Hallem was saying. Glanc-
ing at her, he now saw hope swimming in her eyes, hope and
a giddy, unrestrained, too fragile joy.

Before he had to ask Hallem what he was talking about,
Kevin's father continued. "The boys had a fight, all right,
and that's probably why Kevin was so slow to fess up. He
didn't say so, but I know he wanted to see how much trouble Matt could get himself into because no one had a clue
where he was. Unfortunately, you've got a lot of back-
tracking to do. Cord, Shannon, if we can believe Kevin, and
I believe we can now, your son is determined to climb Copper Mountain."

Chapter 6

Copper. Although he'd climbed the well-known skiing mecca numerous times, today Cord thought of it not as one of the most popular winter sports centers in the state, but as untracked miles punctuated by steep climbs, uncertain footing and, maybe, men with killing on their minds.

"Why would he do that?" Shannon asked Hallem while Cord tried to clamp down on emotions that threatened to get in the way of what he needed to do.

"My guess is, he wants to prove himself, Shannon," Hallem replied, his voice fading a little. "Apparently our sons had a heated disagreement about Matt's ability to walk in his dad's footsteps."

The mountain extended twelve thousand feet above sea level and although it literally swarmed with people in the winter, this was summer. Except for the very occasional hiker, it would remain essentially deserted until the snows began to fall. Deserted except for those determined to take advantage of the isolation to bring down one or more of the wild animals that called the area their home. The need to get back in touch with the sheriff to share what he'd just learned pounded at Cord, but he forced himself to wait. He would protect her from knowing everything. He couldn't give her her son, but he could do this.

"Did Kevin say any more about how much food Matt had with him?" he made himself ask.

"It sounded like a lot, at least it would be if he wasn't expending so much energy. I wish I could tell you more than that, but I really think I've gotten everything out of Kevin this time. He did say that Matt had his determined look on."

Cord knew that look. He'd seen it first when, at ten months, Matt had decided he'd had enough of crawling and was ready to walk. Matt's commitment to his goals, whether they were wise or not, made Cord's heart swell with pride. He walked a fine line between reminding Matt of life's dangers and pitfalls and letting his son know he trusted him. Most of the time his trust in his son's judgment was well placed.

However, there was no question that Matt was out of his element this time. Not only had the boy seriously underestimated the amount of time it would take him to climb Copper, but he hadn't taken the weather into account. Nor had it occurred to him that he might not have the mountain to himself.

After thanking Hallem for his information, Cord turned, looking for Shannon, then stopped. She stood maybe a hundred feet away, her back to him. She'd finally put on a jacket. It followed the lines of her body nearly as faithfully as her blouse did. Her long, dark hair lay in a submissive coil along her spine. Her jeans seemed to have shrunk. They hugged her legs and hips, challenging him, nearly distracting him from what he'd just learned and what was ahead of them.

I'm sorry. I never wanted our son to try to prove himself this way. If anything happens to him—

"Shannon, it's going to take us at least three hours just to reach Copper."

She spun around. "I know. Damn it, I know," she said, her fingers curled into fists. "And after that, we have to climb that damnable mountain because our son is so desperate and determined to win your approval that he's willing to risk his life to do it."

Her eyes threw fire at him, fire and fear and an anger he knew neither of them could control. There'd been no anger in her after Summer's death, only grief and hopelessness. And isolation. He hadn't known what to do with those emotions any more than he knew how to handle what she was feeling right now. Still, he had to try. "What do you want me to say?"

"Nothing." She stalked closer, holding her body as if it was a weapon she might launch at him. "Nothing at all."

Pawnee nickered and bumped his nose against Matt's shoulder in an effort to get at the apple. Matt took two more bites and then gave the core to the gelding.

"You're doing pretty good," he said, not because Pawnee needed to be told that but because he needed to hear a human voice, even if it was only his own. "This rain sucks. And it's steeper than I thought it'd be. You're going to have to go back after a while. You'll go straight home, won't you? Mom'll have a fit if anything happens to you."

He frowned as he tried to come to a conclusion that had eluded him earlier. Although it was impossible to see to the top from where he stood, he'd been high up on the mountain in a ski lift any number of times and it hadn't been all that big a deal. The way he figured it, he would reach the top by evening even with the stupid rain. He'd have to spend the night there, but getting back down in the morning was no big deal. He'd be home right when he told Kevin he would be—if Pawnee was waiting where he left him. But he wasn't sure of his ability to tie Pawnee right. If the gelding got loose and dragged his rope, he might hurt himself and he didn't want that.

He decided to try out the binoculars his dad had given him. After pulling them out of his backpack, he climbed onto a rock and stood as tall as he could while he looked all around. In most directions, he couldn't see anything except for trees that looked as if they were no more than a few inches away, but off to his right the hill turned into a valley and, beyond that, another distant slope so high that no trees grew at the top. He tried to decide how far away the slope was, but with all the ups and downs, it was impossible to know for sure.

In fact, he wasn't all that sure where he was.

Uncomfortable with the thought, he peered through the binoculars again. Although he'd come across a couple of deer trails, he hadn't seen so much as a single squirrel or chipmunk, let alone anything more interesting. Most likely they'd found a dry place to stay until it stopped raining.

Mist rose in puffs and waves just about everywhere he looked, and he told himself it was because the ground was heating, proof that the darn storm was over. The sun couldn't come out soon enough to suit him. Besides, wet rocks were slippery, and he had a lot of climbing to do before he reached the top of Copper.

Wait a minute. Something didn't look quite right out there. Bringing the binoculars back to what had caught his attention, he concentrated. For longer than he wanted to admit, he couldn't figure out what it was, but then he did. Some of the mist or fog didn't look the same as the rest. It was—yeah—darker.

He wanted to move closer, but that would mean leaving Pawnee here on level ground. He had to satisfy himself with simply watching the dark, thin stream of air.

Only it wasn't air. It was smoke.

"That's really dumb," he told Pawnee. "Don't those people know they're not supposed to have fires up here? I ought to tell..." He'd been about to say that he should tell the forest service, but he couldn't because for all he knew, there weren't any on the mountain today.

Wondering at the stupidity of people who didn't know enough to check in before taking off into the wilderness, he took one last look at what was unquestionably smoke. They were probably city slickers, so dumb they'd wind up getting lost and then have to be rescued. Rescued by his dad maybe.

"Wouldn't that be something," he mused. "Dad and me working together to help those people. I bet he'd like that even better than hearing that I got to the top of Copper all by myself. Mom, too. She'd be proud as anything."

A sudden weight in the region of his heart stopped him. Ever since dawn when he'd tried to keep going in the rain, he'd hardly been able to remember why he'd come here. Now, thinking about the look of pride he'd see on his dad's face, he could hardly wait for the climb to be over so he could see his dad again.

And his mom.

Copper Mountain. A place, an actual place. Where they had to go to retrieve their son. Thank God, they at least knew that.

Cord's shirt had worked its way out of his jeans. It now hung down in front and bunched over his right hip. His wet hair lay dark and thick over his forehead like a living curtain. He was walking and leading his horse just as Shannon was, his eyes trained to the ground, his back gracefully bowed.

Because he worked and tracked and stared at what he needed to see, his journey taking him farther and farther emotionally from her, Shannon was unable to look into his eyes and, maybe, gauge what went on inside him. She'd seen dogs on a scent who were no more single-minded and admired his ability to dismiss all discomfort, all feeling while trained on his goal. She wished she could do the same.

They'd ridden their horses hard getting to the base of Copper, but although she was anxious to begin the long climb, she understood that Cord first had to determine what route Matt had taken. Until he'd done that, she could only watch and wait and pray.

Because she carried the memory of Cord rocking his son, she was convinced that this search was more than just another job for him. Still, she would have given a great deal—anything—for him to tell her that his insides, like hers, felt as if they had been ripped open and then put back together a little, simply because they now knew where to begin looking for their son.

Although she now regretted lashing out at him, his reaction had told her things she didn't want to know about the man she'd once loved. Everything had fallen apart for them at Summer's death because for the first time in her life she hadn't been able to express herself. She hadn't been able to reach beyond her own grief, and he had had no idea what was happening inside her. Because he hadn't tried to understand.

Or if he had, she hadn't known.

Today it looked as if the intervening years hadn't changed anything. He was still bottled up inside himself, either holding himself apart from his emotions or, even worse, lacking in that most essential of human qualities.

She could say something to him about what she was feeling and thinking, reveal her still-frightened heart. But if she did, fear might overwhelm her.

"What do you want to do with the horses once we get to where they can't travel?" she asked around the lump caught firmly in her throat. "If you think we're going to need them when we get back down, I'll tether them so they can feed but not get away."

"No." He straightened and looked at her, saying the word slowly as if he'd given it considerable thought. "When and if we need horses, we'll let your folks know. I don't like the idea of these having to wait until who knows when."

Who knows when. The words filled her with dismay. "All right," she said.

"There's something you need to be aware of. It's slow going now. Unfortunately, I can't do anything about that. But when I find where Matt started, it's going to get even slower."

"It is?" She swallowed and wondered how much of her emotions she'd given away. "Why?"

"The rain. Also, he isn't marking his way. He doesn't want or expect to be followed. At least, he didn't when he started."

If this was the way Cord talked to other relatives of missing persons, it was a wonder he didn't have them in hysterics. But what else could he do, lie to her? She had only to stare up at the traitorous clouds, look out at the trees that imprisoned them and defined the sum and substance of their world to understand the reality of their situation. "You— think that might be different now? Are you saying he wants to be found?"

"It probably hasn't happened yet, but it's going to sooner or later. Shannon, he doesn't know what he's let himself in for, but he will when he realizes he can't come close to doing this in two days. I don't think he has any idea how steep it gets in places. The air's thinner up there. It's going to sap his strength.''

She'd already told Cord that Matt might hide if he thought searchers were after him. Now, knowing her son as she did, she had no choice but to face the fact that youthful determination and pride would come before anything else. Those qualities could kill him.

"This kind of thing *has* to have happened before. What did you do then?''

"I didn't give up.''

Cord's answer wasn't nearly complete enough and gave her nothing to hang hope or fear on. "No. You never would. But what I need to know is, what did you do to find whoever you were looking for? I can help more if I understand more.''

He came a step closer, then stopped. Despite the distance between them, she was sure she could smell still-damp cotton and denim. What did she need with other people when he took up her physical world? "You really want to know this?''

"Of course I do. Why wouldn't I?''

"I've had it happen, a lot. Relatives who don't really want to hear the details.''

"Don't you know me any better than that?'' *Stop it,* she admonished herself. *There're already enough walls between us.* "Look, of course I don't want to hear about Matt becoming lost or physically exhausted or hungry or maybe hurt, but those are possibilities, and not saying anything isn't going to change reality. People say you're so successful because you have a sixth sense about whoever you're looking for. Is that it?''

"Maybe I outthink them. I don't know how to explain it exactly. Maybe it is a sensing thing. I've found people a lot more determined to avoid me than Matt is."

"Who?"

"A couple of escaped convicts. A man who'd shot his neighbor and then ran. Those were in Washington, in woods much thicker than these."

She ran her fingers through her hair, long past caring how she looked. "But you had law enforcement with you during those times, didn't you?"

"Yes."

He'd thrown up a barrier between what he knew and what she was trying to find out. How she knew that, she couldn't say, but she had no doubt. She could try to break through to the truth, or she could respect his decision and let him do his job.

She half turned from him, then stopped. She didn't have to look at Cord to know he'd come closer; her nerve endings told her that. When, finally, she faced him, he stood no more than two feet away, close enough for her to see the dark and roughened flesh on his lower arms. Mindless, dangerously, she touched him there with fingers so cool that the tips had become numb. Or at least they'd been that way before she stroked him. Now she felt rawly alive.

"I hate your having to go through this," he whispered.

Oh Cord, thank you. "It's . . . it has to be just as hard for you."

He said nothing, indicated nothing.

"At least we're not fighting right now, bringing up the past." She glanced at her fingers on his forearm and desperately wanted the years and silences to melt into nothing. She wondered how long she'd be able to keep her tears, her fear, at bay. Wondered what, if anything, he was hid-

ing. "I'll get through this. So will you. After... after what
we—"

"Don't think back. Think only about today."

"I'm trying."

"I know you are. It's in your eyes."

Of course it was. Still, she wished she knew how much he
truly sensed about her. There was so much heat contained
within this man. Heat that came from the strong heart that
pumped blood through his veins. Maybe heat he'd pulled
down from the hidden sky and up from the earth's core.

He was looking at her, his eyes gentle yet wary, older than
the mountain looming above them. In that instant she no
longer cared that he was nothing but flesh and blood; her
need to embrace him in remembrance of everything they'd
shared, to be embraced by him and given his courage, was
stronger than any emotion she'd ever experienced.

Still, she fought herself, warned by her soul-deep vulnerability, her fear that once exposed she could never again be
able to keep anything from him. She would not be the only
one to lay herself open! Without saying a word, she gave
him his freedom. But he didn't step away. Instead, he
glanced down at his arm and then met her eyes.

She felt gentled, calmed, by nothing more than his look.

Had they really been divorced seven years? It seemed
much less; it seemed much longer.

Cord hadn't been like the other kids she'd grown up with.

It wasn't that anyone had tried to keep him out of the fun-
loving bunch who thought they ruled the world because they
had a championship basketball team. But he'd kept himself
apart, seeming to need no one, his black, black eyes watching and appraising but never revealing what went on inside
him. Then, somehow, he'd looked at her, and she'd looked
at him, and something happened.

She ran her hand over her horse's neck and lifted her head for a breath of pine-scented air. Even now the memory of that something remained. When the chasm between teenage dreams and grown-up reality became more than she could push aside, she'd usually jump on Pawnee's back and give the young horse his head. But today her son had Pawnee and she couldn't outrun her memories.

It really was too bad Cord hadn't gone out for football, she thought as the ground again claimed his attention. With his solid five foot, eleven inch frame, he could have anchored any defensive line. His palms were so broad and solid that he could manage a revving chain saw one-handed. She knew; she'd seen him do it. And he was quick, the kind of quick that took a person by surprise.

Despite herself, she vividly remembered that windy autumn afternoon just after she turned seventeen when she saw him behind the local grocery store. He'd been squatting on his haunches carrying on a nonconversation with one of the stray cats that lived there. While she stood still and quiet, Cord inched toward a cat with a nasty-looking sore on its side. Suddenly, so fast that she remembered the change from crouch to lunge as nothing but a blur, he'd launched himself forward. Despite warning squalls and nails buried in his forearm, he'd hung on. When he realized she'd seen him, he'd shrugged and then explained he wanted the vet to look at the cat and couldn't think of any other way to get his hands on the animal. That was the first time they'd spoken one on one. It wasn't the last.

Maybe it should have been. If she hadn't started running around with Cord—they didn't date in the usual sense—she wouldn't have been pulled so deeply into his ebony eyes that she would have lost the way out. They wouldn't have gone for long drives in his grandfather's old pickup. They wouldn't have surrendered to the power of teenage hormones.

But they had and that was why they were here today.

Despite telling himself he wanted to turn his back on Shannon and get back to doing what he'd come here for, Cord couldn't put thought into action—not yet, at least.

She stood near the horses, absently running her hand over her gelding's neck. She was muttering something to it, probably some secret to be shared with no one except a big-eyed, big-hearted animal.

The rain had pressed down on her, flattened her hair, plastered her clothes to her until she became part of the environment. The bottom of her jeans hung soddenly down around her boots. She'd stepped on the hems with her boot heels when she walked, fraying the fabric. There were bright splotches of color on her cheeks. By contrast, her nose and mouth looked unnaturally colorless.

His heart went out to her. It went without saying that he didn't want her to be out here looking for their son. But beyond that, he would have given anything to be able to take her back where it was warm and dry.

Maybe she'd put on a little makeup and a soft blouse and a bra that crumpled down to nothing when he held it in his hand. He'd press his lips to her throat and breathe in a hint of roses, a reminder that she was an outdoor woman and he an outdoor man.

That had been a thousand years ago.

A thousand silences ago.

Silent. That's what he had to be today. He hoped she understood.

Forcing his attention away from her and his inability to get far enough away from her to call the sheriff, he again stared at the ground as he looked for indentations made from two shod hoofs. The small craters would be filled with water, but at least the rain hadn't been heavy enough to wash away all of the necessary signs.

That's all he needed. A starting place. Given time and patience, he'd find where his—their—son had spent the night, and then he'd turn into a bloodhound. He'd do the job he'd spent most of his life doing.

That's all he wanted. A job to accomplish.

That and an end to thoughts of what Shannon's hair once felt like against his cheek.

Finally Cord located a small, steeply blanketed clearing where, he said, someone had tethered a horse yesterday. All thoughts of the past quickly vanished from Shannon's mind—all that mattered now was that they were on their way to finding Matt. Cord ran his hands over the ground and told her that the horse was wearing shoes on only its front hoofs. Pawnee!

"Gray Cloud taught me how to use all my senses," Cord said in response to her question about what he was doing squatting on his haunches and staring at mud and rocks. "My eyes tell me most of what I need to know, but sometimes when I lay my hand over a track, I find out more."

She waited for him to say what that was, but he'd straightened and was walking away, head down, once again looking like a bloodhound on a scent. He'd already told her to remain where she was until he'd found what he needed.

He moved as if he had all the time in the world and the patience of the ages, but Shannon knew his demeanor belied his determination.

For several minutes she stared in the direction Cord had gone, then slumped forward slightly, ineffectively trying to wipe the mud off her pants leg.

She understood that tracking required keen concentration, and that Cord was used to working alone. Undoubtedly he knew things he wasn't telling her; he had to be thinking about other times when he'd done this, and the way those situations had turned out. *Talk to me, Cord. Let me in!*

When Cord returned, he simply stood a few feet away, unmoving and impassive, saying nothing. But because she understood at least a little about him, she knew he'd found what he needed.

Handling both horses, she followed after him as he led the way. They'd gone no more than a hundred yards when he stopped near a forked pine surrounded by saplings and pointed to the ground. At first she didn't see anything. Then she made out indentations some six inches apart, one slightly ahead of the other. This was the message her son had left behind. Her knees felt weak; she fought to hold herself erect.

"He's walking white man style," Cord explained, his voice devoid of judgment.

"'White man style.' What does that mean?"

"With his toes pointing out and his feet cutting a wide path. A white man plows through the land. He invades far more space than he needs to."

"Is that good or bad?"

"For tracking him, good. An Indian takes a narrow path, one foot in front of the other. He walks with his thighs and that uses less energy. The way Matt is walking, he'll tire faster."

"Then...maybe he won't have gotten very far," she said.

"Far enough."

He was right, of course. "Do you have any idea how long ago he was here?"

"Yesterday."

Yesterday was a lifetime ago. Not breathing, she wrapped her arms around her middle and took in her surroundings. Copper Mountain loomed over them, beckoning, standing in their way of returning to civilization. Her son was somewhere in that horrible vastness, and she wouldn't leave this massive prison until she'd found him.

"I want to touch him." The words came out a whimper; she couldn't help it. "I need to touch him."

"I know," Cord whispered and stepped, surprisingly heavy-footed, toward her.

"It's the same for both of us," she managed, because that was what she desperately needed to believe. "Only—" She inched closer to him, then stopped, feeling too raw for anything except honest words. "Cord? Please tell me something. This has to be difficult for you, doesn't it? You must have all those memories of times when...when you couldn't do enough."

"Yes." He looked down at her. "It is."

She wanted to weep, to hold and comfort Cord. To absorb his emotions through her senses as she'd never been able to do when they were so young and untested by life.

"Don't think about that," she said after a silence of her own making that went on for a long, long time. "It'll only tie you in knots if you do. At least we now have a starting point. That's what we have to concentrate on."

"I know."

She sucked in air and fought for control over something that threatened to swamp her like a giant wave. "From, uh, from what you can tell about the prints, how is he? I mean, does it look as if he has much energy?"

Cord ducked his head and slipped under a tree branch. His body telegraphed nothing except the message that he knew where he was going—at least for this moment. "A lot of energy."

Chuck Markham shrugged and then shrugged again to re-
position the rifle he carried slung across his shoulders. Finally he made himself face the three men who'd hired him.

Chapter 7

Chuck Markham shrugged and then shrugged again to re-
position the rifle he carried slung across his shoulders. Finally he made himself face the three men who'd hired him.
No one, himself included, had shaved in the past four days.
Neither had any of them changed their clothes, and although he was accustomed to forgoing the so-called neces-
sities for days, even weeks at a time if the conditions
warranted it, his clients had done so much complaining that
he wondered what the hell they thought this hunting trip was
going to be, a resort vacation?

The eldest of the trio, Elliott Lewis, was in the best shape,
and that wasn't saying much. Of course they'd all be doing
a lot better if they hadn't insisted on bringing half their
worldly possessions with them.

Hell, that wasn't his problem. What was, was finding
them something they could shoot and take back home to
mount on a wall, not because he gave a damn about their

macho pride but because satisfied customers sent more business his way.

"Wait just a minute," Elliott insisted when Chuck started walking again. "I'm not taking another miserable step until I know where we're going."

"I told you." Chuck didn't care whether he kept irritation out of his voice or not. If worse came to worst, he'd already gotten half of his fee up front. "After that little stunt Owen pulled, we've got to get to higher elevation."

"Little stunt!" Owen snapped. "I was freezing, just like everyone else, you included. The fire I—"

"The fire you set could have tipped off someone, like a forest ranger or cop, and you know it. And it's so far from freezing that it isn't funny." Stepping closer to Owen, Chuck jutted his chin at the bank executive and stared until Owen dropped his gaze. "One more stunt like that, and I'm pulling the plug on this adventure of yours. You all said you understood the risks, and the necessity of caution. So far I've seen damn little of that. The way you plunge through the woods, it ain't my fault you've scared everything away."

"The hell you're backing out!" Elliott looked as if he was going to shake his fist, but wound up scratching under his chin.

"We're paying you plenty to—"

"I know what you're paying me, but all the money in the world isn't going to get me anywhere if I'm in jail, is it?"

No one had a response for that, which suited him just fine. It was his guess, based on more than fifteen years of experience as a hunting guide, that these white collar types had boasted to everyone they could get to listen that they'd come back with a trophy elk, mountain sheep, bear, or all three if possible. And given the circles these men moved in, no one was likely to blow the whistle on their illegal activities, just give them a hard time about being skunked.

Skunked. They shouldn't be, no way. The game was out there. He'd all but walked them into a black bear's den a couple of days ago, but no, the fools hadn't kept their mouths shut and the bear had bolted. Yesterday five, maybe six deer had done the same. The only thing that could ruin this particularly lucrative expedition was their own stupidity—stupidity that placed a smoking camp fire at the top of the list. Well, he'd let Owen know in no uncertain terms that he'd leave him out in the middle of nowhere if he so much as thought about pulling another stunt like that.

If it wasn't for the money, he wouldn't have anything to do with the men and occasional woman who believed that having the money to do whatever they wanted put them above the law. Not that he could think of any other way he'd rather make a living, not by a long shot. It beat being a mechanic all hollow.

What he did for a living was a game. The biggest challenge out there and a lot safer than robbing banks, which he'd never wanted to do anyway. Him and his clients against the bumbling, ineffective cops and rangers who kept trying to put him out of business. What the law would never understand was that all it got out of this cat and mouse chase was years and years of work followed by a measly pension while he was already rich and getting richer.

And all he had to do to keep the money rolling in was give his clients the hunt of their lives.

"You're sure?" her mother asked as Shannon knew she would. "You really don't want anyone else up there? I mean, now that you know where he is—"

"Mom, there's nothing an army can do that Cord and I can't. Besides, I don't want to embarrass Matt."

"Neither do I. But if his tracks were from yesterday—darn it. I want to hold that boy so much I can hardly stand it."

Shannon felt the same way, maybe even more so. At least the grinding, painful knot in her stomach had eased now that they were on Matt's trail. It would only be a matter of time, just a matter of time. She told her mother that, and her mother agreed. They both played the game so well.

She and Cord had stopped to rest the horses again, and she'd prided herself on having the presence of mind to check on their condition before getting in touch with her folks. It both helped to hear her mother's voice and made her ache with the need to hear another voice, this one younger, louder, enthusiastic about everything.

Catching herself in mid-thought, she realized that her mother was saying something about how it had rained like crazy for about fifteen minutes shortly after they got there this morning but that the signs were getting more and more hopeful. "What about where you are?" Elizabeth asked. "Is it cold?"

"No," she said, although she'd learned she had to keep moving to stay warm. Belatedly she remembered why her parents were at her place and asked how things were going. She was told that most of her customers had canceled their morning rides but so far those set to come in this afternoon still planned to. She apologized for taking her mother from her job with the Summit County tourism association and her dad from what was supposed to have been a day off work to go golfing.

"Don't you worry about us, honey," her dad said, as she knew he would. "I wouldn't have been able to golf in the rain anyway and helping your mom gives me an excuse not to show up at the office."

Finally, at her father's request, she turned the walkie-talkie over to Cord.

Although she tried to let them have as private a conversation as possible, she was aware that Cord's responses were both brief and formal. Once, Cord and her father had called each other friends, but divorce had ended their relationship. She wondered if either man regretted what had been lost.

For a moment, she felt a pang of guilt. It wasn't her fault, was it? She couldn't be expected to stay married to a man who locked himself away from her and her need to have someone to listen to her after their infant daughter died. Could she?

As recently as two years ago she could have thrown back a decisive no in answer to her question. She was no longer so sure. Time had blunted the worst of that awful pain, and lately she'd allowed herself to try to see the past through Cord's eyes, to ask herself what he'd been going through, and whether she'd failed him as much as the other way around.

It didn't matter. Nothing did, except— A distant rumbling caught her attention. Turning in the same direction as Cord, she scanned the gray sky until the sound was directly overhead. She couldn't see the plane for the clouds, but she guessed it wasn't very large, probably belonging to one of several local private pilots.

"What do you suppose he's doing?" she asked Cord as he put the walkie-talkie away. "If it was me, I'd wait until the visibility was better before going out on a sight-seeing flight. Darn, I wish we could reach him and tell him to keep his eye out for Matt. Do you think—"

"I already talked to the sheriff. He said he'd contact the local pilots and the forest service."

She should have thought of that. Where had her brain gone? "I'm glad you did. If Dale hears something, he'll contact you, won't he?"

"Yes. Of course." Cord nodded and then muttered something she didn't catch. She thought to ask him to repeat himself, then decided it didn't matter. The only thing that kept her from dismissing the plane and its pilot, who probably couldn't see the ground because of the storm, was the way Cord kept his head cocked toward the sound until it faded into nothing. She wondered if he would look at her, say something, but he didn't. The sight of his broad back as he returned to work served as the only reminder she needed that leaving him had saved her sanity. At least, she hoped it had.

Cord wondered if Shannon fully understood what he was doing when, occasionally, he stopped and retraced his steps before marking a rectangle left and right, front and back. He could have told her that he'd momentarily lost sight of Matt's and Pawnee's tracks and was picking them up again the way Gray Cloud had taught him. Other times when what he wanted eluded him, he went back to the last print and circled it slowly, concentrating. It didn't matter which method he used as long as he kept picking up the trail. When he did that, Shannon remained where she was so her tracks wouldn't confuse him.

Had she learned that from him? He couldn't remember telling her what her role during a search would have to be. He hadn't often taken her into the wilderness with him, especially not after they'd gotten married and work and school and then a baby took up so much of her time.

Maybe that was when they began losing each other.

Maybe they'd only believed they had something in common because they were so young and in love, so overwhelmed by the exploration of each other's bodies.

He couldn't believe that, not after seeing her standing raw and exposed in front of him when he showed her where their son had stood. Knowing how much of himself he'd handed her.

The emotions wouldn't be so strong if they weren't in some way tapped into each other, would they?

He wouldn't allow himself to be distracted by further thoughts of what he and Shannon once had. His self-preservation depended on it.

Suddenly he stopped, leaned over, then indicated the ground. "He rested here."

"How can you tell?" Shannon asked as she pressed closer.

To him, the signs were as plain as any written message, but he pointed to the broad area of flattened grass that indicated Matt had sat here for a while. Beyond that were a number of heel marks, proof that Matt had scraped his feet over the ground while he rested. Good. There had been energy in his legs.

Shannon squatted in front of the marks and ran her fingers gently over them. "If I touch where he's been, can he tell? Does he know we're here, that . . . that I love him?"

She shouldn't utter those words. When she did, her whispers dug at him and made it nearly impossible for him to concentrate on what he had to do. Still, insanely, he wanted to hold and comfort her, to erase the lost years.

But he couldn't. He didn't know how, and knew better than to try.

"If you believe he can sense you, then maybe he will. Shannon, if you need to cry—"

"Cry? No, Cord. I've done all I'm ever going to do of that."

He tried to touch her because her rough words left him with no choice, but she jerked away. "You don't understand, do you?" She all but threw the words at him. The tears she'd just denied sounded dangerously close to the surface. "The kind of vulnerability I felt when Summer was born and we knew she wasn't going to live—I'm never going to cry alone again."

"Never cry? No one knows what life is going to bring, Shannon. What emotions will build up inside and need release."

She could have pointed out that her exact words were that she wasn't going to cry *alone,* but she didn't because he was right. Although she might wish with all her heart that life wouldn't kick her in the gut again the way it had when Summer died and again when their marriage had ended, no one could look into the future. "What kinds of things build up inside you, Cord? Maybe I should know, but I don't."

"Nothing anyone else doesn't experience."

"I'm not so sure. I'd like to hear about it." Instead of saying anything more, she simply continued to meet his gaze, challenging him to step away from what they'd begun with this conversation.

He started slowly. "I've worked with so many people, seen them go through so much. Sometimes it turns out right, and sometimes it doesn't."

"When it doesn't, who do you talk to about it?"

He didn't answer her, but then, he didn't have to. She knew he had no one. He'd had her for a brief while, and he had Matt; he needed more than that. She wished she'd allowed herself to acknowledge that before now, but there'd always been distance between them. "Cord, I was scared to death when I started my business. Sometimes I'm still scared. If I can tell you that, can't you do the same?''

His body rocked slightly, away from her and then closer again. She heard a rustling in a tree to her left and guessed that there were birds in there. As before, she waited.

''Something happened to me last year,'' he said. ''Something that . . .''

''Something that what?''

''I was in northern Idaho teaching advanced life support to a group of paramedics when we got a call about a sports car that had run into a truck. There were kids in the car, two of them the daughters of the man who'd organized the class.''

''Oh, no.''

''I worked beside him for hours cutting those kids out, getting them stabilized and into helicopters to be air-lifted to the nearest trauma center. Doug couldn't go with his daughters—I drove him the ninety miles.'' Cord ran his fingers through his hair, grabbing still-damp chunks and holding on to them. ''Doug told me about their births, his divorce from their mother, how he'd finally gotten custody of them. The whole time, we didn't know whether the youngest one would live or whether his seventeen-year-old would keep her leg.''

Shannon's heart went out to him.

''By the time we got there, both girls were out of danger. But they had to have surgery that night. It was just Doug and me until morning when his sister got there. The longest night of Doug's life.''

And one of the longest of yours, too, she suspected. ''I'm glad you were there for him, that he wasn't alone.''

''So am I,'' he said on the tail of a long, slow blink. ''When it was over and we knew his daughters would come out of it in one piece, I left Doug with his sister, went outside, walked right past my car in the hospital parking lot, and kept on going."

She held her breath, every piece of her being focused on Cord. "You walked..." she prompted when he simply stood with his eyes now locked on the horizon. *Don't stop now, please!* she begged.

"For miles, hours. And I cried. Relief. Exhaustion. Everything that had boiled up inside me. Sometimes, Shannon, there's nothing to do but cry."

He had cried, this man who hadn't shed a tear at their daughter's death; at least, she hadn't seen him give way to the grief that had consumed her. "It helps," she whispered despite the hard, hot knot in her throat.

"Yeah. It does."

She couldn't think of anything to say after that. Yes, Cord's career brought him in constant contact with life-and-death struggles. He'd seen more of what was raw and basic in the world than most people ever would, but he wouldn't be human if he didn't have some response to those struggles—a response she'd never truly considered before now. Why? Had he been that careful to keep his emotions from her, or hadn't she known how to read the signs?

Too late, a voice inside her head mocked.

Afternoon.

Cord had known that the storm was dying long before the clouds began breaking up. Shannon had cheered when a weak, brief ray of sunlight touched her, but he couldn't share her excitement.

He couldn't sense his son's presence.

True, the trail Matt and Pawnee had left behind was clear enough that he was in no danger of losing it, but the tracks told him that Matt had been walking with the determination of youth, while Cord was hampered by ground that sometimes briefly held secrets and made the search for answers tedious.

Matt would have to spend at least another night on the mountain. If he'd taken his son with him or given him the knowledge he'd already had at that age—

For maybe the fourth time today, Cord tried to shake himself free of the pounding inside his head. He knew how to be a bloodhound, how to walk and work and sacrifice and think of nothing except his goal.

But this was his son, and his son's mother was with him and she, too, would have to endure another night of empty arms.

"Cord? Please, wait a minute."

He straightened and slowly turned around. Because his attention had been focused on the faint road map of Matt's journey left on the ground, it was several seconds before his eyes focused clearly on her. She stood some five feet away with the horses, which she'd been leading on either side of her. Splotches of color still highlighted her cheeks. Her eyes glistened from the effort of sorting through never-ending patterns of light and shadow—and maybe from unspent tears.

"I should be grateful." She shook her head slightly as if she was aware of what her eyes had told him. "It doesn't look as if it's going to rain anymore. The birds have come out of hiding and I saw a butterfly a few minutes ago. If Matt stands in the open where the breeze can get to him, his clothes ought to dry. If the storm had gotten worse, well..."

"A storm's nothing to fear."

"Nothing to fear? Cord, you aren't ten."

"No, I'm not. Still, there's beauty in rain and snow. The forest changes during a storm, becomes one with the wind. If you know to tuck the forest around you, let it absorb you, then a storm surrounds you but doesn't frighten."

Shannon ran the back of her hand impatiently over her forehead. "I don't know who this 'you' you're talking about is, but I didn't come here to be surrounded by rain and wind and cold. I don't want it for my son."

She had an incredible presence. She might say she had no desire to be in the wilderness, but she belonged here. Jeans became her. A cotton blouse fit her as naturally as some women wore silk. And her body—her body with its long, lean limbs, competent hands and slender yet broad shoulders—was made for a life-style beyond walls.

Her breasts and hips and thighs were made for a man. For him.

Despite everything, he had never stopped wanting her.

"I'm trying to make it easier for you," he said in an effort to place a smoke screen over what he was thinking and feeling. "Some children, especially those who've never been told that a storm is something to fear, see one the same way I do."

"Children don't like loud, sudden sounds—like thunder. Lightning frightens them. They don't like being cold and wet and hungry and . . . and lost."

She was right, of course. And as she stood up to him, he realized he had no more defenses against her than a leaf caught in the wind.

With an effort, he turned his attention back to the ground. "What you're following now . . ." she said, "can you tell whether we've made any ground?"

"No." He hated having to say this. "No. We haven't."

She drew in a quick breath and he barely stopped himself from reaching for her. "I'm sorry," he started to say.

A sound, faint as a midnight whisper, pricked at him. He froze. He forgot where he was, what he'd been saying, even who was with him.

A rifle shot. Several miles away, and distorted by the rocks it was echoing off. So faint, most people wouldn't hear it.

The sound was repeated.

For two, nearly three minutes, he remained with his senses open and receptive, but nothing else came to him. Finally, reluctantly, he brought himself back to where he was and ignored his heart's erratic pounding.

"Did you hear something?"

Shannon hadn't made any attempt to keep the combination of tension and anticipation out of her voice. Maybe she was beyond any pretense. He wanted to tell her about the shots; he didn't want to carry this burden alone or have to find a way to battle cold fingers of dread alone. But someone with a rifle was on this mountain and, if possible, he wanted to spare her from knowing what she couldn't do anything about.

"I'm not sure."

"Not sure?" When she leveled him a gaze, he wondered if he could keep anything from her.

"There are a million sounds out there, Shannon." His throat didn't want to work. "I can't be sure of all of them."

"I've never heard you say that before."

Where did she keep those memories of him? "We don't have much more time. It's going to get dark—"

"Not for another four or five hours."

"Five hours isn't going to get us far enough."

In the seconds that followed his words, he could hear her breathing. He didn't need to probe into her to know what she was feeling and battling.

He knew because the same war was raging in his own soul.

This search was different from all the others. Love for a ten-year-old boy had gotten in the way of what he needed and wanted to do. He could fight the emotion, but it would only return, slamming into him just as memories of making love to Shannon did. Because he wasn't up to the battle, he could only force himself to go on, to acknowledge why his heart felt so heavy.

He cared, truly cared for only two people in this world. He was trying to find one before that distant, deadly sound did. The other—

She looked so brave and determined and trapped.

Without moving, without having any control over what was happening, he reached out with his heart and absorbed her emotions.

"What the hell are you doing?"

"A deer! Didn't you see—"

Chuck didn't care what, if anything, Andrew might have been going to say. Cursing, he yanked the rifle out of his client's hands and trained his binoculars in the direction Andrew had shot. Although he stared for several minutes, he didn't see anything, but between the clouds and the sun trying to break out from behind them it was no wonder.

"We'll have to go look," he grumbled. "But I can guarantee you, you didn't kill any damn deer."

"How do you know?"

On the verge of telling Andrew that he couldn't hit the broadside of a barn if he was standing inside it with the door closed, he hoisted Andrew's rifle over his shoulder and started walking. Behind him, the three men chattered like drunken schoolchildren over whether Andrew had indeed made a kill and if he had, what the chances were that it was a trophy buck.

He wished they had. That way he could stop baby-sitting these overgrown morons and pick up some clients who understood that being caught hunting out of season would net him a lot more than a simple fine. He'd already been arrested twice, forfeited his hunting license, and been leveled fines that he'd had no intention of paying. Getting nailed again wasn't what bothered him since bureaucrats were lousy at collecting, but the last thing he wanted was jail time.

Jail time?

He'd shoot all three of these jokers and leave their bodies for the buzzards before he let that happen—them and anyone else who tried to stand in his way.

"Something."

Something. What in God's name did that mean? When Shannon turned anguished eyes on him, Cord gave her a shuttered look, then leaned forward in the saddle, a deeply tanned hand on his horse's neck. His eyes, now trained on their surroundings, grew even darker. His nostrils flared, and she almost thought she could hear him drawing in deep, revealing breaths.

What did he see, smell, hear that others couldn't? Was it possible that *the spirit that moves in all things* spoke to him?

She prayed so.

When Cord moved, it was to slide off the mare and land, silently, on rain-soaked earth. He stepped away from the animal and in a matter of seconds disappeared into the dense forest. She tried to listen, but there were so many sounds that she couldn't begin to sort them out. She thought of how quickly the woods had swallowed Cord and how wonderfully wild he'd looked with evergreens framing him.

Cord hadn't told her to follow him and she knew better than to infringe on his space. She waited, not knowing enough, and yet trusting that eventually he'd come back and tell her what he'd learned. She'd accept whatever it was, just as she accepted this raw and unwanted physical need for the man who'd turned her from a girl into a woman.

Her horse tried to lower its head to eat. She momentarily argued the point and then let it have its way. Cord's mount was wandering away as it searched out fresh outcroppings on the pine needle-blanketed rocks. Shannon concentrated on wind, frogs, her limp and still-damp hair, memories of Cord's faded and body-formed jeans, the wind again. The absence of rain.

How much time had passed? She'd just made up her mind to dismount when Cord's mount lifted its head and snorted. Her horse followed suit, neck arched in interest.

There was no change in the rhyme of the forest, nothing for her ears to decipher. But the horses knew.

A moment later Cord came out of the woods leading Pawnee. Cord seemed to glide, so sure of his footing that he never once took his eyes off her.

Black eyes, dark as midnight. Forever eyes.

Matt's horse!

"That fast?" she managed around her heart's furious beating.

"No," Cord cautioned. "Nothing's changed."

"But you found Pawnee."

Cord shook his head, his incredible eyes so sober that she couldn't fight them, couldn't hold on to her short-lived elation. "Only because Matt either let him loose or didn't tie him well enough. Or— Shannon, on his own, would Pawnee be able to make his way home?"

With an effort, she pulled herself out of endless depths and wild hope and explained that more than once one of her rental horses had wandered back to the corral after an inexperienced rider fell off. Pawnee, however, was full of himself, not as accustomed to life's routines, and as such, more likely to be sidetracked even with an empty belly and memories of food and water.

"I've got to find where Matt and Pawnee parted company."

"How long will that take?"

"As long as it takes."

She bit her tongue to keep from telling Cord not to be flippant. An instant later she knew it wasn't that at all because he was explaining that from the number of tracks he'd found around Pawnee, he knew the animal hadn't been there long. "He's been on the move, running, which means there's no easy way of telling where Matt left him, or where he fell off."

She felt her heart slow, then beat quick and erratic. *No easy way... Fell off.* "Wh-what do you have to do now?"

"Backtrack Pawnee."

It was then that she noticed that Pawnee was wearing his saddle and bridle. The loose reins that had been trailing behind the horse were muddy from dragging. "Maybe Matt ground-tied Pawnee and left him for a few minutes, but something spooked Pawnee."

"Maybe. Look at his legs," Cord observed. "He's been deep in the woods for a while, getting scratched up."

"You said that when you found where the two of them parted company, you'd be able to really start tracking Matt. How are you going to get to that point?"

Cord stepped over to his horse and pulled on the reins, lifting the animal's head. "I'll have to go on foot."

Without another word of explanation, he turned and slipped, silently, into the woods. After a momentary hesitation, she started after him, leading both Pawnee and Cord's horse. She stretched over the neck of the one she rode so the thick-growing branches wouldn't knock her off.

Ahead, Cord walked Indian style, his movements starting in his hips, eyes trained on the ground. She tried to make out what he was concentrating on, but for her there was nothing except the generations of pine needles that thickly carpeted the forest floor. Still, she trusted.

This was Cord's world.

And their son was in it, somewhere.

Safe?

Chapter 8

Afternoon had become evening. The sun was setting. Although he all but had to double over, Cord continued to stare at the ground as he sought out the nuggets of information Matt had left behind. Several times in the past few minutes he'd placed his palm over a faint boot print and let his nerves absorb the silent messages.

Matt had slowed down, and there was no pattern or destination to what he was doing. Like a rabbit, the boy had hopped in one direction for a while before taking off in another. Yes, he continued to climb, but there was no efficiency, no purpose. Cord wasn't sure whether Shannon was aware of how much crisscrossing they'd been doing. He'd explain why once it was too dark to see where he was going, so she wouldn't have to pull the information out of him. If she sounded strong enough, he'd admit that their son was getting tired and toeing out like a fat man in his attempt to keep his body going.

What he wouldn't tell her was that he was certain Pawnee had thrown Matt. The signs had been all too clear, a mass of churned hoof prints, at the middle of a steep slope and, in among those prints, two easily recognizable handprints and two indentations that he was convinced had been made by a pair of knees.

To him, the scenario was spelled out as clearly as if he had a video of the whole accident. Matt had tried to make Pawnee climb the hill and, panicking, Pawnee had begun bucking. Made awkward by his backpack, Matt had fallen off and landed on his hands and knees. Pawnee had run away while Matt had been left behind. Because the ground was rocky and Pawnee had done so much damage to it, it was impossible to know how long Matt had remained there before picking himself up and going on alone.

And maybe Pawnee had been startled by a rifle shot.

At least Matt hadn't been injured enough by the fall that he couldn't move, Cord reminded himself again. But the boy was disoriented. Lost. Were the poachers responsible? If they were . . .

Cord crouched low and extended a shadowed hand over a smear in the pine needles made by a toe dragging over the ground, studying not just the mark but his own hand. The last time he'd seen Matt, they'd shaken hands. Matt had seemed pleased by that, a growing-up boy wanting to say goodbye to his dad man to man.

Why hadn't he clutched that slender yet muscled body to him? Ten wasn't a man yet. Ten was a child. Just because he hadn't thought of himself as one at that age didn't mean he should subject his son to the same standards.

But he had. Somehow, unwittingly, he'd given Matt the message that it was time—past time—for him to become a man.

That's why Matt was out here.

"Cord, please, give it up."

For an instant, he wanted to order Shannon to be silent because he couldn't rest until their son was safe, but she was right. He'd been going more by feel than sight for too long and if he wasn't careful, he might talk himself into believing he'd seen something that wasn't there. When he straightened, he felt a slight pull in the small of his back, but as he'd done many times over the years, he quickly assessed the inconsequential discomfort and dismissed it. It might be different for Matt. His fall from Pawnee might have left him bruised and sore.

"You've done all you can for one day," she said softly. "Get some rest."

"I haven't done enough."

"You aren't superhuman—I'm not asking you to be. Besides, there isn't any go left in me."

His attention was instantly drawn to her. She stood with her legs splayed farther apart then he'd seen them all day. Her mouth was parted, and when she breathed, she straightened slightly, as if needing to increase her lung capacity. Her fingers had swollen a little and he guessed her feet felt the same way.

She hadn't said anything about being tired before. He couldn't remember whether they'd stopped to eat or rest today, something he'd always made part of his agenda before—before his son was the one out there.

"Shannon." He started to lift his hands toward her. After a couple of seconds, he let them drop to his sides. "I should have paced us better. I pushed you too hard."

"No more than you pushed yourself. All I had to do was follow your lead. You're the one who did all the tracking. You're incredible. So determined. So patient. I mean it. No wonder you're in demand."

He could have pointed out that he was used to this life-style and had trained his mind and body to accept what he required of it, but despite the deep shadows, he could see fine lines at the corners of Shannon's eyes, the way her mouth drooped as if she was tired of holding it in place.

Still, she would keep going until she dropped if she believed it would help their son. He didn't dare forget that.

"Rest." His hands felt empty. He had to fight to keep from reaching for her. "I won't do that to you again."

"I don't care. You have to know that."

The world around them had already taken on its night song, cooler, freer somehow than it had during the day. Her voice had risen to blend with it. "Yes, I do," he told her.

"And you feel the same way, don't you?"

"With all my heart."

"Oh, Cord." She touched him, a warm, strong hand on his cheek. Although he didn't move, he felt himself flow into the contact. As when they'd once made love, he lost the distinctions between them.

The caress that wasn't really one continued. He thought about her reaction to his stubble, wanted to protect her from that harshness. Wanted her to know that some things hadn't changed about him and his body would still feel the same to her.

He was full of words. Words that wouldn't come. All he could do was dip his head so that his cheek pressed more firmly against her hand and look into her eyes and wonder what emotions she kept hidden from him.

Maybe none. Maybe a lifetime's worth.

"What are you thinking?" she whispered.

That I want to bury myself in you until there's nothing except us. "I'm not sure I am," he lied.

"I don't believe you. Don't pull back, please. It's all right," she insisted, and he did as she ordered. "I shouldn't have asked. I just— Oh, Cord, I'm such an emotional mess. I guess I was hoping you could tell me how to get through this. My moods are like a roller coaster, up and down until I think I'm going to go crazy."

"He's all right. You've seen his tracks. You know—"

"Yes, I do. I'm just tired. Maybe that makes me think things I shouldn't. Worry more than I should. I mean, look at what we've already accomplished."

"Yes, we have."

"Do you mean it?" she challenged. "I don't want you keeping anything from me. I need you to be honest even if it's bad. Comparing this search to others, is it coming along all right?"

"Much better than many," he told her. If there was any way he could keep her from tapping into everything he was thinking, learning the depth and width of his concerns, he would do it. And if he couldn't—

"That's good." She sighed and stared at her hand as if surprised to see it against his flesh. Stepping back, she let her arm drop to her side. With that gesture, the night seemed to lap against her and take over. "Thank you," she said. "I needed to hear that."

Fifteen minutes later they'd spread out their ground mats and unrolled their separate sleeping bags and Shannon had gotten out the peanut butter and jelly sandwiches she'd made so many hours ago. When Cord caught the smell of peanut butter, his stomach rumbled. Despite that, he picked up the two-way radio and made contact with Shannon's parents because he wanted to give them more details on where they were and what they'd accomplished today.

Despite the strain they couldn't keep out of their voices, Shannon's parents insisted that they were holding up well and were fortunately being kept busy. After telling them about finding Pawnee and having let all three horses go, he turned the radio over to Shannon. His call to the sheriff would have to come later when he was assured of privacy. In the meantime, he'd have to go on fighting himself.

By the time he'd removed his boots, she had told her parents that they could expect the horses to show up at her place sometime tomorrow and that she'd appreciate knowing as soon as they did. After ending the conversation, she handed him his dinner. "Are you tired?" she asked gently.

"Tired? I guess. I try not to think about anything except what I have to do."

"How well do you succeed?"

"Most of the time it works."

"But not now." She tipped her head slightly and studied him intently. "No. You don't have to say anything. I won't push, not tonight. I don't want to have to worry any more than I already am. Does that make me sound like a coward?"

"You're doing what you have to. That's all right."

"Is it?" Stretching her neck, she glanced at the still-darkening sky. "Even if the temperature goes down more, I hope the clouds break up completely tonight. The moon's just about full. If it isn't totally dark, if he can study the moon, it might make him feel better."

"It might."

"But you don't think it's going to make much of a difference because you've shown him there's nothing to fear in the night. I hope you're right, because if you aren't— No! I said I wasn't going to let myself worry." She took a small bite while he studied the shadows' effect on her features. It was becoming harder and harder to separate her from their surroundings.

"My mother made the blackberry jelly I used in the sandwiches," she continued. "She tried to get me to help her, but I guess I'm not as domestic as she, which isn't saying much. What do you think of it?''

"Delicious," he told her although he'd barely tasted what he was eating.

"And the peanut butter will stick to our ribs, not that I have to worry about putting on weight with all the exercise I got today. Listen to me. I keep rambling like—why don't you just tell me to shut up?"

"It's all right," he said as he thought about the miles that separated them from the rest of the world.

"But maybe you have to listen to—"

"I don't," he interrupted. "Matt isn't around here."

"No, he isn't. Just owls and coyotes and crickets and mosquitoes." Closing her eyes, she listened for a minute. "They make quite a lullaby, don't they? I've always loved it." She sighed. "I just hope Matt sees it in the same way."

He almost told her Matt would, but decided not to because that might bring them back to the conversation they'd sidestepped a few minutes ago. "It sounds like this at your place, doesn't it?" he asked.

"Oh, yes. Sometimes when the coyotes get going, they all but drown out the TV."

"Do they ever give you any trouble?"

"No. Actually, I rather like them, a sentiment some of my neighbors don't share. However, you'll notice that I don't keep any chickens or rabbits or anything that might appeal to them. You've seen wolves, haven't you?" Although he couldn't make out her features, he sensed that she was smiling. "I've always wanted to, but with foals around it's probably a good thing there aren't any left around here. Still, I think we've lost something important and basic because they're gone."

He told her that an Alaska fish and game employee had taken him along during a wolf population count a couple of years ago and that he'd watched a pair of adult wolves teach their young how to track and kill.

"The balance of nature," she said when he was finished. "It seems cruel, but predators keep the population of other animals in balance with the available food. Everything works as long as man doesn't interfere. Too bad we couldn't bring along the makings for a steak dinner. I swear I could eat the biggest one out there."

"Do you want more to eat? I've got—"

"No. No, thanks. I'd probably better see how well I digest this." Standing, she told him she was going to make a stab at cleaning up at the creek they'd stopped near. He watched her disappear, flashlight in hand, and then waited a few more minutes before contacting Dale Vollrath at his office. After the briefest of pleasantries Dale explained that he'd been out to the ranch twice to see how Shannon's parents were doing and had let the head of search and rescue know what was going on. So far the press hadn't picked up on what was happening but that might not last long. "Unfortunately, when and if that happens, we're going to be swamped by reporters. I want to work with you, not be interviewed."

"I've found Matt's trail," Cord explained.

"You have? That's great. I'm sure that's a big relief to both of you."

"Not as much as I wish." Keeping his voice as low as he dared, he told Dale about the faint gunshots he'd heard.

"Damn!"

"Yeah, damn. Except for us, is there anyone else on this side of Copper that you know of?"

"The forest service gave me a list of a half dozen hiking groups on the east slope, but that's not what you're talking about, is it?"

"No," he admitted, hating his words. "Has there been any indication that those poachers are still on Breckenridge?"

"I asked about that, too. In fact, trying to get a lead on them has taken most of my day. No one's seen anything, not that that means much. We're talking about a hell of a lot of territory. You're sure about the sound being a shot? You said it was pretty far away."

"I'm sure," he said, and Dale didn't argue the point. Instead, the sheriff promised to do some more snooping around to see if he could come up with anything.

"I'd appreciate that. And, Dale, I want to keep this between you and me."

"In other words, you don't want Shannon knowing. It might not be possible, you know. If something happens..."

He'd seen the result of what happens when a hunter mistakes a human for a deer and knew that that image would stay with him for a long time tonight. Shannon didn't need to carry the same images inside her. Hadn't she told him that she had enough to worry about as it was? Protecting her from anything more was maybe the only thing he could do for her, his only atonement.

Had Cord been talking to someone? Shannon wondered as she returned to their camping spot. She thought she'd heard the murmur of his voice, but maybe she'd only imagined it.

And maybe he'd seen more today than he'd let on and was relaying whatever it was to someone. If Cord knew something he was keeping from her, she would never forgive him. Damn it, they were supposed to be in this together! Forget his natural reserve, his closemouthed nature, his inability to communicate. Angry, she nearly confronted him and insisted he be completely truthful. Instead, she sat down and took off her boots, weariness suddenly overtaking her. Unless Matt set off a keg of dynamite, she didn't think she could move.

At the thought of Matt, she surrendered to a sense of warmth. Fueled by the area's gold history, her son had recently spent a day digging a four-foot-deep hole in the backyard. How could anything bad happen to a boy with dirt on his knees and blisters on his hands and excited talk about all the horses he'd buy her once he had enough gold? Cord had found Pawnee. As the light faded, he'd placed his hand on their son's boot print. They'd find him tomorrow. Her arms would feel full again.

Arms. Hands.

Although it was so dark that she couldn't really see her hand, she held it close to her face. Despite his Ute blood, Cord needed to shave every day. Sometimes when he came back from a search, he hadn't been near a razor for a week or more. When he walked in the door looking like that, she'd think of a bear. A powerful, fearless bear.

And then he'd pull her close to him and she'd forget everything except his body taking over hers. Bringing her to life.

Tonight her palm felt warm and alive. She pressed it against her chest, wondering if the gesture might transfer some of Cord's essence from her hand to her heart. She needed a little of the incredible strength and competence that had saved lives.

That, and more.

Night! She had to face the night alone with him. "Wh-what are you thinking about?" she asked, her voice surprising her. She wasn't sure hearing him speak would give her the necessary distance from her emotions, but she had to try. "At night, when you're on a search, you must think about other searches you've been on."

"Yes."

"And is that happening tonight?"

"More than ever." The answer came too slow.

"Tell me about it," she prompted, although maybe she should leave this particular topic alone.

"You really want—"

"I really want to know, Cord."

As he'd just done, he again paused before speaking. His voice deep and low, he told her about having gone after an escaped convict, an experience that had made national headlines. She remembered; the man had been armed and desperate. What he hadn't been was wise in the ways of the wilderness. By the time Cord tracked him down, the man had lost his fight and had been grateful to have someone take him back to civilization.

"But he was still armed, wasn't he?"

"Yes."

"And yet you walked right up to him?"

Cord chuckled; she'd almost forgotten what that sounded like and wanted to hear it again. "I watched him for a long time and made sure he had no fight left in him before I approached him."

"Approached him? You're not a cop. I don't understand. If someone told me to go hiking off into the middle of nowhere looking for someone who'd already taken one life, I'd tell them to take a flying leap." She shifted position slightly, groaning despite her resolve not to. "Cord, you have a child. Does your life mean that little?"

"My life means a lot to me, Shannon." His voice was somewhere between a whisper and a growl—anger barely kept in check? "But law enforcement couldn't touch that man because of where he was. If I didn't go after him, he might have gotten away and later taken another life. Maybe a child's life the next time.''

Was that why or was it because he was a man who gave up on nothing—except his marriage? ''It's like those newspaper articles say, isn't it? You're invincible. At least, you think of yourself that way.''

Cord didn't say anything, and she wondered if she knew why. He'd never seen himself as anyone except a man who'd been given certain gifts and used those gifts to do a job, a sometimes desperately needed job. She shouldn't have goaded him.

''Look,'' she said. ''I don't mean to press you. Maybe I'm trying to figure out what makes you tick when I have no business doing so.''

''Yes, you do. You need to know if I can find our son.''

She felt a spark, a silent shaft of lightning coming so quickly that she almost didn't recognize it. But in a few words, Cord had shown his ability to step inside her head. He hadn't, she believed, been able to do that back when their marriage was dying. When they'd both given up.

''I don't know if I want to talk to you,'' she admitted. ''I do know I wish with all my heart that we weren't here, that we weren't being forced together like this. That... that I didn't feel so vulnerable.''

She needed to hear him say he understood, but she was wrong because he was going to retrieve their son and life would go back to normal. She also needed to snatch away her raw words and hide behind silence. Silence! That was his domain, a large part of what had destroyed them.

''Cord?'' She took a breath while trying to decide whether to continue. ''When I started my business, I was so scared I wouldn't make it that I couldn't eat. Couldn't sleep. Do you have any idea what I'm talking about? Your stomach never becomes this boulder that weighs more than you can possibly carry, does it? What's it like?" She forced the question. "To not feel fear."

"I don't know."

His answer seemed to drift above them to blend with the night sky and the sounds that defined their existence. She felt both frozen and newly alive as if she'd glimpsed sunlight in the depth of a forest. "There have been times when that boulder feels larger than me."

"Tell me, please," she whispered when he fell silent. *Please let me into that private world of yours.*

"You don't want to hear this."

"Yes, I do. Cord, if I once made you believe I needed you to play the macho role, I'm sorry. It was dumb and immature. I shouldn't have said what I just did. I think I know what you're getting at—searches that seemed like they would never end, the fear you wouldn't get to someone in time."

"That wasn't the worst."

This time she couldn't make a single sound.

"Maybe all new fathers feel the same way—I don't know."

"How...how did you feel?"

"Scared."

"Scared? You?"

"Shannon, I was only eighteen when you got pregnant— when I got you pregnant. The day after you told me, I walked into the forest." His voice trailed away, leaving her feeling as if she was alone in the dark, alone and waiting for him to rejoin her. She felt surrounded by night. "I remember thinking a thousand things, having a thousand fears," he whispered.

"Being in the forest..." she said because she had to say something, "did that help?"

"Not for a long time. I couldn't find the answers inside myself. Finally I asked Gray Cloud's spirit how I was going to put food in my baby's mouth, whether...whether I was what you needed. He didn't answer. I learned, the hard way."

Oh, Cord. "I wish you'd told me," she whispered. *It might have made a difference. Brought us closer.*

"I didn't know how."

And I didn't know how to listen. For a moment she fought the need to walk away from this conversation, the peeling away of too many self-imposed layers.

Then she stood and walked barefoot over to where she knew he was. The night had served them well, she thought as she knelt beside him. Unable to see each other, they'd said things they probably wouldn't have if they'd had to look into each other's eyes. Now she'd made a lie of the darkness by coming to him. Heat, enough to wash through her body, nearly distracted her, but she held on.

"If you'd confided in me..."

"You were the one having the baby. You had enough on your mind."

"But if we'd both known what was going on inside the other, maybe it would have made a difference."

She didn't so much as sense him move. Still, his hands now covered hers and she felt less alone. "I'd like to believe it would have," he said.

Despite the pain that accompanied his word and her inability to turn it into anything else, she now had a deeper understanding of Cord's heart and mind than she'd ever had. *Scared. Her wonderfully brave and masculine lover, scared.* She tried to think back to when they'd faced the consequences of their too young, too innocent lovemaking, but the present—his hands engulfing hers—blocked that out.

"We can't change what happened," she made herself say. "I know that. But..."

He sighed; the gesture lifted his chest and shoulders, lifted her hands. She gripped with the tips of her fingers and pulled even more of his heat into her. "But—" She took a breath and went on. "We've done a lot of growing up, become wiser. At least, I hope we have."

With hands and body, he pulled her around until their shoulders were pressed together. Her heart pounded; she spoke through the sound. "I owe you an apology."

"You owe me?"

"I've spent a great deal of time thinking about what I put you through in the beginning. The way I pressured you to take that horrible, well-paid, dead-end factory job so we would have a roof over our heads. If I'd truly understood you, I never would have done that. Of all the things for you to have to do, being in a windowless room surrounded by machinery had to be the worst."

"I offered. You didn't force me."

He'd taken control of her hands. Now he pulled them near to but not touching his chest. She didn't move away; she couldn't remember how to move. Talking was almost more than she could concentrate on. "Maybe not in so many words, but I remember yelling at you that I wasn't going to spend my life working at minimum wage, and even if you didn't care about an education, I was convinced I had to get one. I wanted to prove to my parents that we were old enough to handle our own lives. I was going to go to college, without their help. When I think of the pressure—"

"You never once yelled, Shannon."

He was confusing her. Or maybe the truth was, their tentative contact was what had her off balance. It didn't matter, she told herself. Not the tangled and twisted words they'd spoken years ago, nor why she couldn't think tonight. She'd come to this isolated place with its night melody of song to look for their son. She hadn't expected to find the man she once loved.

Stripped of everything except raw emotion, she would admit that in some ways she *still* loved Cord Navarro.

Pulling free, she staggered away from him. She expected—wanted—him to call her back so she could tell him that it was dangerous for them to talk about the past when it should be left buried. But he didn't, and now she wanted to throw his silence back at him. Wanted him anywhere but here with her. She knew her night would be filled with memories of their daughter's death and his inability to cry, to feel, to share and understand.

Matt propped himself against a tree and tried to pull his jeans up so he could see his knees but his pant legs were too tight. He probably should stand and take his jeans off, but it seemed like too much of an effort.

What had gotten into Pawnee? Sure, it had been pretty steep back there, but it wasn't as if it was the first time they'd climbed. There was a lot of shale; maybe it had felt slippery under Pawnee's feet and that's what had set him to bucking. Maybe Pawnee had heard something he hadn't.

Bucking. He'd done that all right, so quick and unexpected that Matt had been flying through the air before he knew what was happening. If he hadn't been wearing his backpack, his balance might have been better.

What did it matter? Pawnee had run away and he'd landed on his hands and knees and for a few minutes had been so shook up that he hadn't understood what had happened. Thank heavens he'd been wearing his pack. Otherwise he'd have nothing to eat tonight, not even a bed roll.

He licked the corner of his mouth but there wasn't so much as a taste left of the soggy granola bars he'd had for dinner. Reaching out, he tried to snag his pack to see what else might be in there, but he couldn't reach it without having to move and his knees were already stiff and getting stiffer. Besides, he *had* to quit eating like a pig.

Sighing, he closed his eyes and tried to concentrate on the yapping coyotes, but no matter how hard he tried, it didn't work. This was his second night out and he was nowhere near the top of Copper. In fact, he wasn't at all sure—

But he would be in the morning. All he had to do was find a tall enough tree to climb or scramble up a boulder and then he could figure out where he was and where he needed to go.

You've been saying that all day. So far you haven't—

You think it's so darn easy, you try making sense of all these trees and rocks and hills and valleys and—

Stop it! All right, just stop it!

Feeling exhausted by the argument, he opened his eyes and tried to make out the man in the moon. He thought he saw his grinning face, not that it really mattered. What did matter was getting enough sleep that he could get to the top of the stupid mountain and back down tomorrow before his mom started looking for him.

"Is this what you usually do when you're out on a search?"

Cord looked up from the lazy arcs and circles he was drawing in the dirt with a stick. Shannon had been walking restlessly around the campsite; at the moment she stood barefoot a few inches away. Given the end to their conversation a little while ago, he was surprised she wanted to talk.

"I do a lot of thinking, yes."

She squatted on a rock not far from him. When she spoke, he heard an unexpected smile in her voice. "Drawing in the dirt helps you think? I stare out windows. If I'm not careful, I lose whole hours that way.''

What took hold of her and made her need to spend time within her head? Instead of asking, he told her that for him evenings on a search were spent assessing the information he'd taken in during the day, building on his knowledge of who he was looking for, mapping out tomorrow's strategy.

"You don't have to build on what you know about Matt."

Didn't he? He wasn't sure he'd ever be done exploring his son, or that he'd ever want to. "He's more adventurous than I gave him credit for. And he's not afraid, at least not enough that it gets in the way of what he's doing."

"Not afraid?" Shannon breathed the question, and he felt her struggle to hold back tears. At least that's what he thought she was doing. "That . . . that makes it easier for me."

"I should have told you earlier."

"I should have asked."

"There's something else." He thought about telling her that he'd heard rifle shots and that there'd been poachers on the mountains earlier, because his secrets might drive a wedge between them and he hated carrying his knowledge alone. But he couldn't bring himself to add to her burdens when she'd given him the clear message that she couldn't take much more. Instead, he told her that Matt didn't know where he was going.

"He's lost?"

"Yes."

"Lost but not scared? I don't understand."

"I'm not sure I do, either. I'm thinking he's still confident that he'll be able to get out of this with his pride intact."

She stared at him, eyes dark with concern. For an instant her mouth trembled. Then she pressed her lips together and nodded, a brave mother accepting reality. His respect for her knew no bounds. "Does that make it easier or harder to find him?"

"Different. That's all, just different."

"That doesn't tell me much."

"He isn't panicking. A lot of people do when they realize they have no idea where they are."

"Why isn't he? It's got to be more than dumb self-confidence."

"He knows this country. You've never made it something he should fear."

"I can't take any credit for that. Admit it, Cord. Everything he knows about the wilderness comes from you. He's in such a hurry to grow up. I know he needs the freedom to explore, but sometimes—sometimes he's just a little boy."

Little boy. It wasn't the words so much as the way she said them that touched Cord. Needing to put his mind to something other than the image that conjured up and his unwitting role in Matt's wanting to rush through childhood, he let his attention shift back to her. Her athletic yet feminine form easily caught and held him. He could no more fight her power than he could hold back a storm.

The silence continued. Shannon was looking at him with the night dancing in her eyes; he met her gaze, not knowing what his own eyes revealed. He felt the wilderness surround him, call in its ageless way, engulfing her, as well. They'd come here because of their mutual love for a ten-year-old boy. But this wild land could spin spells over those who listened to its song. He'd always listened. Maybe Shannon would, too, and the experience would change what they were to each other.

Did either of them want that?

"It's hard for boys at this age," she said softly. She hadn't freed him from her gaze. "Half little boy, half near teenager. Matt loves being around horses. When they do what he wants them to, it boosts his confidence and I'm amazed at his patience. Pawnee—"

"He's a beautiful animal, intelligent, independent."

"He is that, all right. But Pawnee sometimes intimidates Matt, although you could never get him to admit it. That animal's a handful. It took Pawnee and me a while before we got our relationship nailed down. I accept Pawnee for what he is, all healthy energy. Matt isn't old enough to understand that energy."

Can you feel my energy? Do you know what you're doing to me? Cord wondered. "It'll come."

"I know. That's why I was willing to let them spend some time together. I just never dreamed it would turn out like this. I feel like the most neglectful mother who ever lived."

"You aren't! Damn it, you aren't!"

She didn't move. Although the night sky remained clear, he felt a storm building—a storm between the two of them.

"Thanks for saying that," she whispered. "I needed to hear it. Matt isn't cautious or easily intimidated."

He hadn't heard that proud, nonjudgmental note in her voice for so long that he'd forgotten it—or convinced himself that he had. "No, he isn't."

"He wants to parachute. Did he tell you that?"

"Yes." Whose voice was that, deep and hollowed out at the same time? He could barely think. Maybe if she moved farther away—"He also wants to take a canoe down a class-five river."

"Not yet." She shook her head and he understood that his words had taken her away from him and back to their son. He was both grateful for the release and disappointed because, dangerous as it was, he needed more of this connection between them.

He reassured her that it would be several years before he'd take Matt down one of the country's wild rivers. Then, needing the safety of words and yet not quite sure how to use them, he told her about exploring the John Day River in eastern Oregon and finding remnants of history in still-standing log cabins and long-discarded arrowheads.

"It sounds wonderful. Matt would love going there with you."

"I know." He'd dropped his stick when Shannon called his attention to it. Now he picked it up and began drawing a crude picture of one of the cabins. "After last Christmas, I know he's ready for that."

"Last Christmas? What happened?"

To his surprise, he found himself chuckling. "Matt informed me that he was too old for a stocking. He wanted me to be the one to tell you because he was afraid of hurting your feelings."

"Why didn't you say anything?"

"I didn't want to hurt your feelings, either."

"I'm tougher than that," she told him. "A little dense when it comes to how fast Matt is growing up, but I'm not going to lose it simply because he doesn't want a stocking anymore. Next year..." No. She refused to give in to fear. There *was* going to be a next year. Cord Navarro wouldn't let her worst nightmare come true. She trusted him in that; she *had* to. "My mother made that stocking, you know. One of her few handmade endeavors. Maybe that's what made telling me hard for Matt."

"Maybe."

Barely aware of what she was doing, she stepped closer and stared down at what he'd been drawing. Her arms dangled at her sides, fingers feeling empty. She sensed him turning toward her, should have had the wisdom to move away, but his dark eyes called out to her, pushed past the barriers and found something vulnerable.

When he took her hand in his and gently squeezed, she squeezed back. The gesture should have conveyed mutual concern for their lost son, nothing more, but she couldn't lie to herself. This was about her and Cord, emotions unfinished, needs. Despite the danger, she allowed him to draw her hand to his mouth so he could kiss the back of her knuckles. She shuddered; maybe he did, too. Words were beyond her.

After crouching for so long, surely he needed to stretch his legs. Instead, he remained where he was and she could neither explain or comprehend why she used her free hand to draw his head against her thigh, or why he let her. For the better part of a minute, neither of them moved or spoke as she absorbed all she could of his strength and more and prayed he could draw something essential from her. Then, because she was afraid of what she might do next, she broke the contact and headed to bed.

She wanted him so badly that she had to fight herself to keep from reaching for him again. She'd gone to stand near him because she hadn't been able to free herself from the realization that a part of her still loved him. Something about his very essence had found its way to her. Into her. Her mouth went dry and her heart hurt each time it beat. She felt so alive and sexually charged that her body seemed like hot liquid.

He could still do that to her. Melt her down with a look, a touch, soft words.

She tried to turn her attention to the seemingly impossible task of finding enough flat ground under her so that she could sleep. But her mind was too filled with memories of their lovemaking, with worries about her son.

Sleep was a long time in coming.

Chapter 9

Risking a call while Shannon was still asleep, Cord learned that the sheriff had spent much of the night trying to discover more about the whereabouts of the suspected poachers but so far had nothing to report. He hoped that would change once people, particularly forest service and ski resort personnel, were up and about. After getting his old friend to repeat his promise that he wouldn't say anything to Shannon, Cord settled back on his sleeping bag and waited for his ex-wife to wake.

It didn't take long, and he wondered whether she'd somehow sensed his scrutiny of her or if dreams of their son had gotten between her and her need for sleep.

"You're up," she said, no surprise in her voice. "I swear, you can get by on less sleep than anyone I've ever known. Either that or—nothing happened, did it?"

"No, nothing did. I'm sorry."

She sat up and he realized that she'd worn a man's undershirt to bed. For a moment, uncertainty and a jealousy he'd never admit surged through him; who had given her the white cotton? Then he remembered. They'd been married only a few months when she discovered how comfortable his shirts felt, especially when her growing belly made it impossible for her to wear many of her clothes and they didn't have the money for a maternity wardrobe. Now, although he was out of her life, she still clung to a piece of the past.

After storing away that piece of information, he asked her how she'd slept. Her answer was noncommittal. She studied him for several seconds until he realized she was trying to decide whether to crawl out of her sleeping bag with him watching. Although he should have done the gentlemanly thing and turned away, he didn't. Instead he made no secret of his interest in her. With a sigh, she threw back the bag and stood. Beneath the shirt, she wore only underpants, which peeked out from under the hem as she pushed herself to her feet. Her legs were as long, as finely muscled as he remembered them. Those muscles, the way she used them to play him, control him, pleasure him . . .

She returned his gaze, waiting until he'd taken his attention from her legs. Then, "When are we going to get going?"

"As soon as you're ready," he told her, his thoughts torn between memories of things better forgotten and the need, the drive, to run his hands along her legs.

"It'll just take a few minutes. Cord, I don't like you looking at me that way. It makes me feel . . ."

"You're a beautiful woman."

She blinked and for a second her mouth sagged. "I'm grungy and stiff, not beautiful." When he didn't say anything, she ran her fingers through her hair, a gesture that looked sensual, which he was sure was the last thing she'd intended. "What's for breakfast?" she asked. "I could kill for some bacon and eggs."

"When we're done with this, I'll make some for you."

"Will you?" She sounded wistful and still off balance. "I'll tell you what. You do the frying. I'll tackle the waffles. Matt loves them—he always has."

"I know. I made them for him when you were in the hospital after Summer's birth. They were the only things he'd eat."

"You did? I neglected Matt so much then. If you hadn't been there— All I could think about was Summer, pray for a miracle."

"Don't," he warned. "Leave her in the past. She doesn't belong with us today."

"Doesn't she?" Shannon retorted. "Cord, you and I had two children. How can you act as if she never existed?"

Suddenly his anger matched hers and, not thinking, he reached into his rear pocket and pulled out the waterproof wallet that held his identification and a few pictures. Stalking over to her, he held one of the pictures out to her. "Maybe I didn't carry her inside me the way you did, Shannon, but I held her in the hospital. I fell in love with her. She'll always be part of me."

Shaken, Shannon ran her fingertips over the faded picture of their infant daughter. She hated seeing the tubes and needles that had been connected to Summer for the five days of her life, but that wasn't what kept her staring at the photograph. She had a picture her folks had taken of Summer, which she kept in her room; she'd never known about this one, or that Cord carried it with him. Memories of that time, of the deadly helplessness and despair in the face of overwhelming birth defects, hit her hard, but she fought them off.

"Did you take this?"

"Yes," he said, and although she wasn't ready, he closed his wallet and put it back in his pocket. "I shouldn't have said anything."

"But you did because I accused you of—" Of what? Of acting as if Summer never existed? Teeth clenched against emotions she didn't understand, she stared up at her ex-husband. "Cord, I . . ."

"It's all right if you cry."

"Cry? I used to," she whispered as his suggestion, his unbelievably gentle suggestion, rocked her. "So many things would set me off. But, Cord, I've learned that tears don't change anything."

"No. They don't. Don't talk about her. Not here. Not this way."

"Don't talk? That won't stop me from thinking about her. Don't you know that?"

He said nothing.

"When Summer died, I thought I'd died with her. I know the doctors told us before she was born that she wouldn't live, but that didn't stop—I couldn't stop myself from loving her."

I fell in love with her. She'll always be part of me. Those words had come not from her but from her ex-husband. "You never shed a tear. I needed you to cry with me, but you didn't."

"Would that have changed anything?"

"I don't know!"

"She's in a better place now. With my grandfather."

She didn't feel strong enough for Cord's words. Self-control might last no longer than a single breath. Still, held there by the reality of Summer's picture, she was incapable of moving. This wasn't the first time she'd heard Cord say what he had about their daughter. The day Summer died, he'd placed his hand on the incubator and mouthed words about the spirit world and Gray Cloud being there to show her the way.

When she and Cord had finished saying their goodbyes to Summer and walked out of the neonatal room, he'd put his arm around her and held her against his hard side. He'd said something, words that rumbled and jumbled, words she couldn't hold on to. She remembered burying her face in his chest and crying until her head pounded and she thought she might die. Maybe he'd gone on talking. Maybe he'd fallen silent.

It didn't matter. She hadn't wanted to hear that Gray Cloud was caring for Summer when her own empty arms ached.

Cord should have known that.

Her husband's arms should have been strong enough to hold back the world.

Instead, two days after the funeral, Cord had gotten a call from the state police in Nevada. He was needed to find an older man who'd wandered away from his fellow campers and was lost somewhere in the stark wilderness around Virginia City. If Cord didn't get there as soon as possible, the man might not survive.

Damn him and his all-consuming career! He'd had that to give his life direction. That and his faith that Gray Cloud would take care of Summer.

What she had was the echo of his stiff goodbye and a nursery with no baby to fill it. How could she possibly study for tests that no longer mattered, be what Matt needed in the way of a mother, think of things to say to Cord when he called?

She hadn't asked him to stay and mourn with her. If he didn't understand that she needed him more than they did the money to pay off Summer's medical bills—

Her bare foot hit a rock and she barely righted herself in time. Biting down on the inside of her mouth, she vowed to think of nothing except finding Matt. But Cord was only a few feet away, his back to her, giving her a view of the pocket where he kept his picture of Summer.

Until this morning she hadn't known he'd taken one.

Maybe, if he'd told her about it and they'd stood together and studied their daughter's features—maybe...

Cord could hear Shannon breathing. It was a whisper sound, a message he understood but didn't know what to do with. It was possible she was now thinking about Matt and had to fight down her fears, but maybe her mind was still on what they'd said, or almost said, to each other a few minutes ago.

She'd said he should have cried with her when Summer died, making it sound like an accusation. Now he wished he'd been able to make her understand that, because of his grandfather's wisdom and teachings, he'd found a peace that transcended grief.

But her grief frightened him, took him back to his sixteenth year. His tears had come the day Gray Cloud wrapped an ancestral doe skin over his frail shoulders and stepped out of the cabin they lived in. It was in Gray Cloud's eyes; he was going away. Going home.

For a night and a day Cord had sat inside the cabin, tears staining his cheeks. Then, when he couldn't cry anymore, he followed his grandfather's tracks into the wilderness. The old man had died curled under the blanket that had been handed down through generations of Utes. He took the blanket because it was now his, buried his grandfather in that peaceful place, and cried again.

Now, suddenly, he stopped, body wire-tight, listening. It took him a moment to sort out what had caught his attention. A deer was hidden maybe thirty feet away. He sig-

naled to let Shannon know. After a few more seconds he
sensed the deer moving away, and went about getting ready
for the day.

Summer lived here. He wondered if Shannon would ever
know that, or why he'd given their daughter an Indian
name. If the time had been right, if she'd ever indicated she
wanted to hear this—if he'd known how to say the words—
he'd have told her about where he'd gone the night after
Summer died. He'd heard his daughter calling to him and
left his sleeping wife, stepped into the night, and gone
looking for her.

Because they'd come back here to be near Shannon's
parents for the birth, he'd wound up at a small, clear pool
of water fed by spring runoff. It was near this spot that he'd
buried Gray Cloud and where he'd spent the night telling his
daughter how much he loved her and that her great-
grandfather would always been there to take care of her.

When he'd taken Summer's picture in the hard-smelling,
too bright hospital, he'd wanted to explode from unspent
tears.

Beside the pool, watched by an owl, talking to two people he loved, he'd lost his grief and found serenity.

But he hadn't been able to guide Shannon to his peace and
now they were trapped together in the wilderness with
nothing in common except the boy who'd been over this
ground yesterday but could be anywhere now.

He needed to find Matt, for himself, and for Shannon.

Because Matt had come across a deer trail and was following it, Cord and Shannon were able to make easy progress. Still, about an hour after they left camp, Cord called
a halt because he wanted to see how well her pack fit. She
turned her back to him and stood passively while he ad-
justed the shoulder straps. He would have believed she felt

nothing, cared nothing for his touch, except that her fingers were tightly clenched.

Lightly clamping his hands over her shoulders, he turned her toward him. "It's going to be a long time before we overtake him," he said. "I want you to know that."

"I do know. And it doesn't matter."

Although he should get started again, he continued to face her. She stood slightly below him on the hill with the sky draped around her, looking smaller than she usually did. She'd run a brush through her hair before rebraiding it and washed up as best she could, her simple chores reminding him of the femininity that simmered—waited—beneath her practical clothes.

"What's going on inside you?" she asked abruptly. "What do you feel? What do you think about when you're trying to find a sign, any sign, that Matt came this way?"

"I don't feel, Shannon." It was a lie, but a necessary one. If he opened so much as a crack to his emotions this morning, she might step boldly inside—might expose herself to too much.

"I feel sorry for you. Sorry and . . . I don't know. Damn it, I don't know!"

"I don't know what more you want me to say."

"I'm sure you don't. I think, finally, I understand that. It's just—maybe I still want different what can't be different. I wish to God I didn't. It would be easier for me, maybe easier for both of us."

"What do you want changed?"

She stared at him as if she had never expected to hear that question from him. Answering her gaze, he looked as deeply into her as he could, but he couldn't reach far enough. If he'd ever once touched her heart, it had been a lifetime ago.

"For us to be able to go back again, to be wiser, honest," she whispered. "Oh, Cord. It should all be behind us, shouldn't it? Okay, I guess I'll always regret that you and I...when we should have clung to each other, shared as we'd never shared before—it didn't happen.''

No. It hadn't. Summer's death had changed something inside Shannon and he'd never truly understood what that was. She'd pulled away from him, buried herself. He'd had no idea how to reach her. ''You never gave us a chance.''

She blinked, looked off balance. Wounded. ''*I* never—You had no idea I might not be there when you came home that last time? That I couldn't stand mourning our daughter alone, that I needed you...''

He couldn't let the conversation continue. Matt was waiting for them to find him. And if Shannon went on, she'd only open wounds she'd spent years healing. He didn't want her hurt any more than she already was. ''You know why I had to be gone.''

''Oh, yes. Yes. We were drowning under medical bills and that had both of us scared. But, Cord, there's another kind of drowning—of the soul. Of love.'' She dragged her hands along her temple and grabbed twin handfuls of hair. ''I'm sorry. I don't want to hurt you. I'm just so raw right now that—''

Although he simply nodded and returned to tracking, he was left with the realization that nothing about their conversation felt complete. The few times she'd spoken to him after that horrible day when he'd walked into an empty apartment stripped of her essence, she'd said only that his silence had been more than she could stand.

Nearly seven years ago they'd gone their separate ways. Neither of them needed any more pain.

But it hadn't all been pain. She'd once been more important to him than life itself. Around her he'd felt whole. Vulnerable and incapable of telling her how much she meant to him, but whole. All she'd had to do was stand in front of him and hold out her arms to him and he would have died for her.

She'd once owned him heart and soul. Didn't she know that?

He closed his eyes and breathed deeply through mouth and nostrils to clear his head of the cobwebs she'd always been able to spin inside him. Matt. Today was about Matt.

Still, because he was tracking with his eyes and not his ears, he didn't need the silence she said she hated. After a few minutes, he drew her attention to a tree trunk that deer used to rub their antlers against, pointed out some black bear sign, and even showed her the entrance to a fox den nestled under a moss-covered boulder.

"How do you know where to look for a newborn fox or where a deer has bedded down?"

"Time and experience. My grandfather. John Muir."

"The naturalist? What are you talking about?"

"He and Gray Cloud spoke the same language. I learned from both of them."

Shannon didn't speak, but he easily absorbed the questioning in her eyes. Looking out across an endless carpet of green, he sought inside himself for an answer. "Muir believed that everything in nature fits into us, becomes part of us."

"You—"

"Not me. There's more to Muir's philosophy than that— about rivers flowing, not past, but through us, vibrating every fiber and cell of our bodies, making them glide and sing. Those aren't the exact words, but it expresses the way I feel when I'm here. Part of nature."

"Part of nature." She breathed the words. "I never knew you had that kind of poetry in you."

Made a little uneasy by what he'd revealed about himself, he gave her a casual—too casual—smile. "I try to hold

on to what Gray Cloud told me because I believe there's a
timelessness to his wisdom.''

"Yes, there is. I've never thought about that before.''

"Not just him. I've found other sources, Indian prayers—
Rachel Carson, William Wordsworth, George Washington
Carver. Carver said that if you love something enough, it
will talk with you. I love being out there where I can hear
nature talking. I can't imagine that ever changing.''

"That's—'' Her eyes glistened. "Beautiful.''

Without knowing he was going to do it, he touched a tear
caught in her right lashes. She smiled, a slight, shy gesture.
"Anyone can become tuned in with nature,'' he went on,
the words tumbling out of him simply because she'd smiled
at him through tears he was responsible for. "All they have
to do is listen and observe and love that world. You live out
of doors. You must know what I'm talking about.''

"I...think so. I don't have the words you do to draw on,
but they touch me.'' She blinked away her tears and tried
another smile. "Obviously they do.''

Although he turned to gaze at his green and brown and
blue world, he sensed her eyes still on him.

"I don't think you would have done that at eighteen,'' she
whispered. "Told anyone, not even me, about the poetry
that has meaning for you.''

"No,'' he admitted. "I wouldn't have.''

"Maybe it's because you were still finding out who you
are. I say that because I felt the same way. Growing up takes
longer than we think it's going to, doesn't it? Eighteen isn't
nearly as mature as we'd like it to be.''

"No. It isn't.''

After a few minutes of silence, she began talking about
caring for orphan rabbits and a fawn whose mother had
been hit by a car. Then, when he thought she might have run
out of anything to say, she told him she'd seen so many deer

this year that she barely paid any attention to them. But she could never dismiss the sight of an elk. Matt, too, had a fixation about them and when one occasionally came into the pasture with the horses, he considered his day complete.

Then, when the trail they were on briefly became as clear as a highway, she admitted she wanted to buy a mountain bike so she could find and explore paths like this. She said she enjoyed most of her customers. A few had unrealistic expectations of what horseback riding on a well-worn trail was like and she'd had to learn how to deal with her customers' reactions.

His attention spread between her and Matt's erratic progress, he told her about competition between different law enforcement agencies and how that sometimes complicated his work.

He described the untouched view of natural forest land from his deck. She smiled, a little wistfully, he thought, then asked if he'd ever gotten the wide-angle lens for his camera he'd been talking about. He had, he said, surprised that she'd remembered.

As the day dragged on, he learned more about Shannon's interests than he'd ever known and felt gifted because she wanted him to understand those things about her. Listening to her talk about her admiration of a local wildlife photographer, he was again struck by her enthusiasm for life.

That was what he'd fallen in love with—that and the way she'd freely given him her body and, he'd thought, her heart. What had scared him back when he was too young to truly understand the complexity of love had been the totality of his response to her body. Even with her walking behind him, out of sight much of the time, his body remembered.

Getting his work off the ground had put a great deal of strain on their marriage, but it had been nothing compared to the aftereffects of Summer's death. Was it possible to mend what they'd once had? Maybe he—they—shouldn't try. After all, they'd each built new lives for themselves. However, life had brought them back together, at least briefly.

He was halfway through telling her about his reaction to spotting a massive grizzly while being flown into Denali Park in Alaska by a ground-scraping bush pilot when he spotted a series of unexpected prints. Because he'd stopped to study his surroundings innumerable times, he didn't think she would be alarmed when he did it again. Still, he was glad she couldn't see inside his head.

Three or four people—men, probably, by the size of the prints—had been here in the past couple of days. The rain had washed away some of their tracks but not enough that he couldn't draw out the information he needed but didn't want. Their boots were new; they carried considerable weight on their backs, which altered their stance; they walked not like people out for a leisurely stroll, but cautiously and with purpose in mind.

Hunters?

The men followed the deer trail for another fifty yards before veering away from it. Although he continued to look for them, the prints didn't reappear. Hadn't they known what they'd come upon? he wondered. He wanted to go back to where he'd last seen the tracks, but if he did, Shannon would ask why he'd left the trail, and he'd have to tell her he was being forced to ask himself whether it was more important to find Matt or men with rifles.

Matt, his heart decided for him. Besides, the men had been here before his son. They might be miles away by now and no longer representing a danger to Matt.

Maybe.

And if they were, all the police in the world couldn't do any more than he was. But was it enough?

"There."

Shannon had waited hours to hear Cord say that. Now it was nearly dark; there was precious little strength left in her legs, and the thin air at this altitude had given her a headache. She stood near Cord and watched him spread his fingers over what looked to her like nothing except a thousand years of forest litter. "What? What is it?"

"Where he spent last night."

Last night seemed so incredibly long ago. Hadn't they gotten any closer than that? "That's all you know? That he slept here?"

"He slept well. He barely moved."

"Oh. Thank heavens." She sank to her knees beside Cord and, as she'd done before, touched the ground he indicated. No matter that she was deluding herself. For a few seconds at least, she could pretend Matt had left some of his heat behind for her. What had Cord said earlier? That if someone loved something enough, it would speak to that person without words. He'd been referring to nature; she thought of Matt. And of Cord. "He seems so far away."

"I know."

Despite everything that was going on inside her, her thoughts caught on the emotion laced through Cord's words. They shared a parent's love for a child, and that love would bond them for as long as they lived. Why had she not allowed herself to see that earlier? "I feel cheated," she admitted. "There ought to be a string attached to him. I should be able to pull on it and bring him back to me."

"I know."

"That's how you feel? As if he's just out of reach?"

"More than just. Damn it, much more."

"Cord? Don't, please."

"Don't what?"

"Talk like that. It scares me."

"What do you want, then?" He spoke with his hands on his thighs and his head turned toward her, but his face was in the shadows, making it impossible for her to read his emotions. She would have to go by what he said, and that wasn't enough; his few words had never been enough. "I can't tell you I'm not frustrated. You have to know that."

He sounded much more than just frustrated. He'd told her that everything in nature could fit inside the human heart, but right now he didn't sound at peace with either himself or the world they were in. Was it because he'd piled the long, disappointing day on his shoulders and didn't know how to shake it off?

Or maybe he knew more than he'd told her.

Concerned now more for him than for herself, she took his hand and pressed it to her waist. She was dimly aware of how unwise the gesture was, but she could no more stop herself than she could tell her lungs to cease breathing. This man was the other half of her son's existence.

Still a vital part of her life.

"I do know how frustrating this is," she told him gently. "But, Cord, you found his trail and where he spent last night."

"Yes."

"Then think about that, not what you still have to do."

"I can't help it."

No one had ever heard that raw and uncensored tone from him. She was certain of it. She accepted his honesty both as a gift for her alone and as proof of how much this search had taken out of him. "Tell me what you're thinking now. Please."

He tensed and then released the tension in a long, deep sigh. She felt the hand she held move and accepted it when he laced his fingers through hers. The sun was nearly done with its work for the day and the moon hadn't come out yet. She thought of their son having to look up at the sky alone, with the universe surrounding him, and then tore her mind free. She couldn't help Matt tonight, couldn't do anything more than send him a silent message of love. His father was here and maybe Cord needed her as much as she needed him. Had he ever before? Had she ever asked herself the question? "I have to know what's going on inside you," she begged. "I know I keep asking you for that, but, please..."

For a long time he simply stared at her in the deepening gloom. Then he turned his attention to their intertwined fingers. He lifted her hand toward him and touched his mouth to her knuckles.

"You really want to know what I'm thinking?"

"Yes." She kept her eyes off their hands, breathed, tried to think. *He kissed me.* And the night—the night was for them alone. "Yes, I do. Cord, I know so much about your silences, I've tried to reach beyond them. Please, no more, not tonight."

For the second time in a matter of seconds, he kissed her wind-chapped knuckle. A jolt filled with equal sparks of ice and heat raced through her. She breathed again; it didn't help.

"You saw my silence as a barrier?" he asked.

Incapable of speech, she nodded.

"I wish you'd told me before," he said.

"I wish I'd known how to, gently, without carving a wedge between us. Cord, please."

His mouth worked; she all but tasted his effort. "I'm comfortable not saying much," he told her. "It's what I grew up with, what I was taught." Still holding on to her, he shifted position until he was sitting cross-legged, so close that their knees touched. "You know that."

"Yes, I do. But, Cord, so many times I didn't know what to do with your silence. I needed you to talk to me. I still need that. Try—that's all I'm asking."

He began by telling her about the first time he saw his grandfather. He'd been six or seven, living hand to mouth with his mother, when they went to visit this strange old man who lived all by himself in a cabin without electricity or running water.

"I could hardly wait to leave," he admitted. "He kept looking at me without so much as acknowledging my presence. I barely understood anything he said. Later, my mother told me Gray Cloud spent so much time by himself that he didn't know how to carry on a conversation. She understood him, at least a little, because he'd passed in and out of her childhood, but she had to work at it. And she told me that sometimes she didn't like what he said."

"What did he say?"

Cord released her hand, shrugged off his backpack and helped her out of hers. Only when he was done and they were back to sitting with their knees touching did he go on.

"I think he was critical of the way she lived," he said. "Because she wasn't interested in the old ways."

"A generation gap."

"That and other things. He and my grandmother were divorced when my mother was very young. I don't know what went wrong between them—he never said."

"No. I imagine he didn't."

"I'm sure my grandmother's family didn't want him around. It hurt him deeply not to be in touch with his child—maybe that's why he had so little to do with people. I don't think he knew what to do with his grown daughter. I remember the criticism in her voice when she told me he didn't understand that the world was changing and she couldn't live in a hut and spend most of her time in the wilderness."

"But you did. And it worked for you." Her body belonged to her again, but she didn't trust it to remain that way. She wanted their time together to go on forever.

"Yes, it did. Once, not long before Gray Cloud died, I asked him why he took me in after my dad split and my mom died. He said it was in my eyes—that mine were the same as his."

"Yes, I think they were."

"Do you? I don't know whether he had legal custody of me—I don't think that kind of thing concerned him. He said I had to go to school because that's what every other child was doing, but he had little use for the institution. He never once let anyone tell him how I should be raised. People, like principals and social workers, tried—he ignored them. He never told me why he'd changed his life for me, shared it with me—just that there was something in my eyes."

She became aware of the way her heart was beating. It seemed to work in fits and starts, sometimes strong, sometimes weak, always making its presence known. Hurting and yet singing at the same time. She'd gone beyond tears simply because Cord had said more to her tonight than he ever had before. "He never told you he loved you, did he?"

"No."

Cord's simple word seemed to echo in the now-solid night. Mindless of the danger, she took his hand and once again held it to her middle. She *felt* him looking at her. What did it matter? She no longer cared that she'd begun to strip herself naked to him. "It hurt, didn't it?"

"Hurt?"

"Surely you wanted to hear words of affection from him. You had a right, the right of every child."

"I knew. It was in the way he treated me, the things he taught me. What we shared."

Tonight it sounded precious. "What did you share?"

"Things. So many things. Listening together. Sitting in the mountains, melting into them, watching nature go about its life. We did that together."

Shivering, she fought for words. "But a child needs to hear certain words from the people in his life. You tell Matt you love him. You know what he needs."

"I learned from you."

She went hot; ice touched fire again. Tears raged inside her but she fought them.

He leaned forward slightly and increased the pressure of knee against knee. "It came so naturally to you. Nursing Matt. Holding and rocking him in that comfortable old rocking chair you bought. Singing to him. Showing him that it was wonderful to smile. I'd watch the two of you, the way he studied your face as if it was the most fascinating thing he'd ever seen. Then he'd smile and you'd show him how to make it bigger."

She shivered, fought a sob. "What about love, Cord?" *Silent? Cord Navarro? Not tonight, not for these few precious seconds.* "What did I do that guided you?"

He hesitated, as if leery of entrusting her with too much of himself, but she held on with hand and heat and heart, desperate to keep the suddenly precious channel between them open.

"What you said to him. And to me. Actions as much as words." He took a deep breath and she could tell that he was looking around at his surroundings. Then he stared at her again and she was glad it was only the two of them.

"There was no way you could stop yourself from expressing what was in your heart," he said. "That love boiled up inside you and spilled over to engulf Matt. And, for a while, me."

A sob again slashed through her. She fought it, only barely aware of her fingers boring into his flesh. "Cord?" The word came out a whimper. When she tried again, it sounded the same. "Cord? Why didn't you say this to me before?"

She felt his forefinger rubbing against the back of her hand, a strong, yet gentle gesture. "Maybe what I felt was caught too deep."

Someone else might have laughed at his hesitant explanation, but she understood. It went back to Gray Cloud and before that a mother overwhelmed by the responsibility of a child. In her mind and heart she saw the little boy he once was, a boy desperate for love and clinging as best he could to what was given him. Or maybe he'd been born self-contained, self-confident. It didn't matter, did it? "Why is it different tonight?"

By way of answer, he looked upward. The moon had just begun its journey over the tips of the shadow trees. The cool, distant source of light was a little more than half full with a gentle rounding on one side that gave promise of more to come. It struck her that Cord was like that, much more than a thin sliver of emotion but not yet having reached what he was—she hoped—capable of.

"It still isn't easy for you, is it?" she whispered. "Talking about emotions."

He grunted.

"Cord, nature speaks to you. Shares its secrets with you. Sharing with another human being isn't any different, not deep down. I'm trying to be that person, at least for now, listening in ways I didn't . . . wasn't capable of before."

He was fighting within himself, at war with something she could only guess at. She wondered if he understood how much she wanted to give him of herself, now. Finally. For long, hungry minutes she waited for him to give her another glimpse of himself so she could do the same in turn and damn the consequences.

Instead, "He should have enough food. Kevin said—"

"Kevin? We're talking about you, not Kevin."

"We're here because of Matt."

His words, his undeniable words, stripped her of anger as quickly as the emotion had assaulted her. "I know," she said. "Oh, God, I know." The sounds eddied and she didn't bother repeating herself. No longer caring—or maybe caring too much, about everything—she reached out as if to grab her pack with its food supply.

He stopped her. Filled with the strength that had brought him here, he gripped her arms and pulled her close. She should have been prepared for her body's reaction. Hadn't she felt the contrast of heat and cold twice already tonight and known of the danger? But when he touched her, she became nothing and everything just the way she had all those years ago when she blindly, naively loved him so much she didn't know if she could stand it.

"We can't fight," he whispered. "We don't dare."

She knew that, but with the sound of his heart pulsing through her and his capable hands holding her so near, she was aware of precious little except him.

I need you. Senseless, insane, I need you. She tried to pull away. He wouldn't let her. She ended the battle she hadn't wanted. "Cord?"

"Shannon? Please, I need to ask you something."

"What?"

"Is it my fault?"

"Your fault?"

"That Matt's out here? Never mind. I don't have to ask. I'm the one responsible for his wanting to prove himself and not having the necessary skills to accomplish that. What I need to know is, how do you feel about it?''

She struggled to make sense of his words. He'd opened himself up to her and was asking for honesty in return. She wanted to give him that and erase a little of the distances that separated them.

But another distance, or rather the lack of one, had made its impact.

He felt far warmer than any summer night she'd ever known. Cooler than the moon that had briefly vied for her attention. There he sat with his incomplete and yet incredibly honest words, his life-hardened body, his mouth so close that its very nearness robbed her of a certain will and made her desperately hungry. She hadn't exorcised him from her body after all, had she? What had made her think that possible?

He sat there looking as if he didn't quite believe he'd taken hold of her, his eyes saying he was ready for her to resist him. But night sounds and sights and smells had begun to sweep over her and claim her for their own.

Most of all, there was him.

She leaned into him, asking with her body, shutting off her mind, accepting the truth about herself. He answered by standing and pulling her against him until they were pressed together chest to hips. So long—how long had she wanted this?

He hadn't moved and his body continued to call to her and there wasn't a half inch of her that didn't know what that call of his felt like. She had only one answer in her.

She felt the stretch in her neck as she rose to meet his mouth. He covered her lips with his, a simple, complex, life-giving kiss that raced through her until the message in their embrace touched her heart. She was instantly flooded with memories—memories of that other lifetime when youth and wonder and love and physical hunger had her in their grip.

He'd met her with barely parted lips, but that soon changed. She felt his mouth open, slowly, tantalizingly. To give herself strength, she clamped her arms around his neck and waited. On fire, she waited.

He gave her access. Still mindless, she touched her tongue to his teeth and asked entrance. Something cool lapped at the back of her neck, but she ignored the unexpected breeze. For the past hour, her feet had been aching. Now the warmth boiling from deep inside her laced a slow trail down her legs until even her toes felt the impact.

Trusting that he wouldn't leave her, she released his neck and slowly ran her fingers into his thick, coarse hair. In silent response, he pressed his palms into the small of her back. He'd done that a thousand times in the distant past when just looking at each other had stripped away the world. She arched herself toward him, stopping only when his hard body gave no more.

Sealed together.

Could she remember what he needed most in a kiss? She tried to put her mind to the massive question but it snaked out of reach.

His exploring tongue slowly worked its way into her. She closed her teeth gently around him and gave herself up to the magic of the other ways she'd once surrounded him.

Lovemaking. The promise was within her grasp—a teasing, testing memory that felt like hot coals applied to the heat already pulsing through her.

He'd once known her body, explored it as he explored his beloved wilderness. Maybe cherished both in the same way.

But that was yesterday. Years ago. Tonight his fingers and hands and tongue and lips felt totally new. Surely he'd never filled her so full of life before. She would have remembered that.

She would have learned how to control her reaction.

But those lessons, if they'd once been hers, rushed away like butterflies caught in the wind.

She felt fingers along the side of her neck. She leaned into him, thinking to surround him, but went weak instead.

With her hands still in his hair and her palms resting over the pulsing veins at his temple, she covered his mouth and chin and cheeks with hummingbird kisses. Her body, needing more, fought her, but she refused to listen to its cry.

"Shannon?"

Her name on his lips. She touched her tongue there as if doing so could draw the sound deep inside her. She wanted to be able to say something that might reach him in the same way, but years of silence and distance stood between them, and she didn't know how to begin to bridge that. What she could do was let him know how she felt about him at this moment—gentle and tentative and frightened and eager, wondering if there was a journey to begin, asking him to help with the decision.

He didn't speak again. His hands inched lower until he'd cupped them around her buttocks and pulled her against him. He was ready to capture her, hard and alive and urgent.

She fought her own urgency, her mind nearly screaming in its need for that precious first step.

First step? A mountain to climb? Maybe. A bottomless ravine? Maybe.

With an awful wrench, she resisted him. At the same time, fighting herself, she continued her whispering kisses. She prayed he understood how dangerous what they were doing was and how it might explode at any moment. She should be able to tell him, to get him to go at the pace she was trying to set so they wouldn't lose it all.

But they'd lost so many years, so much love. Maybe they should remain buried behind those years. If not, if there was something to their time together, the journey needed to be taken slowly.

Didn't it?

Why couldn't she think?

He pushed her away from him until she could no longer cover him with her questioning kisses. She felt his eyes dig into her, felt his own battle.

Understood, suddenly, the true meaning of danger.

"We can't—it isn't—" she began.

"You don't want..."

No. Not that. Surely not that. "Cord? What we're doing, it's—we're insane. We know better. We should."

"And you don't want it."

If he'd asked a question she could have told him how wrong he was, but he'd misinterpreted and she suddenly felt too exhausted to try to explain. Wondering how long it would take her body to release his memory, she twisted away from him until a full foot of night air separated them.

"You're wrong," she whispered. "I want. Oh, how I want."

Chapter 10

Matt pulled off his boot and twisted his foot around so he could stare at his heel, but the moon wasn't bright enough to be much help. Despite his aching knees, he'd felt the blister all the time he was walking today and had hoped it wouldn't pop. Well, it had. As an owl complained about something, he tried to remember what his mother had said about how to take care of a blister.

Mom wasn't here. He'd have to figure out what to do on his own. After a moment he had an idea. He'd clean the blister in the little creek he'd come across just before dark and then leave it open to the air during the night. Air was good for a lot of things, wasn't it? That had to be why Mom blew on his scrapes and scratches.

Had Mom called around to see what he was up to after all? Sure, she'd said she wasn't going to because she knew he would be safe at the campground, but she sometimes still thought of him as a little kid. If she learned—

Learned what? Kevin promised he wouldn't tell.

Kevin's a jerk. Besides, if she so much as sees him, she'll know something happened.

She won't. She promised.

Yeah. And you promised you'd go to that dumb old campground with Kevin.

Sick of what was going on inside him, he scurried on hands and knees to the tree he'd decided to spend the night under. The moon was glinting off the little bit of water just enough to turn the darkness there a real interesting-looking silver. Maybe in the morning he'd spot a fish and figure out a way to catch it. He wasn't sure what he'd do with the fish once he had it, but he'd seen his father cut some open and hoped he'd remember how.

What was he thinking? There wouldn't be any creek here if it wasn't for the last bit of snow runoff. Fish weren't in it, just some little insects and maybe frogs. Besides, he didn't have any way of cooking anything and he'd never kill something he didn't have a use for. That's what his dad always said, don't kill anything if there's any other way. He wanted his dad to be proud of him.

Wait a minute! Maybe Dad was looking for him. Oh, gosh! If Mom had somehow learned that he'd decided to climb Copper, she would have found a way to get in touch with Dad.

He couldn't let his dad find him. No way! For a moment, he nearly changed his mind; he didn't like how that stupid old owl kept hooting as if he was laughing at him. But he'd fallen asleep last night listening to an owl and his father's calm voice inside his head and hadn't woken up even once. There wasn't anything to be afraid of in an owl. Or in a bear. His dad had told him that years ago and he hadn't forgotten, still believed.

Just the same, he looked around, wondering despite himself if he might see little bear eyes staring at him. Instead he heard more owls and buzzing insects and other things he didn't recognize and the wind slapping away at the pine needles in the trees. And then he noticed something glowing off in the distance. Maybe someone a long way away had a powerful flashlight, maybe one of those heavy things he'd seen police carry.

Seeing proof that he wasn't alone up here reminded him of the smoke he'd noticed yesterday. There had been a lot of smoke, too much in fact. If he had a match and it was all right to build one here, he sure wouldn't make one like that. If those people—whoever they were—weren't careful and started another fire, they might set the woods on fire.

His dad would never do anything like that. Cord Navarro knew how to build a fire that used just the littlest bit of wood and hardly made any smoke but would keep a person warm for hours. Indians did neat stuff like that, and his dad knew more about the woods and fire building and bears and stuff than any of the Indians he'd ever seen on TV or at the movies.

If his dad was anywhere around, he sure wasn't with whoever had the flashlight. He was positive of that because his dad would have somehow sensed he wasn't alone out here—would know how close his son was.

Those guys, whoever they were, must be hikers. What other reason would they have to be way up here on Copper?

"What the hell are you doing?"

Whirling, Owen tucked the flashlight against his soft belly as if trying to protect both it and him. "Nothing."

What was it with Owen? Chuck Markham thought. The man had to be at least forty and yet he acted like some lamebrain kid. "You're going to use up that damn thing."

He indicated the flashlight, not caring that both Elliot and Andrew had stopped their conversation to listen.

"I heard something." Owen pointed at the trees. "I was trying to figure out what it was."

"Owls." Chuck snorted. "You heard owls. This area's lousy with them."

"That's about the only thing." Elliot spoke up. "Look, the three of us have been talking. So far the only thing we've gotten out of this hunting trip is blisters and a lot of hype from you, plus too damn much criticism. If you think you're going to get more out of us by dragging things out, you've got another think coming."

"Is that what you think?" Chuck challenged. Flashlight still tucked against his belly, Owen had sidled closer to Elliot and Andrew, leaving him standing alone. "I thought you said you'd checked out my reputation before signing on with me. If you didn't like what you heard, what are you doing here?"

Elliot laughed, his voice going high at the end. "You know better than we do that the country's not exactly crawling with guides willing to give us what we want."

What Elliot was saying was that not many people had the guts to risk imprisonment because a sizable chunk of money was waved under their chin. Fine. He didn't mind being one of a kind. "We'll find what you're after," he said. "Keep those rifles loaded, gentlemen. You're about to get what you came for."

"Cord? My mother wants to talk to you."

Surprised, Cord took the two-way radio from Shannon. Elizabeth's voice sounded slightly hollow and jerky, but despite the distance that separated them, he heard everything she said. "I didn't have time to talk to you before you started after Matt," she said. "And when we talked earlier it was pretty businesslike. I hope you haven't settled down for the night."

He wasn't sure whether he'd be able to sleep tonight, not unless he could shut off memories of those risky moments he and Shannon had spent in each other's arms. That and men's footprints. "Not yet," he told his former mother-in-law.

"I just want you to know," Elizabeth continued. "I'm sure you've heard this already—but I'm so glad it's you up there. Cord, there's no doubt? You're sure it's my grandson you're tracking?"

He told her he had no doubt, then waited for what else she needed to say. Last Christmas when he'd come by to pick up Matt, he'd felt awkward being in the same room with Shannon's parents while Matt unwrapped his presents. Christmas was family time and he wasn't part of their family anymore. Since the divorce, he'd kept his contact with Matt's grandparents to a minimum, assuming that was what they wanted.

Tonight none of that mattered.

"I know I shouldn't allow myself to think about everything that can go wrong," Elizabeth was saying. "Everyone tells me to think positive. And I do—but..."

He didn't need further explanation. Wasn't his own mind full of thoughts of what might happen if Matt had an accident or the poachers mistook his son for some animal? "Elizabeth, just before it got dark, Shannon and I placed our hands over the mark Matt made sleeping last night. What I've seen this afternoon convinces me he's in good shape physically." *Except that he's limping.* "We'll find him." *If a bullet doesn't first.*

"You promise me?"

Not once in his career had he allowed himself to be backed into making a commitment beyond his control. But it was different this time. Elizabeth was asking her former son-in-law, the man who'd gotten her teenage daughter pregnant, to take responsibility for the result of that pregnancy in a way far more important than any that had gone before.

"I promise," he said when he knew he might not be able to make good on his words.

"Oh...Cord? It helps to hear you say that. I can't tell you how much."

He didn't have to be told; he heard it in her voice. Careful to keep emotion out of his voice, he said that from what he'd been able to tell, Matt wasn't frightened. Lost but not scared. "You should be proud of him. I am. A lot of children in his position frighten themselves. Their fear works against them."

"If he's not afraid, it's because of what you've taught him."

I haven't taught him enough. "I hope so," he told her honestly. In the few minutes they'd been talking, her voice had lost its taut tone. *I'm sorry,* he wanted to tell her. *Sorry I robbed your daughter of the last of her girlhood and made her a woman too soon. Sorry I didn't turn out to be what she needed.*

"Cord? Just bring him back to me, please. Holding him is the only thing I want in life. Shannon, too—I'm sure of that."

The only thing she wants in life. Of course. Nothing else mattered.

In the half hour since they'd pulled out of each other's arms, he had busied himself with tending to their boots and taking mental pictures of their surroundings in an effort to determine where Matt was most likely to be. He'd told Shannon what he was doing because he knew she needed to hear that, but he'd barely been able to put the words together. Too much energy had gone into trying to make his body forget what holding her had done to his self-control. She'd wanted and needed the embrace as much as he did; he'd never doubt that. They'd been like birds about to take flight, testing the wind, eager for that incredible sense of freedom. But they'd both seen the danger in time.

He acknowledged what remained of his need for her and again cast it off. That time in each other's arms had been insanity, the result of too much tension and isolation.

Maybe not insanity. Maybe echoes of something they'd once had but had died long ago.

An ache behind his right temple served as the distraction he needed. This wasn't the time for letting the past overtake him. He *had* to concentrate on his surroundings, and learn who might be sharing it with them.

And when he had that information, he would have to tell Shannon. Somehow.

Shannon could only guess at Cord's reaction to what her mother had said to him. Obviously something had hit a nerve with him. Nothing else would have made him walk out into the dark until, if it hadn't been for the moon, he would have disappeared completely.

Earlier tonight she hadn't been able to look at him without remembering the seemingly endless dance of their lovemaking, wanting back what had brought them together all those years ago. She'd always accepted his silence in bed. What had she needed with words back then when his body spoke for him? Only, time and wisdom and experience had taught her that a body wasn't enough. The holes in him, his incomplete heart, his inability to see into her and understand that she needed more than sex—needed compassion and emotional honesty, those were the things that had torn them apart. And what had taken him from her side tonight.

Unmindful of her bare feet, she stood and started toward him. She wasn't sure why, just that she sensed that something precious was in danger of fading into the night and if she didn't reach out for it, she might spend the rest of her life regretting it. Talking about Summer, learning that he carried their daughter's picture, had caused some of her melancholy. As for the rest—

She tried to walk silently the way Cord had done several times today when observing some wild creature. It seemed to her that she didn't make any sound, but if Cord could sense the presence of fox kits hidden beneath the ground, surely he sensed her.

Still, he didn't turn. Maybe he didn't care. Maybe... Knowing she might be risking a return to what had been so hard to break free from earlier, she touched his back. He didn't move and yet she sensed something change deep within him. "My mother said something that's bothering you, didn't she? I wish you'd talk to me about it," she whispered. There was just the two of them in this world of night and wilderness sounds. Just this man who had embraced and been embraced by that wilderness.

He remained still, not speaking for so long that she began to break inside. Then, "She said that having Matt back is the only thing she wants in life. You, too."

Her mother's words hit her with the force of a blow. They must have done the same to Cord, and that's why he'd let darkness absorb him. "It's the truth."

"I know."

"But... didn't you expect that from her?"

Through her fingers, she felt him draw in a deep breath. "I didn't expect her to be that honest with me."

Why? Oh, Cord, what does it feel like to be set apart from others this way? "My mother believes in keeping her opinions to herself, not that I have to tell you that. It took this for her to break through all those polite layers."

She thought that might turn him around, but he continued to stare off at nothing. Only the night wasn't nothing for him. He knew which creatures embraced it, who hunted and who was hunted. Lost in thoughts of his place in a mountain night, she ran his shirt fabric between her fingers. He shifted his weight so that he now angled himself toward her slightly. "Why did you come back here?" he asked.

"To Summit County?" *Is this what we're going to talk about? Decisions from the past?*

"You were so eager to leave it. When we got married, you told me you needed to move away so you could get an education and make use of it."

"I did say that, didn't I?" Almost before the words were out of her mouth, she winced. After everything they'd shared in the past few days, she didn't want to skirt around his question. "I don't know why I returned. At least, I didn't know what I was going to do when I packed my bags and . . . and—"

"When you walked out of the apartment we were living in."

We? He'd hardly ever been there. Although she now felt petty saying it, she reminded him that she'd paid the utilities and rent before leaving, even stocked the refrigerator for him.

"I never spent another night in it."

She hadn't known that. "Why not?"

"The memories."

Memories. "I should have—I didn't know how to handle any of that."

He nodded. "Neither did I."

"Oh. Oh."

He turned fully around, presenting himself to her, taking over everything. "Did your parents want you to live near them?"

"They...had nothing to do with my decision." She didn't dare acknowledge his gaze; she might forget what she wanted him to understand. "I got in the car and started driving. This is where I wound up. Of course, my folks were happy and for a while I let them spoil me. But—"

"But you don't like it when someone tries to take care of you."

He knew that about her. What else hadn't the years erased? "No. I don't." She thought about rubbing warmth into her arms, but he might guess she felt uncomfortable in her body. She finally gripped her right elbow with her left hand. "I think, when I realized I couldn't spend another night waiting for you to be there for me—to look at you and think of you as a stranger—nothing but home called to me."

"Your childhood home, not the one we'd made."

"We didn't have a home. Not what I needed, thought I needed. Oh, Cord, I was so confused. Hurting. All I knew was, I would lose my mind if I didn't do something. I knew I needed space around me. That apartment you felt penned up in, it got that way for me, too. I needed to smell pines and look at mountains and . . . and support Matt and myself doing something I loved. I needed to go on with life." *Put you behind me.*

"You've done well," he said softly. "You've made a success of your business."

She'd been concentrating on where his voice came from for so long that her mind filled in what her eyes couldn't see in the dark. She knew he'd removed his boots and was walking around barefoot just like her. It wouldn't take much for the wilderness to absorb him; if it did, would she ever find him again? "It's been a lot of work, but then, I don't have to tell you what it's like to be self-employed. You know about the sacrifices, the uncertainty."

"Yes." His voice threatened to encircle her. She started to fight it, but that single word was so quickly followed by others that she remained off balance. "Only, when it's something you truly want to do, or feel compelled to do, it doesn't feel like a sacrifice, does it?"

"No. It doesn't."

"Matt's proud of you."

Warmth at Matt's endorsement spread through her, followed by even more realization of how much communication took place between father and son. Maybe Matt even sensed his father's presence tonight. She could at least hope. "He can see what I'm doing on a daily basis. A lot of kids can't say that."

"I know."

She thought she understood what was behind Cord's pensive tone, that he envied what she had. She nearly told him so, but everything they said to each other seemed so complex and she was worn out from trying to deal with her reaction to being here, alone, with him. She shifted her weight onto her right leg and began absently rubbing her hand up and down her arm. "I thought Matt might balk at having to help with the horses. A lot of his friends don't have any real responsibilities and have a lot more free time. But I don't think he minds. At least, he's never said."

"He doesn't mind."

"He told you that?"

"Yes," Cord said softly. She thought he'd said something else but just then an owl let out with an indignant call that momentarily stopped all conversation.

"Maybe we're disturbing him," she ventured a few seconds later. "After all, he was here first."

"He's passing along information to other owls."

"What kind of information? That there are intruders around?"

"Yes."

"Then—Cord, if the owls are talking about Matt as well as us, would you know?"

"No. Not unless he was close."

She knew she'd been grasping at straws when she asked her question. Still, his denial depressed her more than it should.

Unsure what to do with herself now, she made a move as if to turn back to her bed roll.

"Shannon?"

"Yes?"

"There's something..."

"Something? What?" she prompted.

"We aren't... there are—does... does it bother you that it's just us looking for him? You haven't said."

That's not what he'd started out to say. She knew that instinctively. But because she understood all too well the folly of pressing Cord to reveal something he didn't want to, she told him she trusted his judgment in this. He was following Matt's tracks. There wasn't anything a hundred searchers could do that wasn't being done by them.

But what she felt went deeper than practical considerations. It was somehow fitting that they were the ones intent on bringing their son back where he belonged. In this world of complex organizations, rules and regulations, sometimes parents simply needed to be the ones doing the job that instinct and love and commitment had prepared them for. "I want us to find him, for us to be the first people he sees when he realizes he's no longer lost. A kind of bonding."

"Bonding?"

"Yes. No matter what you and I are to each other, we created a child. Two children. That's precious."

When he didn't say anything else and she couldn't find a way around the emotion that clogged her entire being, she turned her attention to where she was going to spend the night. Although she stepped on a pinecone and felt a stab of pain in her instep, she managed to make her way back to her bed. She sat down, aware that her brain wasn't nearly as tired as her body and that sleep might be hours away.

They'd created a child. Two children.

And Cord carried pictures of both of them.

He'd left his shelter of darkness. She could hear him moving around. "Does it bother you, not having a fire?" he asked.

"If I thought Matt would see it, I'd have already set the woods afire. But you're sure he's far enough away that he couldn't see one, aren't you?"

"I'm sorry."

The words were simple enough but there was nothing un-cluttered in the emotion behind them. As if drawn to Cord by what was going on inside him, she got up and walked over to stand beside him. The moonlight had made its impact on his features. He was now a dark, brooding, silver-touched melody of shadow. She was unable to do more than guess at what was going on behind the dark center of his eyes, so she took her cue from what she knew about him.

He was lost deep in that place he went when she'd never been able to reach him. Too many times she'd asked for an explanation of what he was thinking about and had to settle for what little he'd been willing or able to give her. Tonight she wouldn't try, not because she didn't care but because for once she didn't need words from him.

She'd simply stand beside him and share a little of herself. And she wouldn't listen to her body's restless hum. Somehow.

"I think, if I wasn't doing what I am, I might want to be an astronomer," she told him. She was grasping at the first thing to come to mind. "I don't know what qualifications I'd have to bring to the job—probably a lot more schooling. But I love the idea of discovering some unknown moon, maybe a whole galaxy. I'd engage in lofty discussions with other scientists about whether there's more intelligent life out there."

"I hope there is."

"Because maybe they've come up with some solutions we haven't?"

"That's part of it. And because I want to see if they have big heads and eyes and long, thin fingers."

His attempt at humor made her smile. "What about you? Are you at all interested in doing anything else?"

"Archaeology."

"You're serious? You'd really like to dig in the dirt for signs of ancient life?"

"Yeah. I would." He sounded pensive.

"Why?" she prompted. She'd had to push him so many times in the past that it came instinctively.

"Curiosity, I guess. Maybe I'm looking for my roots."

Gray Cloud had been his only roots. "You never told me that."

"I never used to think about it, but... There's a place in California's Saline Valley where the Shoshone Indians once had a winter camp. Their civilization may have been over six thousand years old when the white man came. Six thousand years." Wonder painted his tone. "I was there once on a search and stayed an extra week talking to BLM archaeologists about Shoshone art and religious beliefs."

"A week? It must have made quite an impression to keep you in one place that long."

"It did. And it made me aware of how little I know about a great deal of my own heritage. Since then I've been intrigued by what ancient civilizations left behind. Nevada, southeastern Oregon, the four corners area, all that and more is rich with remnants of the past, if people who know what they're looking for can get to it before vandals do."

"I hope that happens. I mean it, I've never heard you talk about this kind of thing before."

"I think, until just a while ago, I was too young to be interested in the past. Really interested."

And now he was. Circumstances had taken him to part of the country and an experience that excited him and opened him up to interests he'd never expected. Would that continue throughout his life, or was he reaching into the past because his present felt incomplete?

With a silent groan, she shook off the heavy thought. "I love looking at stars." She was barely aware of what she was saying. "There's an endlessness about them. A permanence. And yet they're so illusive, so mysterious. I know it's been said a million times, but I feel as if I could reach out and touch one."

"What would you do if you could?"

The question was so totally unlike Cord to ask that it turned her toward him. He waited in dark as old and enduring as the stars. This mountain was his place, the night with its stars and moon created for him. "Do?"

"I'm trying to picture you standing on the top of a mountain holding a star in your hand."

Oh, Cord. "You are?"

"Yes."

"Why?"

"Why? Being here with you . . ."

She didn't want him to say anything that might make her feel even more off balance than she already did. Another word, a whisper, a touch, and she'd spin off into eternity. Still— "What about our being here together?"

"I think you know."

He'd sounded unsure of himself a few heartbeats ago. Now he was once again the strong, confident man she'd fallen in love with and—in many ways—still loved. She wanted to be like him, to have control over her emotions, but how could she if they were alone, together, and the night had them in its embrace?

"Do you?" he pressed.

Do I what? Your voice—just your voice. "Cord? Cord, there isn't enough of me left over to try to deal with anything except Matt." *Liar.*

He rocked forward slightly and then back. The movement did beautiful and mysterious things to his features as the moon caressed him. He looked unreal, a mountain man created from wilderness and wind. She didn't know how to stop her reaction or even if she wanted to. But to tell him?

Only an insane woman would try to touch a bolt of lightning.

Chapter 11

Feeling more peaceful than she had since the ordeal had begun, Shannon watched the early morning sun touch the sky and turn it from black to a soft gold. It was going to be warm, summer's promise seeping through deeply shaded valleys and touching them with life—heating their son's body.

"He's all right," she said, her voice still filled with sleep. "I'd know it if he wasn't."

She fully expected Cord to tell her she couldn't possibly be sure about what she'd just said. If he did, she wouldn't argue with him because it was nothing except her mother's heart speaking. Instead, he nodded, stretched, and began rolling up his sleeping bag. He'd worn only briefs to sleep in. Although they'd settled down some ten feet from each other, she plainly saw the dark dusting of hair that covered his thighs and calves. Once she'd run her fingers, toes, lips over his legs, lost in wonder at the belief that he loved her.

Now all she could do was look and remember.

When he stepped into his jeans and sat to put on his boots, she tried to eat a few bites of dried apple, but her stomach seemed to have lost all interest in food. Maybe she was becoming more and more like Cord. As long as she searched for their son, she wouldn't be aware of her body.

Only, that wasn't it. At least, not all of it. She didn't even have to be near Cord for her body to pick up signals from him.

He seemed unnaturally quiet this morning. Maybe it was only her need to be diverted from the disjointed and disturbing thoughts flitting through her that made her ache for conversation, but she didn't think so. Giving up on her breakfast, she reached for her own jeans. She wondered if his attention might be drawn to her legs, but he'd stopped what he was doing and was sitting with his head cocked to one side, his fingers clamped tightly over his knees. She felt as if she could reach out and touch the tension in him, and struggled to hear anything except the stiff breeze, the way the birds welcomed the morning. Cord had exceptional hearing; she'd been impressed by it from the beginning. She longed to ask if he might be able to hear Matt, but if that had been the case, he surely would have told her.

When the radio squawked to life, she momentarily resented the intrusion, then watched intently as Cord picked it up. It was Kevin's dad reporting that he'd been in contact with the sheriff during the night and that Dale, who was off doing something Hallem didn't explain, wanted Cord to know that he would be getting in touch with him as soon as possible.

"What is that about?" she asked after Hallem and Cord had spoken for several minutes. "What's Dale up to? Are you thinking about bringing in more help? I thought—"

Cord barely glanced at her, making her wonder if he was really aware of her presence. "Even if they could be of assistance, it'd take them too long to get here. Damn. I wish Dale had been there."

"Why? Was there something the two of you needed to talk about?" She rolled her bag into a tight bundle and secured it, then stuffed it into her pack.

"What? Nothing important."

"If it isn't important, why are you so upset?"

By way of answer, not that it was one, he pushed himself to his feet and stared out at his surroundings. She wanted to concentrate on the conversation and try to force him to tell her everything, but high above the tops of the trees she spotted an eagle silhouetted against the morning sky. For reasons she couldn't pretend to understand, the eagle distracted her from the need for confrontation. "What do we do now?" she asked. "Where do we go?"

Still taking in his quiet, clean world, he pointed in the direction they'd been heading when it got too dark to travel last night. She waited for him to say something, but he seemed caught within his own thoughts, as far from her as if he'd been in another state. She'd seen that look on him before and felt helpless to transcend it. In the past she'd believed he was deliberately holding himself apart from her. Now she knew it was more complicated than that.

"Are you ready to start?" he asked after nearly a minute of silence.

By way of answer, she walked over to him and gave her pack a final shrug. She supposed she could have asked him for help in getting into it, but then she'd feel compelled to do the same for him and right now touching him wasn't wise; maybe it never would be. He hadn't asked whether she was up to another long day of walking and looking, but then he didn't need to. Surely he knew that as long as there was life in her, she'd search for Matt.

His pace bothered her. She'd picked up enough from watching him in the past few days to know how much work it took to find a faint mark in the dirt. She admired his patience and tenacity, but today there seemed to be a new sense of urgency to what he was doing. As she concentrated on both keeping up with him and not distracting him, she fought off the persistent question of whether he knew something about Matt's condition he wasn't willing to tell her. Again and again she teetered on the brink of asking him what he was thinking, demand he leave nothing locked up inside him, but each time she held back. If he gave weight to her worst fears, she might panic.

And she didn't dare. If she did, she would be no good to him. Or to their son.

Shannon stepped on a loose section of shale. When the rock broke apart and skittered down the slope away from them, Cord stopped long enough to assure himself that she hadn't injured herself.

From the sun's position, he knew they'd been traveling, without rest, for nearly four hours. Heat pressed down on him and taunted him to surrender to lethargy, but he fought it just as he fought the distraction of elk sign, floating hawks, the song of insects. With each step they were getting closer to Matt, but that gave him scant comfort. Matt's prints had begun to smear, proof that he was occasionally dragging his feet. Still, there was a fierce determination to the way his son walked that said overtaking him wouldn't be easy.

He was proud of Matt, so proud that his heart ached with the need to tell the boy that. Matt hadn't given up, hadn't let weariness or hunger or fear, if he was afraid, get the upper hand. Obviously he was determined to prove he didn't need rescuing; maybe it hadn't so much as occurred to him that he couldn't get back home, eventually, without help. But if Matt went without listening to his body's needs for much longer, he could set himself up for injury or accident.

That wasn't the worst of it. Just after he woke up this morning and looked across the space that separated him from Shannon, he had once again heard the one sound capable of chilling him. He'd listened again a little later, unsuccessfully this time, which had only drawn Shannon's attention to him.

The hunters were still out there, still engaged in their deadly sport. And with the way the rifle shot bounced off the peaks, he could only guess at where they were. For all he knew, they could have found their prey—or Matt.

Ignoring the sun that beat down on the back of his neck, he leaned forward, briefly confused. Part of his confusion came, he knew, because he couldn't dismiss the father in him who wanted nothing more in life than to have his son back again. But it was more complex than that. For the past half hour Matt had been traveling as directly northeast as the terrain would allow. Now, suddenly, he'd changed directions. To make sure he hadn't misinterpreted the sign, he made a slow circle while Shannon waited off to one side.

"I don't know what he's doing," he muttered.

"What do you mean?"

Her question startled him. He didn't remember speaking out loud. "The way he was going, I thought he'd made a decision. But he's lost confidence in himself again."

"Oh, no. The poor boy."

"It happens," he told her without risking the distraction of looking at her. He'd seen her in her undershirt this morning, and although he'd already gone four hours trying to shake off the memory of her long, tanned legs, it hadn't been enough. "Lost people sometimes convince themselves that they know what they're doing. Then they see or don't see something and it throws them off balance."

"Does he know he's lost? Can you tell?"

"No, I don't think he does."

"How... how do you know?"

"Most lost children stay where they are, especially if they've been going as long as he has."

"In other words, Matt's trying to convince himself that he knows what he's doing."

"Yes."

"Because..." Even when her voice trailed off, he didn't look at her. Still, because of the years they'd spent together, he knew what he'd see in her eyes. "Because he's Cord Navarro's son and any son of his couldn't possibly be in this much trouble."

"I can't help it, Shannon! Don't you think I'd change this if I could?"

She didn't say anything, and although he regretted his outburst, maybe it was better that they'd gotten this out in the open even if it drove yet another wedge between them. Still, as he reassured himself that he'd properly read his son's tracks, he made a vow not to react to anything else she said. She needed him to find their son, nothing more. He'd done this before, and he could do it again.

"I hate this. I absolutely hate this."

He'd glanced over his shoulder at her before he'd had time to warn himself of the folly of such a move. Her cheeks looked slightly wind-chapped, her shirt wrinkled. He wanted to wrap her in silk and give her a rainbow. "The walking?"

"No. Of course not. If I thought it would help, I'd walk until I came to the end of the world. It's the damn stuff that keeps going through my head. I know you know what I'm talking about. You're going through the same thing."

"Yes. I am," he said, although his thoughts, compounded by past experiences of failed rescues and his knowledge of who else they shared the mountain with, made it even harder. "There's only one thing we can do, Shannon. Follow him until we find him."

"We've been looking for days. What the hell good has it done us?"

Shannon never swore. Now she'd done it twice in less than a minute. The words were enough to swing him back around toward her.

Her eyes said it all. They were sunken deeper into their sockets and the flesh there was now shadowed almost as if she'd bruised herself. There were lines at the corners of her mouth he'd never noticed before and her shoulders seemed to sag a little.

Still, determination ruled her.

"I didn't mean to say that," she apologized. "I'm just giving in to frustration, that's all. Please don't stop for me. No matter where you go or how fast, I'll keep up."

"This isn't a race."

"Yes, it is. A race to save our son. I lost one child, Cord. I can't do it again."

She'd spoken the words as if they meant no more to her than a million other words had, but her eyes gave her away. She wasn't crying. He sensed how fiercely she'd guarded against letting that happen. But for reasons she might not fully understand, everything had boiled over for her and the only thing she could do was fight her way around a mother's worst fears, a father's nightmare.

"He's all right," he told her.

"You don't know that. Don't fill me with false hope."

"I'm telling you the truth." *At least it was when he walked this way.* "It's in his signs."

That took the fight out of her; he didn't know he was capable of hurting her so deeply with a few words. Anger—at her tears, at the wilderness that defied them—had whipped through her and met head-on with fear and defeat.

"Shannon, listen to me, please. The Taos Indians have a saying, a prayer. There's a lot of wisdom in it. Maybe it'll help you. I know it does me."

"Does it?"

"Yes," he said, although he knew she was simply going through the gestures of keeping the conversation going. "They believe that the Mother of us all is earth, the Father is the sun, the Grandfather, the creator who bathed us with his mind and gave life to all things. Our Brother is the beasts and trees, Sister is that with wings."

She stared, blinked, stared.

"We, the Taos believe, are the children of earth. That's what Matt is. A child of the earth." *And so is Summer.*

"Of the earth? Safe?"

"Safe," he told her, believing, at least for the moment.

She held out a trembling hand, and he took it, pulled her to him, embraced both her and her pack. She'd again attempted to braid her hair this morning but hadn't been able to capture all the strands. Now one teased the corner of his mouth. Barely aware of what he was doing, he gave her his chest to cry into if that's what she needed, fought the thousand emotions that had built and then splintered inside him. Fought more than that.

"It's all right to be afraid," he whispered.

"Is it? Fighting fear so it won't take over everything is so hard, takes so damn much energy."

She was right; he knew that better than she. "Pretending it doesn't exist is even worse."

He felt more than heard a deep sob tear through her. Clutching her to him, he thought to shield her from the worst of her pain. If only he could think of the words to say, but if he wasn't careful, his own fear would spill out.

She needed him to be strong, to be there for her when she couldn't do it on her own.

He clamped down on his anxiety and denied it. Buried it. Hid from it.

"It's all right," he whispered while she fought to gain control over her tears. "It's all right to cry."

She didn't argue with him this time. In fact, if he was correctly reading her body's silent messages, she was grateful he'd given her license to acknowledge what she'd been holding inside her.

Shannon worked with her fear, accepted it with tears that dampened his shirt and again made him long to spirit her away from this place, this journey. This nightmare. Feeling awkward and inadequate, he held on.

Still, a quiet, insistent part of his brain continued to listen, to assess their world.

Her loss of control didn't last long. After half a dozen shuddering breaths and a raw sound deep in her throat, her body found its strength again.

"What else do the Taos believe?" she asked. "I think I need to hear it all."

He kissed her forehead, wondering if that simple gesture might convey everything he felt at this moment and whether exposing his vulnerability, his need for her, was dangerous. It didn't matter because he was past holding himself in. "That everyone—man, beasts, trees, birds, earth, all share the same breath."

Her chest heaved with the effort of a deep breath. "It sounds so simple, too simple of course, but I want to believe that. Oh, God, how I want to believe."

"You will. If you listen to what nature has to say."

"Maybe—will you help me do that?"

Overwhelmed by her need for him, at least at this moment, he nodded.

"I'm sorry I caved in like that," she whispered. "I—I didn't know I was going to."

"It's all right."

"That's what you already said. Cord? I want you to tell me...to tell me I can trust you, that you'll make it all come out the way we want and need it to. We've been through hell once—surely we won't be asked to survive a child's loss again."

He brushed her hair away from her throat, came within a whisper of covering her trembling lips with his own and letting her feel his—everything.

"But you can't, can you?" she whispered.

"No."

Despite his hard truth, she held on with fingers that bit into his forearms. "I don't want to hear you say that. You know that, don't you?"

"Yes." *More than you could possibly understand.*

"No. Yes." She echoed him while still holding on. "That's all you're going to say, isn't it?"

"Yes." He winced at the word but it was too late.

"It's all right," she said, surprising him. "There really aren't any other words."

Because he felt the need to be doing something and remembered that the gesture used to calm her at the end of a long day, he slid his fingers around to the back of her neck and began massaging the top of her spine.

She rolled her shoulders backward and sighed. "You're so good at that. I'd forgotten."

"I hadn't."

"Oh, Cord, where did it all fall apart for us? Was it because of what happened to Summer and the way I isolated myself, the way we both did? Or was there more to it than that?''

"I don't know."

"I think you do. More than we've talked about, anyway. But it doesn't matter. Darn it, nothing does except getting our son back."

No, he thought. Maybe nothing did except Matt's safety. And yet ... And yet he wanted affirmation that life would go on and he would hold on if ... He couldn't make himself finish.

As her tears dried, she continued to look at him and he had to tell himself she had no idea what was going on inside him. The strong lines of her mouth softened and he again fought the desire to take her—both of them—to places that once had been so easy to reach. Places that would take him away from the reality of today.

"Why do I keep beating myself up trying to reinvent the past?" she moaned before he'd ended his battle. "The past doesn't matter—I just want it buried."

Can you? Can either of us?

"I'm trying to remember something," she said after a silence that had become uncomfortable. "Matt came across it at school and brought it home to me. How does it go? 'The earth does not belong to man—man belongs to the earth. Whatever befalls the earth befalls the sons of the earth. Man did not weave the web of life—he is merely a strand in it.' Yes. That's it."

Cord smiled, feeling incredibly close to her again and knowing how fragile it was. "Every part of this earth is sacred to my people," he continued for her. "Every shining pine needle, every sandy shore, every mist in the dark woods, every clearing and humming insect is holy in the memory and experience of my people. Those were Chief Seattle's words. At least, I'd like to believe they were. He was trying to explain to President Pierce why his people would never understand the concept of selling land. Matt told you about that?''

"Yes." Her voice trembled slightly. "He said that's the way you feel. He knows you very well, doesn't he?"

"Yes, he does."

"Better than I do."

Because he couldn't let her go, he pressed her close to him and hoped that his body would say what he didn't have words for. After a long minute of holding, rocking, giving, he caught the softest of sounds escape her lips, a sound far different from the sobs that had claimed her a few minutes ago.

The whisper told him everything, let him believe what he wanted. She'd let him place his arms around her because she was weary of carrying her burden alone. He'd been able to assume enough of that weight that she could now listen to what else was going on inside her. He struggled to find the words to tell her that everything and anything she felt was right, but no matter how he worked them, they seemed inadequate and half formed.

Maybe the truth was that with her pressed against him, no words would come.

Without regret, he gave up the fight and, beyond that, the need to learn whether hunters had found their son. Her mouth had once belonged to him; she'd given it to him freely. He'd lost any claim to her years ago, but for this moment, time had been stripped away and he could bury himself in what her body offered.

She couldn't close her mouth. He sensed the tiny tremble that signaled her effort. Then she gave up and accepted. Invited.

So long—he'd waited so long for this. He had his arms firmly on her so that her arms were half trapped between their bodies. She pulled them free and wrapped them around his neck in an incredibly graceful gesture that made him hungry for something he hadn't allowed himself to think about for too long—maybe forever. He felt her fingertips on his sunburned flesh. Somehow they cooled and heated at the same time.

Twisting slightly to the side, he eased her cheek against his shoulder and began stroking her hair. His groin pulsed in need, but the rest of him—heart and head—needed more than sex.

Needed to love this woman.

Shannon. Shannon. Slight, strong, built for climbing mountains and making love and raising children and watching eagles and—and loving me. Making me feel whole, no longer alone.

She repeated her chest-deep whimpering sound. He pulled it into him through his pores. Physical need grew, and he knew the folly of fighting that. He'd been sleeping by himself for a long time and no matter what he demanded of his body through his work, it wasn't enough to still that primitive need.

If—they could—she would—

He opened his eyes, only dimly comprehending that he'd shut out the world. A desperate need to lay himself open to her surged through him and for a few beats of his heart separated him from years of work and training. After what they'd gone through and still had to weather, self-preservation didn't matter. With Shannon he would be vulnerable, more open than—

No.

His heart and body screamed at him to close his eyes again and lose himself in the sensual, equally needful woman who waited for him, but the father part of him, the scared father part had just seen something that turned him cold.

The sun glinting off something in the distance—a rifle barrel?

"Cord?" Shannon clutched at him with insistent fingers. "Cord, what is it?"

"What?" He couldn't take his eyes off the horizon. Again that deadly dancing shaft.

"What? You—you're like steel."

He felt tension radiating throughout his body and knew he couldn't do anything about it. How could she not be aware of it? What should he say, that he'd just seen something that scared the hell out of him and was going to do the same to her?

Instead he said, "We have to get going. Now."

"Now? You're— Without lunch?"

She'd already pulled out of his embrace and was staring up at him, her need-hazed eyes filled with question, doubt, a return to fear, distrust of everything about him. She didn't care any more about food than he did.

"Go ahead. Eat. I've got—"

"You've got to what? Damn it, Cord! For once in your life be honest with me! I can't take any more of this!"

It could be a hiker, a ranger. The human or humans out there weren't necessarily killers. "Don't you want to find him?"

Her look, hard and cold and hot all at the same time sliced into him. He already regretted what he'd said, but the words had spewed from him in a knee-jerk attempt to distance himself from her outburst. Although he readied himself for more of her anger, she whirled away and stood with her back to him, fists knotted at her side. "Do it, Cord," she snapped. "Find him so I can get away from you."

* * *

Although her head pounded, Shannon gave no thought to asking Cord to stop and allow her to rest. Something had happened to him, changed him, just as they were on the brink of— On the brink of what? If only she could think beyond her own emotions, but she should know better than to even try. Cord brought out so much in her, made her crazy.

Maybe, she thought without seeing any humor in it, she was already crazy and had been since the day he walked into her life.

There was incredible danger in thinking back to what had nearly happened between them earlier today, but putting their embrace and what went with it, and the words she'd thrown at him, behind her was impossible. She should know that by now.

They'd come close, so close that it scared her. She'd needed his understanding and compassion and love, needed it desperately. She no more could have kept that from him than she could have once not told him she loved him.

When he'd trusted her with what he carried inside him of the wisdom of the Taos Indians, he'd given her a precious gift she'd just begun to understand. She'd acknowledged his offer in the only way her heart had known, by showing him that she, too, believed in the wisdom of his people.

And then something had happened. He'd heard, or seen, or remembered, and something had ripped him from her and she'd lashed out.

Only something to do with Matt could have done that.

She'd thought his pace relentless earlier but his determination now frightened her so much that she couldn't remember what she'd said to him, just that those words had been the last they'd spoken to each other. His forward progress was only slightly faster than it had been before because every few feet he had to search and reassess.

During those times when his entire attention was focused on the ground and his hands knotted and his knuckles turned white, she almost begged him to tell her the truth. But every time the words pushed their way to the surface, she held them back.

She didn't want to know.

Instead she watched Cord and wondered when she'd have the words to ask his forgiveness. Not until he could concentrate on her. He moved so quietly that if she hadn't been directly behind him, she wouldn't know he was here. Because he said nothing, he left her free to listen to the voice of the earth around her. Its sound reached her as an ebbing and flowing wave, notes both high and shrill from a scolding chipmunk or deep and low as the wind worked its ageless way through the trees. Her world smelled of hot bark and dirt. They'd recently gone through a burned area and she'd been struck by the earth's ability to repair and renew itself. She could spend her life here surrounded by the colors of the wilderness—finding herself.

What had Cord said, that the Grandfather is the creator who bathed everyone with his mind and gave life to all things? What incredibly eloquent words.

"He's still limping."

Cord hadn't said anything for so long. Instantly she lost her sense of peace. "You're sure?"

He pointed at something on the littered ground that made little sense to her. Then in a tone so controlled that she could nearly touch the effort of his keeping it so, he explained that Matt was putting more weight on one leg than the other and occasionally dragging that leg.

"It'll slow him down, won't it?" she made herself ask.

'Yes."

Yes. There was that single eloquent word again. "Cord, when do you think we'll overtake him?"

"Soon."

Soon meant in a few minutes or tomorrow, or maybe the day after that. He had to give her more to cling to than that. As weakness hit her, she fought to brace herself. "If we called to him—"

"No."

He'd been talking with his body angled away from her. She grabbed his arm and pulled him around; he let her. "Why not?"

Although the silence that trailed after her question nearly drove her crazy, she refused to push. Finally, "He's trying to get home on his own. If he hears us, he might try to hide. In fact, I can guarantee it. He could get careless and hurt himself."

"Oh."

"One time—" He glanced away and then met her gaze again. "Once early in my career I went after an older woman who'd gotten separated from a group of senior citizens. She was out there for two nights. Everyone was calling, me included. Finally we found her down a ravine with a broken leg. She'd heard us, gotten disoriented, convinced herself she had to hurry or we'd leave. She didn't see the drop-off."

"She panicked. Matt wouldn't."

"Wouldn't he?"

She freed herself from Cord's gaze long enough to focus on their son's footprint. Matt was hopelessly lost, now with an injured leg or foot. What would it do to him to hear his parents' voices echoing off a hundred boulders? She also didn't dare let herself forget his damnable pride, his determination to complete what he'd set out to accomplish. "So. . . so, what do we do?"

"Come to him gently."

He shouldn't have pushed her the way he had, Cord admonished himself as he watched Shannon sink onto her knees when night stopped them. Without saying a word, he helped her out of her backpack and then knelt in front of her so he could untie her boots. She was watching his hands, maybe seeing something in the way they worked that he should be keeping from her.

All afternoon he'd waited for a rifle shot, and when it hadn't come, he'd asked himself if he maybe shouldn't have taken a chance on trying to call out to the hunters, if that's what they were, and let them know that a little boy was out there. But they were too far away and if they were poaching, they might hide from him. Besides, Shannon would hear—would realize that he'd already heard sounds that might have spelled their son's death.

"We're close," he told her. The words were more for himself than her. "Much closer to him than we were last night."

"You promise?"

"I promise." He finished pulling off her boots and began massaging her right instep. She continued to watch him through half-closed eyes, her body rocking slightly as if she could barely keep it erect. After the way she'd snapped at him earlier today, he hadn't known what to expect from her tonight, but she seemed to have put her outburst behind her.

Maybe. And maybe he'd been given a sample of her true feelings toward him. It didn't matter, not with why they were here and how it might play out. He didn't dare forget that— as if he could.

Five minutes later he was still kneading, only now he'd pushed her pant leg as high as it would go and had pressed fingers and thumb against her calf. She'd braced herself with her hands behind her. Her eyes were closed and she breathed lightly through slightly parted lips and he managed to quiet the hammering questions about Matt's safety, the boy's life even.

He'd surrendered to those lips twice already. He knew how hard resisting now, and later tonight, would be. Earlier, he'd been distracted from making love to the mother of his son first by a flash of light and then by her anger, but it was dark now and they were locked within nature's dark world.

Only, first he had to make contact with another world.

Without trying to explain why he was leaving her when that was the last thing he wanted to do, he removed the walkie-talkie from his pack. She didn't open her eyes when he told her he needed to climb to a higher elevation where natural obstructions would be less likely to interfere with transmission. She told him to tell her parents she was going to take a quick nap, and then stretched out on the ground.

Still he didn't attempt to make contact with her family until he was sure he was out of Shannon's earshot in case the sheriff was with them. Her father answered. The first words out of his mouth were to ask if they'd found Matt. No, he had to tell his former father-in-law, but tomorrow—

"I hope to God you're right. If that boy has any idea how hard this is on all of us... What does that matter? It's got to be much harder on him."

His throat tight, Cord agreed and then explained what they'd accomplished today. He could only pray they were still talking about a living child. Halfway through the conversation, Shannon's father told him the sheriff wanted to talk to him.

"It's not good," Dale Vollrath said when Cord reached him at his house. "I figured I'd better wait until you contacted me. I take it Shannon still isn't part of this?"

"No."

"You ready? Hell, what choice do you have? I've finally learned the identity of who owns a plane that's been at the airport for about a week."

"Tell me."

"The guy's name is Chuck Markham. It probably doesn't mean anything to you, but this isn't the first time I've heard of this joker. He gets around all right, anywhere there's game."

"Game?"

"Sorry, Cord. Markham has a record—the proverbial mile-long rap sheet, starting with hunting out of season, as a teenager. Since then he's pretty much made a career of flaunting the law. He's been stopped a number of times, even served time twice. Mostly he gets a slap on the wrist and, I'm assuming, goes right back to work the next day."

"Work?" Cord asked, although he was pretty sure he already knew the answer.

"He's graduated to the big time, at least that's what he's done in the past and I have no reason to believe he's turned over a new leaf and is here simply to commune with nature. Hell, why should he take up a different line of work when this one has been so profitable?"

"He's poaching, right?"

"Yeah, not that that's what he tells the IRS. And he has three other men with him, which means—"

"Which means he's probably acting as their guide."

"Bingo. Damn. If I had more time, I might be able to learn who's with him, but at this point it doesn't particularly matter."

No, it didn't. This wasn't the first time he'd been involved with hunters who believed that money gave them the
right to bring down whatever they wanted, whenever they
wanted. Men like that didn't have a conscience, at least not
the kind that made any kind of sense to him. This morning
they'd shot at something—maybe a child, his child.

"I've alerted all the rangers in the area," Dale was saying. "Not that there are that many of them on Copper right
now. One thing I can promise you, Markham and his em-
ployers won't get back to their plane without our knowing
it."

That was some consolation, although by the time those
men tried to leave the mountains, they might have already
accomplished what they'd set out to, namely illegally killed
one or more wild animals. And, if they shot without first
getting a good look at their so-called prey, they might put a
bullet into an innocent boy.

Holding that thought at bay with all the willpower in him,
he told Dale about the early morning shot and the glint of
sunlight he'd seen this afternoon. His throat still tight, he
asked Dale to keep him informed.

"You better believe it. The thing is, these jokers are going to do everything they can to stay out of sight of any
rangers or deputies. They might be carrying radios. If they
are, they could be listening to us right now and getting the
message, but I wouldn't count on that."

"I'm not."

"I'm sorry as hell about this, Cord. Damn it, you've already got enough to worry about."

"It's all right."

"Hmm. You haven't told her yet, have you?"

"No."

"Look, man, she's—"

"I can't!" he blurted. "She's already going through hell."

"No more than you are. What happens if—when—she hears a rifle shot or comes face-to-face with those jokers— or with what they've already done? She's going to take one look at you and know you were anticipating this. What's she going to do then?"

He didn't know.

Chapter 12

Cord had been sitting on that rocky outcropping for a long time, hadn't he? Although the need to rest continued to pull at her, Shannon stood and slowly made her way up the hill to him. He acknowledged her with a look that didn't quite connect. The sense that he was part and parcel of his surroundings hit her with the same force it had earlier. He would always belong to the mountains. No matter what life brought, he could renew himself here.

"What happened?" she asked. "My folks? Are they all right?"

"They're holding up."

The top button on his cotton shirt had come off. He sat with one shoulder resting against a rock. His position pulled the fabric away from his chest. She felt her hand begin to tingle and knew why. If she touched him, she would be filled with warmth and strength—his warmth, his strength.

Why now when she felt so tired that all she wanted to do was fall into bed? She should have been attracted to him earlier today, when for hours there'd been precious little to look at except him and nothing else safe to think about.

Safe? No, not at all.

"What did you tell them?" she made herself ask, and then listened as he relayed the essence of the conversation he'd had with her father. "I should have talked to him. Maybe I'll call him back and—"

"Don't. Please."

She thought she caught a warning note in his voice, but before she could question it, he explained that her father had sounded deeply tired himself, and when he suggested he get some rest, her father had agreed. "If your folks and you start talking about Matt, they might not be able to sleep."

That made sense, enough that she dismissed her nagging sense that Cord had left certain words and emotions untouched. He was trying to shelter her from the world; she'd be a fool not to, at least briefly, accept the gift.

"I must have fallen asleep down there." Her legs began to tremble and she lowered herself, less than gracefully, near him. She'd been right; his warmth was enough to reach her. *Ah, Cord, you are beautiful, beautiful and competent and primitively sexy.* "Then— I don't know what was going through me, something unsettling. It woke me."

"You were thinking about Matt."

Of course she was, but enough pieces of her dream remained that she had to admit it was more than that—something to do with Cord, his body, whispered words, coming together. Unsettling didn't say the half of it.

"I hope he's asleep."

"I'm sure he is."

He was saying that for her sake; she was unbelievably grateful to him for that. "He always sleeps curled up on his right side," she began. "Do you remember when he couldn't go to bed without that teddy bear my mother bought him cuddled in his arms?''

''He still has it, doesn't he?''

''Yes. In a dresser drawer. He doesn't want his friends to see it, and I don't think he looks at it very much, but...he's growing up so fast.''

''Too fast. I miss— How many times did you sit with him in that rocker your folks gave you, trying to get him to fall back asleep? I'd get up in the middle of the night and find you and Matt rocking in the dark. You humming. Him playing with your chin.''

''You remember that?''

''You looked so content, tired but content. And beautiful. The chair always groaned a little. I asked if you wanted me to fix it, but you said the sound lulled Matt.''

Momentarily stripped of words, she rested her head on his shoulder. When he wrapped his arm around her, she struggled to keep the sound inside her confined to a sigh. He called her beautiful? What he'd just told her was exquisite.

''It was good then, wasn't it?''

''Yes.''

''I want...I want—I have this unbearable need to send him some kind of message,'' she tried around what boiled inside her. ''Tell him we're getting closer, and if he'd stop moving, it won't take nearly as long for us to find him.''

''He wants to do this on his own.''

''I know he does. He's made that clear, hasn't he?'' She shouldn't run her hand inside his shirt and spread her palm over his chest, but the gesture seemed so natural. So right and necessary. Yes. It had been good between them, once. ''He—am I a terrible person for saying this? All I've thought about for days now is Matt. I'm tired of it. Tired of being scared and upset, my stomach in a knot. I just want to go back to what it was before.''

"No. You aren't crazy."

Before she could think what, if anything, she needed to say in response to his incredible wisdom, he cupped his hand over hers and pulled it off his chest. With her fingers still cradled inside his, he held her palm close to his face and covered it with light kisses.

"Every emotion you have, no matter what it is, is all right."

What about what I'm feeling now, Cord? How are you going to deal with it? How am I?

"I don't know what my emotions are, not really." She tried the words, but they didn't feel right. Maybe nothing she said would. After a minute, during which he touched his lips to the back of her hand, she forced herself to straighten.

Never in her life had she felt more isolated. It wasn't just the surroundings and the reason they were here. But over the past seven years, there'd always been something to keep her from concentrating totally on Cord and that hollow place deep inside her that refused to heal. She wanted it that way, fought to keep him locked away where he couldn't reach her. When they talked about such things as shared custody and the particular stage Matt was going through and where Cord had just been, she hadn't let herself think about him and her. About what remained of her love for him.

Tonight she couldn't tap into the world beyond Copper Mountain, and she didn't dare let her thoughts go to Matt. That left only Cord and stars and the moon, trees that had been growing for hundreds of years, memories of ancient Indian tribes, Mother earth, Father sun, breathing with everything that made up the incredible wilderness.

Cord.

She'd never told him this, but she followed his career with the devotion of a loyal fan. She didn't cut out newspaper clippings or keep the article in *People* magazine because...

Maybe because that would mean acknowledging something she didn't want to. But she'd committed those accounts to memory. Because, if he possibly could, he always called Matt before leaving on a rescue, and she'd know when to start listening to the news for word of him, when to worry about his safety.

This time she didn't have to listen and read and wait for a phone call. She had Cord next to her.

"I love the night sky." She'd said that last night; she was sure of it. But she needed to hear the sound of her voice and learn how Cord might respond to it. Forget danger. Forget everything except need and hunger and the two of us alone, together. "Those city lights we used to look out at when we were in that stupid, cramped little apartment? How could I think they were exciting?"

"They are to some people."

"But not to us." *Us.* "Cord?" She heard her voice speaking his name but couldn't think what she'd been about to say, if anything. "Cord?" she tried again. "I am so glad you're here."

"Are you?"

"Yes."

She expected him to assume that she needed his expertise to locate Matt and that's why she wanted him on the mountain with her. If he'd said that, would she have let it go at that?

But he didn't speak. Instead, he freed her hand and with weathered fingers and palm began an exploration of her throat. She sat as motionless as his caress would allow. Her mind drifted, briefly, flitting into the past, touching on a thousand restless nights when she slept alone. There'd been two men she'd thought she'd begun to care for, but they hadn't touched her soul in that way only Cord had.

She should have put him behind her. They were divorced, finished.

But they weren't.

There was no need to ask permission. His touch had already told her everything she needed to know about his reaction to tonight and them. When she bracketed his face with her hands and pulled herself close to kiss him, she felt a deep shudder that might have come from either or both of them.

He met her open-mouthed; his breath rushed against her.

Her body came alive.

Bold, so bold that there was no questioning the move, she slid her hands down him, unbuttoning and pulling at the same time until she'd laid his chest bare. Although he tried to continue their kiss, she pulled free so she could run her mouth over his chin, down his throat, to the soft mat of hair that covered his chest. With her tongue she worked her way through the slight barrier until she could take his taste, his essence even, deep into her.

She felt his body tense.

She still needed words and emotions from him. She would always need those things. But tonight she could forget what had torn them apart and lose herself in what was both achingly familiar and so new that her heart sang with discovery.

He'd caught a few strands of hair that dropped along the side of her neck and was letting them slide lazily through his fingers. She concentrated on the slight tugging followed by a sensation of release. He held her hair in the shelter of his hand. Played with her. Promised.

Feeling hot and wild, free beyond belief, she ran her fingers around his waist until she touched the hard ridge of his backbone. It was both sheltered and surrounded by muscle and flesh and hers to explore. Simply searching that part of him dug a molten path through her.

Words flitted through her, questions, a promise freely given that tonight meant as much to him as it did to her. She opened her mouth to ask him to gift her with that, spotted the moon cradled between great tree shadows, lost the ability to speak.

When he ran his thumb along her collarbone, she again leaned forward, twisting her head at the same time. She took his right nipple between her teeth.

She felt his shudder, heard the rumble of his groan. Accepted when he freed himself.

Quickly, gently, almost tentatively, he concentrated on her blouse buttons. She worked with him as he slid the garment off her shoulders. She felt a cool rush of air at the base of her throat and across her back, but he must have known that was going to happen because before the cold could distract her, he pulled her against him. She thought he might want to stop with yet another embrace and wondered how long she could keep her body still, but he soon let her know that his needs went beyond that—matched hers.

He unfastened her bra with an ease that made a lie of the last seven years. With the heels of his hands brushing, always brushing against her, he pulled the garment off and dropped it on top of her blouse. Through eyes that wouldn't focus, she stared at the moon and stars. The points of light blurred, came together.

Together. Like her and Cord.

Alive. The word, the emotion, melted through her. She lapped at his breast and then quivered when he held her in his strong hands so he could do the same to her. She felt her breasts swell and the tips harden, felt him draw her breast into his mouth as she would soon...soon take him into her.

I need this, Cord. Need you loving me. Giving yourself to me.

Without you I might die.

When he pulled back, leaving her dampened flesh vulnerable to the air, she moaned. Then, with indistinct vision, she watched as he spread their shirts out on the ground. She trembled, feeling like a sixteen-year-old virgin. He touched the base of her throat; it was the touch of a sixteen-year-old boy bombarded by emotions beyond his comprehension.

Then he leaned into her, eased her onto her back, and followed her down.

With one hand bracing himself, he worked at her jeans' zipper. She arched her hips upward, helping. When her jeans caught around her hips and he had to work at pulling the denim off her, she whimpered at the delay. Night air found her newly naked thighs; the heat in her body surged to the surface, kept her hot.

The sound of a zipper slicing downward caught her attention. While she'd been lost in what he'd already done to her, he had stood and stepped out of his jeans. He started to reach for his briefs, but she reared up and grabbed his hands, stopping him. She needed his help to reach a kneeling position, then she finished the act of disrobing him while he stood with the night surrounding him and his eyes staring down at her, dark as midnight. He was a mountain, part of their untamed surroundings. *Take me! Carry me to the horizon! Together we'll find yesterday, tomorrow, a place without time!*

He knelt in front of her, thighs and hands and breasts touching. Then he gripped the fragile elastic that held her panties in place and began a slow downward journey. When he could go no further, he stretched her out on their shirts and lifted first one leg and then the other, the gesture both practiced and new.

She lay naked beneath him, no longer existing anywhere else. The breeze, now like cool lace, brushed against flesh that felt touched by moonlight and lightning and, most of all, by Cord.

I need this, Cord. Need you loving me.

He seemed to hesitate. Could he, a man who saw the vast wilderness as his home, be afraid of making love with his wife? What little remained of her rational mind knew she hadn't been his wife for a long, long time, but that didn't matter.

Tonight they were right for each other, or if not right, beyond caring.

She held out her hands, accepted the swirling ball of heat deep inside her, and issued a silent invitation.

He heard, came, slowly at first, then with a sense of urgency that matched hers. There was no more foreplay, no more time wasted erasing the years.

She spread herself for him, took him into her. Lost herself against him.

And she cried, tears without meaning or understanding.

Sometime during the night, they left where they'd made love and, shivering a little, returned to their sleeping bags. She started to lower herself to her bed, but he stopped her with a touch and she responded. They made love again, just as silent and frenzied.

In the morning, she woke with the weight of his arm over her breast.

She opened her eyes to look at him. In the newborn day, she saw that he was already gazing at her. His eyes asked if she had any regrets, and because she couldn't answer him or herself, she didn't speak.

Instead she kissed his powerful shoulder, the tanned hollow at the base of his throat, answered his silent kiss, and then, because he'd already taken too much of her, she slid away from him.

Now he was getting dressed and she was trying to remember how to braid her hair and regret swirled around her like a free-moving river.

She'd spent so many years and so much energy getting to that hard-won place where she believed she no longer loved Cord and couldn't be hurt by him. Last night, twice, he'd made a lie of that belief and it would take years to undo two acts of lovemaking.

But he wasn't the only one responsible for the way her heart felt this morning; she couldn't blame him for that. She'd let it out of its quiet, cushioned prison and learned that the years had changed nothing of what she felt for him after all.

The realization terrified her.

"Shannon, there's a small elk herd around here. We aren't that far from a spring they've been using. If Matt finds it, he might follow it down."

Although she wasn't ready for this or any other conversation, she agreed that what he said made sense and should make sense to Matt, too—if the boy had given up on his goal of making it to the top of the mountain. She asked if that meant he intended to stop following their son's tracks.

"No. That's the last thing I'd do. His footprints are our only tie to him."

Only. "It scares me when you say that."

He kicked into his boot and stepped closer to her. She thought she read the slightest hint of fear in his eyes, but couldn't begin to comprehend its source. Not once during the hard past few days had he truly given her access to what was going on inside him. She'd come to expect that curtain to remain in place and could only guess at the changes inside him that had allowed it to momentarily slip away.

If he was afraid for Matt, she didn't want to hear about it. If what happened between them last night had changed him in some way he had no control over and left him vulnerable, honest about Matt's chances, she didn't want to know that, either.

Cord was the mountain. Strong, invincible, the man she'd charged with bringing her son back to her.

Not a frail, insecure, sometimes helpless human being. Like her.

"I don't want you to be scared. If I could, I'd take you out of here so you wouldn't have to go through this."

"I wish you could, too, but the only way I'll leave is when we find Matt."

"I know. And we will."

When? she wanted to shout at him, but didn't ask, just as she hadn't pushed for the reason behind what lurked in his eyes. As she watched him turn his attention to what little needed to be done before they could get going, she struggled for a memory of anything that had happened in her life before coming here with him. Nothing surfaced and after a minute she gave up the search.

Her body needed his touch. If he reached for her, the gesture might put an end to the unease that flowed through her. But he, like she, must have decided that reaching for any more of what they'd experienced last night would only throw them into more turmoil.

She took a handful of nuts and dried fruit and began chewing. Neither had any flavor. When Cord approached, she handed him the bag and told him that she wasn't sure she but she thought the fruit was apple.

"You made wonderful apple pies," he told her around a healthy bite. His eyes settled on her, dark, keeping their secrets. "I tried making one a couple of times, but the dough I bought didn't taste anything like yours."

Needing relief from his intensity, she pretended to be shocked. "Packaged dough? Did you ever see me use that?"

Frowning, he shook his head. "I should have paid more attention to how you did it."

"I guess you should have."

He ate as if it was something he knew he had to do but which concerned him little. She remembered pressing against his right hip last night and noting how quickly he'd pulled away. He must have bruised himself during one of those times when he'd scrambled over rocks, but like fueling his body, bruises didn't concern him.

Despite herself, she couldn't help wondering if he'd dismissed their lovemaking just as easily. If that's why he was able to stand near her and talk about apple pies and now look around him instead of into her eyes; she hurt for both of them.

But maybe it wasn't like that at all. Maybe, as for her, last night still bombarded him.

"There's going to be a wind," he said. "Coming from the north and probably lasting all day."

"Does that make a difference?"

"It might make it harder for us to hear Matt."

She nodded, barely understanding herself because talk and thoughts of how Matt was doing no longer brought her to the brink of tears. Had she been through so many emotions that they'd all been washed away? Maybe without knowing it, she'd become so tired that her system simply couldn't reach to anything.

And maybe making love with Cord had left such an impact that precious little else could penetrate. "We aren't going to talk about it, are we?" she asked as he watched her adjust the straps on her pack.

"About what?"

"Last night." He stood so close that she would only have to take a single step to touch him. There wasn't a square inch of her that didn't want to answer her heart's demand. Still, she remained where she was—standing safe and alone and untouched. "Cord, we can't pretend we didn't make love."

"I'm not going to apologize."

Was that what he thought she wanted? Surely he knew her better than that. She shut her eyes and lost herself in darkness until she began to feel dizzy. The question repeated inside her. Maybe he didn't know her at all anymore. Maybe she didn't know him. "I didn't expect you to apologize." She spoke with her teeth clenched and her eyes barely open. "Maybe what I want is a better understanding of why we wound up in each other's arms."

"Why?"

"Don't you?" This argument, if that's what they were having, was insane. "Is that the difference between us? I've surrounded myself with emotion. I need to know the strength, the boundaries of that emotion. You—maybe you just act."

"Is that what you believe?"

She'd asked him an impossible question. Now he'd thrown the same back at her. "I don't know." She forced herself to relax and took a step designed to let him know she was ready to get started. "I don't know what goes on inside you."

Only his hair, buffeted by the breeze, moved. She couldn't free herself from the power and probe of his eyes. Had her words wounded him? Was that why he was reacting this way? She couldn't begin to guess what she might say or do to drag an answer out of him. It was easier to rock back on her heels and incline her head in the direction she believed they would be heading. Something dark and cloudlike drifted over his features, but she couldn't penetrate that anymore than she'd ever been able to penetrate his silences.

He started to turn away. She felt the keen stab of disappointment at the realization that he was actually going to do what she wanted him to. Then, letting the gesture speak for him, he reached out and brushed his hand over her cheek.

"The first peace is that which comes within the souls of people when they realize their oneness with the universe and all its powers."

"Cord, what are you—"

"Not me. The Sioux. They believe that the Great Spirit dwells at the center of the universe, that this center is everywhere, and is within each of us."

Not philosophy! Not ancient words! I need—you. And yet I'm afraid.

They should have gone camping more. If she'd made the time, Cord might have taught her how to build a shelter from branches and leaves and limbs and she'd know how to start a fire without matches.

She'd have a greater understanding of Sioux beliefs and why Cord had learned so much about them.

She might know why his simple yet eloquent words had stripped her down to nothing except emotion.

They'd been walking for nearly two hours now. The ground was steep and almost barren here, all but the hardiest of trees below them. From a distance, one would believe it easy to spot another human being, but the land was deceptive. It contained deep pockets of shade where the sun seldom touched, and rocky outcroppings impossible to see around. She felt surrounded by rocks and boulders and seldom saw the prints that guided Cord slowly but well.

She could see only his powerful shoulders and muscular legs, learn how to walk herself from the sure way he kept his footing. His eyes took in everything, his head almost constantly in motion. A few days ago she'd tried to see everything he did, but that no longer seemed important.

No longer pressed through the web of emotion that last night and this morning had left in her.

If they'd been born generations ago, he would have been an Indian scout and her a mountain woman. They'd weave their lives around the elements. They wouldn't need much; enough food to fill their bellies, a shelter when the weather became too raw for even Cord Navarro. She'd make their clothes from deer hide and he'd create exquisite arrowheads to place on strong, straight shafts. Their friends would be other Indians or the few mountain men who traveled through their wilderness.

They'd raise their children here, make love under stars and moon.

And whether or not they used words to communicate, they'd always understand each other.

In that misty world where everything was right.

Shaken by the depth of her need, she forced herself to focus on her surroundings. The effort succeeded for maybe two minutes, then Cord extended his hand to help her over loose shale.

She stood beside him on their precarious perch, unable to remember how to work her muscles to free her hand. His shoulder was now molded to hers, a mountain of strength. They hadn't spoken for hours. Other than pointing occasionally at wildlife or uncertain ground, he'd done nothing to make her think she was on his mind. But now, although he could have easily moved away, he didn't. Instead, he turned her slightly so she could see what he'd been looking at. Just below them, maybe no more than two hundred feet away, a spring bubbled up from the earth. Overflow trickled downward to be lost among grass and shrubs. Between

them and the spring she could see several distinct tracks—
the tracks they'd been following for days.

"We're close."

Her heart skittered and then caught. "How...close."

"Very. The grass he stepped on is still bent."

Feeling weak, she slid her free arm around his waist and
continued to stare at the fragile proof of their son's existence. He held her to him and brushed his lips over her
forehead. There was no imagining it; she knew she could
hear his heart beating. She prayed he could hear hers, as
well.

She had no words in her, nothing that could possibly express what she felt at this moment. When his breath caught
as he tried to inhale, she knew the same emotion had entered him. She continued to cling, sharing in the only way
she had. Their son was near; they'd soon find him; he'd feel
his parents' love.

"Do...do you want him to know?" she whispered.

"Not yet. I want to make sure he's safe first."

Tears built behind her eyes, but with an effort, she managed to keep them there. Cord had done the impossible,
brought her to her son—their son.

"Where?"

"I can't say for sure. From the angle of his prints, its obvious he was headed toward the spring."

"He...he's thinking he'll have to follow the creek all the
way to the bottom, isn't he?"

"Yes."

A sudden sense of urgency washed over her. With all her
heart, she wanted to be able to cut the bruise out of the re-
maining apple and feed it to Matt. She wanted to watch as
Cord clutched his son to his chest.

Only two things held her back: realization that the thick
brush around the little creek could accommodate a child but

prove daunting to adults, and the belief that no one else in the world except Cord could possibly know what she was experiencing at this moment.

"I thought..." She shuddered. "I tried so hard not to think about it, but I couldn't help— There've been times when I was terrified of what we'd find."

"So was I."

No. Cord wasn't supposed to have nightmare thoughts. Although she'd accused him of having buried his emotions so deep that he might have lost them, she needed him to be as strong and confident as her mythical Indian scout, a miracle-working machine.

"You? You were—"

What was that?

Cord started, suddenly gripping her with a strength that took her breath away.

A rifle shot!

Comprehension of what she'd heard came so close on the heels of Cord's reaction that she couldn't separate the two. Her blood seemed to stop in her veins; her heart skittered; her lungs screamed with the need for breath but she couldn't remember how to accomplish that incredibly difficult task.

Another shot! A rifle blast echoing, at the same time sounding so close that if Matt hadn't been more important than her own life, she would have dropped to the ground.

"No!" Cord's deep scream all but shattered her senses. "Oh, God, no!"

Chapter 13

"Cord! Wha—"

"Poachers."

How did he know? Cord didn't give her half a second in which to ask. Whirling away, he plunged into the thick shrubbery. Alive with fear, she followed his lead. He was already deep in the underbrush and making more noise than she'd ever heard from him, but it wasn't the sound that made her plow after him.

He'd begun yelling Matt's name.

She shoved herself around a stunted evergreen and struggled to keep up with him. "Cord, stop it! You'll scare—"

"Hunters! If they've shot...Matt! Matt! Stay where you are!"

Shot! Her legs weakened, but she refused to give in to the dread that instantly replaced all other emotion.

When they reached the narrow, ambling water, there were enough rocks on either side that brush had been unable to get much of a toehold on the bank. She could run without worrying that some sharp branch might slap her face; still she was unable to keep up. Foot by foot, Cord increased the distance between them. Still, the air felt alive with his fear.

"Matt! I'm here! Mom, too. Matt, please! Where are you?"

Once more she heard the horrible explosion of sound she so hated during hunting season. Cord stared over his shoulder at her; whatever he was experiencing had so altered his features, she barely recognized him.

What she saw terrified her.

"Cord?" she sobbed. "Cord, please!"

Instead of answering her insane plea, he yanked off his pack without losing stride and kept running. She jumped over it, nearly lost her footing, and struggled with her own burden. By the time she'd flung it off, Cord had disappeared.

A thousand emotions boiled up inside her—rage at whoever might have cost Matt his life, a desperate plea to give Cord the strength and speed to get to their son before it was too late. Prayers to God, to Gray Cloud's Great Spirit.

Guided by a trail that might not have been one to any other eyes, she followed Cord. Her heart beat so rapidly that it robbed her of the breath she needed, but she didn't stop. She couldn't. Nor did she waste time in cries Cord wouldn't pay attention to and Matt might no longer be able to hear.

Sweat broke out on her temple. Angry, she wiped it away. The rest of the time, she kept her hands close to her body so a branch wouldn't snag her—Indian style, the way Cord had taught her.

And she prayed to *the spirit that moves in all things* to shelter and protect a ten-year-old boy.

Had she lost sight of the creek? For a moment, the sudden change in terrain confused her. Then she realized she was back on rocks where precious little growth could take root. Blinking back tears of desperation, she stared at her surroundings.

She could see for a hundred, maybe a hundred and fifty feet. At the far end of the unexpected clearing, she caught a glimpse of faded denim and white cotton.

Cord. Kneeling over something, eyes trained on his surroundings, body ready, not for flight, but fight.

She didn't know she'd shoved her fist in her mouth until she tasted blood. Somehow she forced herself to stop clenching her teeth, but now she couldn't make herself move.

She'd turn around. Walk away.

That way she'd never have to see if her son had been killed.

But she was, above everything else in life, a mother. No matter what had happened, she couldn't leave.

When she started running again, her legs felt so heavy that twice she stumbled. Still, she couldn't take her eyes off Cord's hunched form now holding something—someone.

Don't let him die, Cord. For me, for you, for the rest of our lives—don't let him die.

"Mommy!"

Matt's voice washed over her like a sudden, brilliant sunrise. Stripped of muscle and bone, she dropped to her knees beside father and son.

"Mommy!"

Eyes wide and deep and boiling with emotion, Cord clutched Matt tightly to his chest. All she could do was touch her son's back, run her fingers into his hair, draw in the smell of little-boy sweat. Sob in relief.

"Are you all right? Oh, Matt . . . Cord?"

"They didn't hit him. Thank God, they didn't . . ." Cord gaped at her, then stared at his surroundings.

Her heart ached. Only embracing Matt would take away the pain. Yet Matt had his arms around Cord's neck, his face buried against his father and was crying a little, muttering, "I'm sorry, I'm sorry," over and over, and she knew that no other sound on earth would ever mean as much as hearing his voice at this moment did.

Hot tears burned their way down her cheeks. She should wipe them away, blunt a little of her fear and relief so Matt would recognize her as his mother and not a half-insane woman, but she couldn't take her hands off him long enough for that.

"I tried. Dad, I wanted you to be proud of me."

"I know you did."

"But I got lost. You're never lost."

All too soon she became aware of the cadence of silence. Cord should say something to his son, some words of reassurance and love. Instead, he simply knelt on dirt and rocks and held Matt. She couldn't see his face now, could only guess at what was going on inside him.

"It's all right." She spoke for her ex-husband. "You did a wonderful job, honey. You were so brave, so strong, so—"

"Mommy?"

Matt hadn't called her "Mommy" since he'd started school. Wise in the way of growing boys, she'd learned to respond to a casual "Mom." Now he was taking her back to when a little boy needed his mother's loving reassurance.

That's what she'd think about—not the bullets that had nearly ended his life.

"What, honey?"

"You've been looking a long time, haven't you?"

"Yes." She ran her hand over his small, wiry shoulders, down his straight back. His shirt was torn and filthy. The warmth beneath the ruined fabric made it possible for her heart to go on beating.

"Just you and Dad?"

"Yes."

Matt lifted his head off his father's chest to look at her. His face was wind-chapped and sunburned, and she wasn't sure any shampoo would repair the damage to his hair. He had a few mosquito bites and two parallel scratches near his right eye.

This wasn't the ten-year-old boy she'd been going to make pizza for a few days ago. Dirt and tangled hair and chapped skin made him look older.

Only, it wasn't the outward signs of his ordeal that had matured him. His eyes—Cord's dark eyes—were different somehow. Wiser. Experienced.

"I'm proud of you," she whispered when he did nothing except stare at her with those newly mature eyes that so reminded her of the man she'd made love to last night. "So very proud."

"You aren't going to punish me?"

"No. Oh, no. Did you think I would?"

Instead of answering, Matt planted his hands on his father's chest and pushed back just enough so he could look into Cord's eyes. The very forest seemed to pause, almost stop its rhythm. From where she knelt, she was privy to the emotion going through her son and understood it in a way she'd seldom understood anything else. He might have called her "Mommy" and asked if she was going to punish him, but it was his father's reaction he sought and needed. She had no will or strength to fight her tears; Matt would simply have to see them. If he was as wise as she now believed, he'd understand that her tears traced the depth of her love for him.

Cord's hands were at Matt's waist; maybe Matt could feel something intangible and vital through that silent contact, and maybe Matt hadn't stopped staring at his father because he didn't know enough.

Please, Cord. Say something.

"Just you and Mom?" Matt's voice was still that of a little boy's. "There's no search and rescue?"

"No."

She thought Matt would ask why not. He simply nodded. "You followed my tracks?"

"Your dad did, yes."

"All—I didn't do so good. I got pretty lost."

Cord didn't speak, didn't move. His eyes still locked with his father's, Matt slowly pulled free and pushed himself to his feet. He glanced down at his dirty boots. "Mom? I'm sorry I scared you."

A thousand words rolled through her, but she didn't try to sort through them. She stood and held out her hands. *Cord, please! Say something!*

"It's all right," she managed as Matt buried himself against her. "You're alive. That's all that matters."

He felt wonderful! A dirty, tired bundle of bone and muscle now pressed against her. His arms slid around her waist; she gripped his shoulders, buried her face in his matted hair, and wondered how much longer she would be able to look down at him.

Matt, alive and well.

Matt, not a victim of some hunter's gun.

Matt, given back to her by Cord.

Cord, who now stood a few feet away looking as if he didn't know what to do with his body.

Talk to him, Cord. Tell him you love him.

Cord spun and stalked away from them. She nearly screamed at him before she spotted what had caught his attention. Standing at the edge of a bushy thicket were four men, all of them armed with rifles. *Cord! No, don't! They might—*

He couldn't hear her silent warning, and even if he had, his long, purposeful stride told her he was beyond listening. Without saying a word, he walked up to them and grabbed the rifle from one of the men before slamming it to the ground.

"Damn you! Damn you! You almost—"

The rifleless man turned toward one of his companions, a shorter man in a faded red-and-white checked shirt and a face like sun-dried leather. "Chuck! You said it was an elk!"

"That 'elk' was my son." Cord's strong fingers had become fists. He kept them at his side, just barely. "You're hunting out of season, shooting at anything that moves. If you'd been a decent shot . . ." Although close to a hundred feet separated her and Matt from the others, she saw Cord shudder. He concentrated on the man with the checkered shirt. "Chuck?" he asked. "Chuck Markham?"

"Yeah?" To her horror, instead of lowering his rifle, the way the other two men were doing, Chuck kept it firm and steady in his arms—aimed at Cord's chest. "What of it?"

"Nothing matters to you except getting what you want, does it?" Cord stalked closer.

"What's it to you? Your kid's safe, isn't he?"

What's it to you? If she hadn't been so focused on the weapon and her ex-husband, she might have flung the words at the horrible man.

"You almost killed him." Cord's voice was either without emotion or so laden that he could barely get the words out; she didn't know which. "Damn it, you could have killed my son."

"Look." Shifting the rifle slightly but not lowering it, Chuck leaned closer to Cord. "There's elk all over here. I've been following their signs for days. How the hell was I supposed to know there was a kid out here?''

If Chuck expected an answer from Cord, he didn't get it. Cord just continued to stare at the hunter—poacher—whatever he was. As had happened so many times during their days and nights together, his surroundings seemed to lap at him, take over until she wasn't sure there was anything civilized left in him.

"Look," Chuck repeated. "It wasn't me who shot at him anyway. You want to blame someone, blame Owen."

The man Cord had taken the rifle from spun toward Chuck. "Wait a minute," he spluttered. "You're the one who got us here. You planned this whole damn thing. I'm not—"

Shannon couldn't concentrate on the balding man's words. What did it matter who was responsible for the poachers'—that's what they were, all right—being here? The bottom line was, their greed had nearly cost her son his life. With a start, she realized that all four men were talking at once. Cord's silence stood in sharp contrast to the babble of words. Someone, the oldest of the group she guessed, was offering Cord an obscene amount of money in exchange for a promise not to say anything to the authorities. Owen started toward her and Matt, but Cord stopped him with a cold stare. Neither Cord nor Chuck had altered their defensive stances. Nor had Chuck lowered his weapon.

"Shut up, Elliott!" Chuck ordered. "You don't get it, do you? I know him." He jabbed the rifle at Cord. "Know his reputation, anyway. He's the next thing to the law, works with them all the time. There's no way he'll take your money and keep his mouth shut."

She'd once seen a massive dog that had been cornered by several men after it had killed a couple of lambs. The dog had been backed into a corner, but she hadn't for a second believed it was giving up. When one of the men made the mistake of getting too close, the dog had lunged at him. If the others hadn't pulled the dog off its victim, the man would have had his throat torn out.

Chuck reminded her of that dog.

"Cord," she warned, realizing too late that she shouldn't try to distract him from the poacher.

Chuck acknowledged her with a look, the contact lasting less than a second but leaving her with the impression that no sense of humanity, of compassion, of regret, even of relief, existed in the man. She waited for him to say something, but when he didn't, his silence was as telling as the dog's growls had been.

"Mom?" Matt whispered. She stopped him by pressing him against her side.

No matter how much she wanted to become part of the confrontation, this was between Cord and the man he'd called Chuck. Although the others were nearby, they, like her, were simply bit players in the drama.

"Put it down," Cord ordered, his voice as deep and low as the wind finding its way through a canyon. "Now."

"You know who I am? How did—"

"It doesn't matter."

"No," Chuck admitted. "It doesn't. Nothing does except . . ."

She wanted to scream at him to finish because right now nothing mattered more than getting inside Chuck Markham's head. He had to at least care about an innocent boy's life, didn't he? He couldn't possibly be thinking of taking the father's life. As if in answer to her question, Chuck curled himself around his weapon, became part of it.

"No!"

Everything became a blur of movement, Cord striking out and throwing himself to the ground at the same time, a shattering blast of sound, cursing, Matt screaming and clutching her, a woman's wailing cry. She fought to escape her son's grasp, but he held on with fierce and desperate fingers, and she was afraid of hurting him.

Cord went down hard, his body bouncing off the earth. For a horrible instant, he lay limp as a fallen leaf. Then, although she wasn't sure he was capable of rational thought or action, he reached out and grabbed Chuck around the ankles. Grunting, Chuck fell on top of him, the rifle trapped between them. She was terrified that in one, no more than two seconds, strength and maybe life itself would pour out of Cord and she would see her ex-husband die before her eyes.

"No. No. No." She had to stop sounding like a wounded animal, but how? Dragging Matt with her, she stumbled over rocks and uneven ground until she'd covered about half of the distance. The two men were still locked together as they fought for control of the weapon. Cord wasn't a killer, but if it came to his own life—

She couldn't help him this way.

"Matt! Please," she begged. "Let me go."

"No! He'll kill—they'll kill you."

"No, they won't," she said, although she might be lying to both herself and her son. The other men were staring fixedly at Cord and Chuck, briefly drawing her attention from her still-forming plan. Chuck, although shorter, outweighed Cord by maybe thirty pounds. That would slow him and make him clumsy, but he could also use his heft to advantage, especially if Cord was injured.

At the moment, it looked as if her awful prediction had come true. Chuck had straddled Cord and was using the rifle like a wedge to drive him into the ground. She saw—no!—saw that blood soaked the side of Cord's head.

"Matt! Hide! Don't move until I tell you to."

"But—"

"Now!"

Her scream captured her son's attention, but he was still staring at her when she whirled and ran back the way she'd come. For a desperate moment she couldn't find Cord's pack, then spotted it on a litter of grass and dead leaves. Dropping to her knees, she rummaged through it until she found the two-way radio.

"Dad!" she screamed into it. "Dad! Where are you?"

"Here, honey. What—"

"We need help! Now!"

"Matt?"

"Matt's alive," she told him as she hurried back toward the men, determined to let them hear and see. "But there are poachers—they have guns. They tried—I think one of them shot Cord." *Cord? Please, Cord!*

Fortunately her father didn't ask any more questions. Instead, he informed her that Sheriff Vollrath was with him and immediately turned the radio over to him. Unable to keep herself from babbling, she gave the sheriff a brief sketch of what was happening. The three other men watched her intently, but if either Clint or Cord heard, they gave no indication. Now Chuck was trying to get free while Cord struggled to keep him with him.

She was vaguely aware that Dale didn't sound surprised by the presence of poachers, but that didn't matter. The only thing that did was giving him as accurate a description of where they were as possible. To her overwhelming relief, Dale said he could get a forest service helicopter in the air in a matter of minutes.

Still clutching the now-silent radio, she looked around for Matt. She couldn't see him and prayed he'd obeyed her command to hide.

"I've called the police!" she yelled at the men. "They're on their way." *Please let that be the truth.* "They know who you are." *Do they?* "Stop it!" She indicated the fighters. "Make them stop!"

For what seemed forever but couldn't be, no one moved. She heard furious breathing and a grunt of pain that tore into her. It was all she could do not to jump into the middle of the battle, but what if something happened to her? Matt could be left with nothing—no one.

Finally, cursing, first one man and then the other two reached, not for Cord as she feared, but for Chuck.

"Leave me alone!" Chuck bellowed. "This ain't none of your business!"

"The hell it isn't," the man called Elliott retorted. "It's over, damn it. Over." He wrapped his arm around Chuck's neck and hauled him back. At the same time, Owen grabbed the rifle and wrenched it out of Chuck's grip. It clattered to the ground near Cord; to her immense relief, it didn't fire.

"The cops are on their way," Owen rasped, his attention riveted on the rifle. "I can't— Oh, God, I can't believe this is happening."

"Then I'm out of here," Chuck insisted as he struggled to free himself from Elliott. "You guys will get your hands slapped. Me, I'm looking at jail time."

Cord forced himself to his feet and stood with his legs wide apart, swaying slightly. "Where do you think you could go?" He took a deep, hard-won breath. "The sheriff knows about your plane. He'll be looking for you. Everyone will be."

"Not if I—"

"Didn't you hear me?" she insisted. "There's a helicopter on its way. You'll never get away. You can't—"

"Owen! Think, damn it!" Chuck snarled. "You want to be charged with attempted murder? If we get out of here, no one will ever—"

"You're crazy. Insane," Elliott interrupted. "Do you really think we're going to let you dump this on us? Even if you somehow managed to disappear, the rest of us can't. We've got businesses. Families."

"Owen!" Chuck tried to jerk free. "Attempted murder? Do you want that?"

Owen's rifle lay on the ground where Cord had thrown it, but he could reach it before anyone stopped him. In a strangely detached way, she wondered if she could place herself between Owen and Cord before he finished what Chuck had begun.

"I'm no killer. Never so much as hunted anything before this. I thought...thought it would..." Owen's face contorted. "I almost shot a boy," he whimpered, and kicked at his weapon. "I don't ever—don't ever want to touch that thing again."

"You're going to go to jail," Chuck insisted. "And take me with you. Damn you, I—"

"Enough."

Cord's voice was like a cold wind on a hot day and instantly commanded her attention. How she couldn't have noticed that he'd picked up Chuck's rifle, she didn't know. He held it with the barrel aimed at Chuck's chest; despite what was wrong with the side of his head, he'd found the strength to keep it level. Something terrible and wild and dangerous came to life in his ebony eyes, and for the first time in her life she understood how fine the line could be between civilization and the law of the wild. By the other men's reactions, she knew she wasn't the only one aware of how close Cord was to crossing that line.

"You don't want to do this, man," Elliott said. At the same time, he released Chuck and stepped away from him, leaving the poacher to face the rifle alone. "You don't want to kill him."

Cord didn't answer, but then she already knew he wouldn't. He was aware of nothing and no one except Chuck. Although Owen had been the one who'd nearly hit their son, Chuck had shot at Cord and her ex-husband obviously held him responsible for everything that had happened. The same need for revenge that pulsed inside Cord lapped at her, and for a moment she wanted to be the one to put an end to Chuck.

But if she did—if Cord did—their son would know.

"No, Cord, no!"

His attention flickered toward her. When he blinked, she knew she'd reached him. "You can't," she said, speaking more softly now. "It doesn't matter what he's done, you can't lower yourself to his level."

"He's been killing wild animals for years."

"Let the courts deal with him. They might not be perfect, but they're all we have."

"I have this." Cord indicated the rifle.

"If you use it, you'll lose your son. You might spend your life behind bars."

"My son," Cord whispered as if the possibility of prison meant nothing to him. Then, while the others waited without breathing, he handed the weapon to her. She still had to fight her own desire for revenge, but the words she'd thrown at Cord were for her, too. After unloading the rifle, she tossed the bullets into the brush, grabbed the weapon by the barrel and swung it as hard as she could against the nearest boulder.

"What the—" Chuck began.

"Shut up." Cord spoke without emotion. "Just shut up."

Although he continued to glare, the fight went out of Chuck. Still, she was glad the men had grabbed his arms; that way she could dismiss him and concentrate on what really mattered.

Cord wasn't staring at the men or her. He still looked as angry and untamed as she'd ever seen him, but after a few minutes, a little of the tension, or maybe it was his strength, seeped out of him. He no longer reminded her of an elk ready for battle. He was more like the man she might spend the rest of her life trying to understand.

"You need help." She whispered because she could barely get her voice to work. "A doctor."

"I'm fine. I hit my head on a rock, that's all."

"You're not fine." Ignoring the others, she gently pushed aside Cord's hair so she could look at his injury. A ragged gash bled freely from his scalp; she could only pray he hadn't sustained a concussion. With sudden, sickening clarity she understood that if the bullet had hit him, it would have killed him since it had been designed to bring down an animal weighing several times what he did.

"I'll call Dale back and tell him to send along a paramedic," she told Cord.

"I'm a paramedic," he said with the slightest of smiles. "It stunned me, that's all."

Then, to her concern and relief, he sat on the nearest rock and lowered his head. With trembling hands, she rubbed the back of his neck until he straightened and looked at her. His eyes were clear, his pupils normal size. Still, more emotions than she could possibly contend with threatened to explode inside her, but until they did, she would act in a calm and responsible way.

She continued to watch the men out of the corner of her eye, but what they heard and saw and thought didn't matter. If Chuck made a run for it, the others would either re-

capture him or not. If they didn't, he might spend the rest
of his life up here on the mountain because he didn't dare
come down to where law enforcement waited.

The primitive, vengeful woman who'd nearly lost the two
most important people in her life hoped he would take off—
unarmed and without so much as a match or handful of trail
mix. He wasn't Cord Navarro. He'd starve in country that
could sustain Cord for as long as he needed it to.

"Mom?"

Matt had joined them and was carrying his father's first-
aid kit. With less than steady hands, she took it from him
and removed what she needed to clean the gash. Much as
she wanted to shield Matt from the sight of all that blood,
it was too late. Besides, Matt wasn't a little boy to be protected from reality.

"Dad? I'm sorry. You almost—"

"I'm all right," Cord said softly, and she could tell that
Matt believed him. "What about you?"

"Me? I was scared. When I heard that sound, I—"

"You did right," she reassured him. Cord didn't so much
as move a muscle as she started working on him; maybe he
wasn't aware of his body, of her. "Exactly right."

"You had no idea they were around?" Cord asked.

"I felt like, you know, someone was watching me.
Maybe—maybe I knew you were coming."

"Maybe you did," she whispered when Cord didn't
speak.

Cord continued to stare at Matt, his face all but expres-
sionless. She'd seen his fury at the men who had risked
Matt's life, his need for revenge, a raw moment of un-
adorned relief when he realized his son was all right. Now
he was doing what he must think was expected of him—letting his son believe this had been nothing more than another search for him, one with a successful ending.

Something began building inside her. She couldn't put a name to the emotion; neither could she fight the growing storm. "You knew that man's name. How long have you known they were up here? How long, Cord?"

"Days."

"Days? And you didn't tell me? Why not?"

In the distance a crow squawked. The hard sound echoed what she heard in her voice.

"Why not?" she repeated.

"You had enough to worry about."

"Enough?" The rolling wave of emotion expanded and became more than she could control. "You didn't think I was strong enough, did you? Cord, what you did—" Matt was staring at her with alarm in his eyes. Still, she couldn't stop, didn't even try. "You don't have any idea how much I hate your damnable silence, do you? The strong, silent Indian. Keeping emotions, if you have them, from your wi—from me."

"I wanted to spare you."

"Spare?" She threw the word back at him. How dare he sit there with the wind tossing his hair and sunlight glinting in his beautiful black eyes while she worked on the injury that held proof of...of what? "Spare?" She didn't care whether the men or Matt heard; she had no control over what came out of her and didn't want it back until she'd said what she had to. "I survived Summer's death, our divorce, days and nights of looking for Matt. Don't you have any idea how strong I am?"

"You couldn't have done anything if you'd known."

"You and I searched for Matt because he's the most important human being in both our lives. At least, he is in mine. I've been honest with you about everything I've felt. Every emotion. But you—what the hell does it matter?"

"Mom?"

Matt shouldn't hear his parents fighting—hear her yelling at his father. But she and Cord had made love deep in his beloved wilderness. How could he not know her heart?

Cord said nothing; she didn't expect or want anything from him, couldn't imagine ever wanting to speak to him again. When, after an awkward moment, Cord told Matt to take off his boots and sit down so he could see his foot, she simply stood back, watching father and son.

There were no words between them. Only touching.

There were things she had to do, like keeping pressure on the wound so it would stop bleeding. Her parents deserved to know what had happened since her desperate call. She should ask Dale when she could expect the helicopter and tell him how many prisoners—was that what they were?—there were. Maybe Matt needed something to eat. But he was looking from her to his father and then back again, clearly uneasy.

Feeling both dead inside and more alive than she'd ever been, she concentrated on her son. "Your dad said...he said he didn't think you were afraid. We found where you slept, you barely moved."

"I wasn't scared, not after a while." Matt tried to rub some dirt off his hand by scrubbing it along his jeans. "Dad, I remember you telling me there wasn't anything to be afraid of in the woods."

"I—I'm glad you remembered," she whispered.

Ignoring his bare foot, Matt kicked at the ground and then stole a glance at his father. "I wanted you to be proud of me."

"I am."

"I should have gotten unlost without your help."

She didn't feel like laughing. Still, she heard herself do just that. "That's what your dad said, that you wanted to prove you could climb Copper all by yourself. That's what made tracking you so hard.''

''Not so hard. You found me. Dad, I wanted to be like you.''

No, you don't, son.

Chapter 14

The helicopter's whirling blades kicked up dust and debris as it took off with a full load consisting of the pilot, Dale, and the four poachers, Chuck in handcuffs. Dale had been concerned about Cord, but he'd assured the sheriff that he didn't have so much as a headache and seeing a doctor could wait. As the screaming sound eased, Shannon faced the fact that she, Matt, and Cord would be alone until it returned.

If only she and Matt had gone down first; that way she wouldn't have to speak to Cord, could put off telling him that he'd destroyed something inside her because, as too many times before, he'd hidden behind silence.

Matt hadn't seemed to mind. Had he been too distracted to notice how little his father said to him, or did he somehow know something she didn't?

No, that couldn't be.

Cord had known the poachers were up there, but he hadn't told her because he believed she couldn't handle it.

Despite everything she'd been through in life, he didn't believe she was strong enough—either that, or communicating with her hadn't been that important to him. She hadn't wanted to be spared; she would never want that.

Over and over again she'd told Matt how much she loved him, held him until he grew restless and embarrassed because others were watching. When he and his father talked, it had been about the fight with Chuck, how fast the helicopter could travel and how much weight it could carry, tracking techniques. Cord hadn't said a word about a father's fears, his love for his son.

That's all she wanted, for Cord to tell Matt how much he loved him. If he could at least do that...

And if he couldn't...

Matt was asleep. It took her several seconds to realize her son was no longer simply resting by leaning against a rock. Because he'd slid over to one side and was slowly sinking to the ground, she helped him the rest of the way. Only then did she acknowledge that Cord was watching her.

Although she wanted to stay with Matt, she walked away from him, left him to his peace. "I don't know what those men are going to be charged with," she said when she'd gotten as close to Cord as she dared, not that the words mattered. "Whatever it is, we will probably have to testify. Of course, if you're off on another rescue..." She felt a sharp pain in her left forearm and realized she'd been gripping it with all the strength in her.

"I'm proud of you," he said.

"You are? For keeping up with you?"

"For not falling apart."

"Apart? I—"

"I know. You aren't a woman who caves in. I shouldn't have tried to protect you the way I did."

"No," she said, surprised at his admission. "You shouldn't have."

"But you wanted me to."

"What?"

"Don't deny it, Shannon. The things you said, the look in your eyes, I knew."

She had; she couldn't lie to him about that. "But for you to have to weather what you did alone, why?"

"Because looking for Matt is the hardest thing you've ever done."

"No, Cord." Her arms dropped by her side. She couldn't make them move. Couldn't let him go this easily, couldn't stop the words inside her. "Not the hardest."

Although he stared at her without blinking for the better part of a minute, he said nothing. Nothing. "Do you have any idea what I'm talking about?"

He took a long, deep breath. "Summer."

Now it was her turn to stare. Cord looked weary and she wondered if he might collapse, but he simply widened his stance and went on meeting her gaze. "I remember what you were like then," he said softly.

She didn't want this conversation. Not now and maybe not ever. "Thank God, things ended the way they did for Matt," she blurted. "I think he's going to look back at it with a sense of pride. I couldn't have stood it if...if—" *Stop babbling.*

"If you'd lost Matt, too."

"Yes. Summer..."

"What about her?"

"She—I never got to hold her, Cord, not really."

Despite the turmoil of her thoughts, she was aware that he'd taken a few steps toward her. "Finally." He breathed the word.

"Finally, what?"

"We're going to talk about our daughter."

After everything she'd been through, she didn't know how she could handle this, but before she could escape, he continued. "*We* should have said more before. So much more."

When? What was he talking about? She tried to think how to ask the question, but he was so close, and despite her exhaustion, she wanted him, wild and unthinking.

Oh, yes, unthinking. Unwise.

"I felt Summer's spirit all the time we were following Matt," he said. "I'd like you to know that."

Summer is in the wilderness with Gray Cloud. That's what he had said years ago when she desperately needed him to mourn with her. "I'm glad you did."

"Shannon, don't."

"Don't what?"

"Shut me out."

Stop this conversation, now! Before it's too late. "That's how you felt? Shut out?"

"Yes."

He scared her, or maybe it was herself she was afraid of. "I didn't know. You never told me."

"Neither of us told the other what we should have."

His words rocked her, forced her beyond herself. Had she failed him as badly as he'd failed her? "Maybe...maybe we didn't. There weren't any guidelines, no one telling us how to say goodbye to our baby daughter."

"Tell me now. What was it like for you?"

He was wounded and weak, maybe as tired as Matt. If she told him that, maybe she could back away from what stirred and simmered between them, but if she did ... "Do you remember what the doctors said, that she didn't have a chance? That we were lucky she lived such a short time."

"I remember."

"They were right. She would have never really known what it was like to be alive. She'd...she'd never ride a horse or go hiking with you or trail after her big brother."

"I know."

"Do you? Cord, do you remember what you said to the doctors the day she was born?"

Instead of answering, he simply looked at her until she felt the words boil out of her. "You said that some things weren't meant to be."

"Sometimes they aren't."

She wanted to lash out at him. If she could feel anger, maybe saying this would be easier. But he'd given her back Matt, and they'd made love last night and she could never hate him. "I carried her inside me, Cord. Before we knew what was wrong with her, I'd lie there at night feeling her move. I had so many dreams—so much...I felt her being born. Me. Not you."

"I gave her a name."

She felt bombarded and off balance. Felt like crying all over again. "I...yes. You did. A beautiful name. And you took that picture of her, the one you carry. Why didn't you show it to me before?"

"Shannon, you were locked up inside yourself. I didn't know how to reach you, didn't even know how to begin. I was afraid that no matter what I did or said, it would be the wrong thing."

Because we were so young? Because neither of us knew how to communicate, not just you? She started to touch him, then pulled back, afraid of the risk.

"I held you when she died," he told her in a tone that sounded as hollow as the wind racing across a barren plain. "It was the only thing I could think to do."

"I cried. You didn't."

"I didn't need to."

"Didn't need . . ."

"I tried to tell you that. Tried and failed. I know that now. Through Gray Cloud, I found peace, something I was unable to give you. I wish it could have been different, that your grief hadn't scared me."

"Scared? Peace?"

"Shannon, I went into the woods right after she died because I needed answers, a way to deal with what had happened. I asked Gray Cloud to take care of our daughter. He told me she was in the air, the earth, water. She would always be in those places, always be safe and happy."

It hurt to speak. "You told me Summer was with him and I shouldn't be sad. Cord, I didn't have your belief in Gray Cloud and his world. I needed more than words about her being with her great-grandfather. I needed you."

He looked as if she'd slapped him. Still, he didn't lean away. "I had—"

"I know. You had to work so you could pay the bills. I understand that much better now than I did then. But—"

"But I shouldn't have let it take me away from you. I wanted to talk to you, wanted to help you start talking, but I was afraid that whatever I said, it would be the wrong thing."

"You did?"

"I knew how you felt about my being gone. I thought I knew how much you hurt. I didn't want us to dwell on that. I thought—I wanted to avoid causing you any more pain. Only, that was the wrong thing to do. I know that now."

"Cord, I just saw you with that man. You aren't afraid of anything."

"Back then I was afraid of your emotions, your grief. My inability to give you the sense of peace I'd found." He continued slowly, his voice rough. "I can't be anything except who I am. I was shaped, to a large extent, by my grandfather."

"I know that."

"Do you? Really?"

Not sure what he wanted from her, she waited.

"Gray Cloud came to the hospital just before my mother died. He found me in an empty room where I'd gone to hide and told me I was going to live with him. Then he took me to see my mother. She opened her eyes and looked at him and he looked back, but they didn't say anything. After she died, he held me, but he didn't say a word. I don't think he ever spoke her name again."

"Why...not?"

"It was too hard for him. I knew that, in my heart. He'd be watching me and I'd see something in his eyes that told me he was thinking of her. Mourning lost years. He'd touch me or we'd go off into the mountains together and I'd know that was his way of being close to her. And of bringing us together without having to talk about it."

As she stood listening to the breeze and unseen birds with Cord beside her but not touching, she felt exhaustion seep into her very being. He'd told her something important, something that might, finally, allow her to understand him. But searching for and finding their son had stripped away her ability to think. To feel.

"Cord, we need to get off this mountain. Maybe then..."

He gazed at her for long seconds, then let his attention shift to Matt's huddled form. Looking at him, she was once again filled with an urgent need to put distance between them. She'd nearly died when their marriage collapsed around her; she couldn't handle any more emotion. Couldn't handle anything.

Without telling Cord what she was doing, she walked over to where he and Chuck had fought. She wasn't sure whether she could see his blood or not; it didn't matter. What did was facing the fact that Cord had risked his life and now she felt nothing, absolutely nothing. Their marriage had ended seven years ago. It *had* to remain buried.

When a full minute passed without Cord having said or done anything, she turned back around. He wasn't where she'd left him. Where—

A sound so light she couldn't be sure she'd heard it pulled her attention toward Matt. Cord was standing over him, looking so much a part of his surroundings that she wasn't sure whether he was real. He stared down at his son.

She heard the sound again, a human being in pain. Matt? No. Matt was dead to the world.

Cord. The sound came from him.

She began to tremble but forced herself to remain a silent observer. Slowly, shoulders heaving, he lifted a hand to his face and pressed it against his forehead. Then he dropped to his knees, his body hunched over his son's sleeping form.

Grabbing blindly for something to hold on to, she snagged her palm on a branch but ignored the pain. Cord's entire body shook, deep spasms wrenched from his soul. She felt heat in her eyes and had no desire to try to stem her own emotion.

Cord, crying for his son.

Alone.

As she closed the distance between them, her left foot brushed against a rotting branch. She kicked it aside, blinked to clear her vision, and kept going. Then when she was only a few inches from him, she stopped. Maybe he didn't want to share this moment with anyone. If she'd been the one in his place, she'd want and need privacy.

But the two of them already shared the child responsible for his tears.

"Cord?" Feeling as if she'd never touched him before, she laid her right hand along the side of his neck. "He's all right."

Silence. Only this one she understood as clearly as she understood the beating of her own heart.

"You found him. No one—no one but you could have done that. He's alive. Thank God, he's alive."

Cord's body quieted a little. Still, his every breath took incredible effort. Acting instinctively, she leaned forward and kissed the top of his head. He placed a hand on Matt's cheek; his fingers began a restless, aimless movement over smooth young flesh.

"He's fine, safe."

Cord still did nothing to acknowledge her presence. Or rather, if she hadn't known him—known him in a way she hadn't comprehended until this moment—she wouldn't have been aware of the change in him. But although he continued to struggle to control the emotion that had him in its grip, she felt him begin to relax. To find peace within himself.

"Why didn't you tell me how scared you were?"

"Scared? It wasn't . . . that."

No. It wasn't. He'd been terrified when he heard the rifle and undoubtedly uneasy from the moment he knew who shared Copper Mountain with them. But his tears had been born of emotion far deeper than fear—love for his son.

"I know," she whispered. "I know."

She felt the effort it took for him to push himself to his feet, half saw, half felt him turn toward her, and wondered if he cared that she could see his tears. As soon as he touched her cheek, the question evaporated.

"There's nothing else in life like it." His unsteady fingers slid under her chin, found the side of her neck and covered the vein there. "No feeling in the world like what we feel for our children, is there?"

"No, Cord. There isn't."

"Love. There aren't any words."

Cord's love for Matt. She'd just seen that in all its beautiful intensity. "No. There aren't. Sometimes it becomes so powerful there's nothing to do but cry."

He nodded. "I love Summer. As much as you do."

"I know that now."

"I'm sorry. I wish I'd been able to convey everything I felt and thought when our marriage depended on it."

"I wish you had, too. No." Her body became restless; she didn't know what to do with herself. "That's a horrible thing for me to say. What you felt for her was there all the time, but I'd wrapped myself into a tight ball and wouldn't let anything touch me, most of all you. If I'd understood what you were saying when you told me you'd entrusted her to Gray Cloud, if I hadn't tied myself up in knots—"

"Don't."

She spoke with her eyes closed, tracing each word as it flowed from her heart. "Everyone—man, beasts, trees, birds, earth, all share the same breath." She opened her eyes. "You said that to me earlier today. You tried to tell me the same thing years ago. I heard you today. I should have the first time."

"I gave you Gray Cloud's words, not mine, because I didn't know how to tell you what was in my heart. Shannon?" When he paused, she sensed his struggle and waited him out. "I don't ever want to do that to you again. I didn't want to break down. I fought it because—stupid!—I thought I had to keep that to myself."

"You didn't."

"No, I don't," he whispered. His eyes darkened, asked her to come into the depths with him. "Shannon, Matt and I don't always need words."

"I understand. Now."

"But he deserves to hear—to see how precious he is to me. Just as I want you to."

Cord. "You . . ."

He brushed her hair back from her temple. "You have beautiful eyes. Green like the forest. I fell back in love with you during our search. Or maybe I finally realized I'd never stopped loving you."

"Oh, Cord."

"I want you to know that, tonight, tomorrow, for the rest of our lives."

"The rest—"

His forefinger, steady now, rested on the pulse at the side of her throat. "I love you."

He was the one with the beautiful eyes, dark like a midnight forest. "And . . . and I love you." Her heart sang the words. She stood on tiptoe, offering her mouth, her heart, to the only man she'd ever loved.

Epilogue

"I love you, little one. Do you understand? Your daddy loves you with all his heart."

Tears blurred Shannon's vision. Despite muscles that trembled as a result of the hours of labor and delivery, she eased onto her side so she could study the interplay between Cord and the infant in his arms. Looking totally relaxed, one-hour-old Autumn Navarro yawned and stared wide-eyed at her father's face.

"You are so beautiful," he whispered. "So precious. So innocent and helpless. I'm here for you. I will always be here for you, I promise you that."

Shannon touched Cord's wrist. Smiling, his eyes misted, he eased his chair closer so she could run her fingers over the silky black hair curling over their daughter's head—hair as dark and rich as Cord's. "We were right. We did have a girl." Like her husband, she could barely form words.

Cord glanced at her, then returned his attention to the pink wrapped bundle snuggled against his strong body. "Do

you understand what we're saying, little one? Your mommy
and daddy knew everything about you long before you were
born. We didn't need an ultrasound, didn't need to pick out
a boy's name just in case. From the moment we realized you
were on the way, we had your name waiting for you.''

Autumn had been named for the season of her birth, just
as Summer had been. When she was old enough, Autumn
would be told that she had a sister who lived with the an-
gels, a fragile, beautiful girl who still held a place in her
parents' hearts.

"She looks so small in your arms," Shannon said. "So
right there. I hoped her hair would be black like yours."

"There's so much of it." Cord caught a curl between his
thumb and forefinger and studied it for a long minute. Re-
leasing it, he laid his little finger against his daughter's hand.
Autumn reached out and clamped her fist around it.

"What a grip you have there, young lady." He laughed,
the sound rich and full. "I bet you think you're stronger
than your father. You probably are. Even if I wanted to,
there's no way I could free my heart from your hold on it.
Do you have any idea of the power you have? How totally
and completely I love you?"

Cord spoke in a sing-song whisper that touched her heart.
He'd been there for Autumn's birth, breathing with her,
encouraging, cooling her with damp cloths, giving her
courage and strength and will to bring their daughter into
the world. They hadn't talked about it much during her
pregnancy, but as they were leaving for the hospital last
night, he'd confessed that he was thinking about Summer's
birth. Although they'd been assured that this child was
healthy, he couldn't quite make himself believe it until he
held her in his arms.

Now with the morning sun streaming in the window behind him, he had his wish. And she had everything she wanted in life.

"I've been thinking," he said. For the first time since the nurse handed Autumn to him, he looked at her fully, his dark eyes alive with love. "You got to hold her for nine months. Now it's my turn."

"I'll remind you of that at 2:00 a.m. Cord?"

"What?"

"I—I hope I never forget the way the two of you look right now."

Shifting Autumn so she now rested in the crook of his arm, he leaned forward, his mouth inches from hers. "I love you, Shannon. I never stopped loving you. I know I've told you that, but I want to say it again."

"Thank you," she whispered. "You mean everything to me. Everything." Then their lips met, joined, sealed and words were no longer necessary. She locked her arms around his neck and caught their daughter between them. She felt Autumn squirm and give a little yelp of sound that made them both chuckle.

Her parents would be here in a few minutes with Matt, but although she was looking forward to seeing their son's reaction to his baby sister, she could wait.

For now there was only her and Cord and the new life they'd created; a healthy, giving marriage; love. So much love expressed fully and openly.

* * * * *

Concluding in November from Silhouette books...

This exciting new cross-line continuity series unites five of your favorite authors as they weave five connected novels about love, marriage—and Daddy's unexpected need for a baby carriage!

🥕🥕🥕🥕🥕🥕🥕🥕

You fell in love with the wonderful characters in:

THE BABY NOTION by Dixie Browning (Desire 7/96)

BABY IN A BASKET by Helen R. Myers
(Romance 8/96)

MARRIED...WITH TWINS! by Jennifer Mikels
(Special Edition 9/96)

HOW TO HOOK A HUSBAND (AND A BABY)
by Carolyn Zane (Yours Truly 10/96)

And now all of your questions will finally be answered in

DISCOVERED: DADDY
by Marilyn Pappano (Intimate Moments 11/96)

Everybody is still wondering...who's the father of prim and proper Faith Harper's baby? But Faith isn't letting anyone in on her secret—not until she informs the daddy-to-be. Trouble is, *he* doesn't seem to remember her....

Don't miss the exciting conclusion of
DADDY KNOWS LAST...only in Silhouette books!

DKL-IM

MILLION DOLLAR SWEEPSTAKES

SWP-M96

As seen on TV!
Free Gift Offer

With a Free Gift proof-of-purchase from any Silhouette® book,
you can receive a beautiful cubic zirconia pendant.

This gorgeous marquise-shaped stone is a genuine cubic
zirconia—accented by an 18" gold tone necklace.

(Approximate retail value $19.95)

Send for yours today...
compliments of *Silhouette*®

To receive your free gift, a cubic zirconia pendant, send us one original proof-of-purchase, photocopies not accepted, from the back of any Silhouette Romance™, Silhouette Desire®, Silhouette Special Edition®, Silhouette Intimate Moments® or Silhouette Yours Truly™ title available in August, September, October, November and December at your favorite retail outlet, together with the Free Gift Certificate, plus a check or money order for $1.65 U.S./$2.15 CAN. (do not send cash) to cover postage and handling, payable to Silhouette Free Gift Offer. We will send you the specified gift. Allow 6 to 8 weeks for delivery. Offer good until December 31, 1996 or while quantities last. Offer valid in the U.S. and Canada only.

Free Gift Certificate

Name: _____

Address: _____

City: _____ State/Province: _____ Zip/Postal Code: _____

Mail this certificate, one proof-of-purchase and a check or money order for postage and handling to: SILHOUETTE FREE GIFT OFFER 1996. In the U.S.: 3010 Walden Avenue, P.O. Box 9077, Buffalo NY 14269-9077. In Canada: P.O. Box 613, Fort Erie, Ontario L2Z 5X3.

FREE GIFT OFFER   084-KMD
ONE PROOF-OF-PURCHASE
To collect your fabulous FREE GIFT, a cubic zirconia pendant, you must include this
original proof-of-purchase for each gift with the properly completed Free Gift Certificate.

084-KMD-R

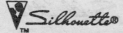